# the four way reader

#2

poetry/fiction/memoir
# the four way reader

edited by carlen arnett,
jane brox, dzvinia orlowsky,
and martha rhodes

four way books

marshfield, vermont
new york, new york

Copyright © 2001 Four Way Books

No part of this book may be used or reproduced in any manner without written permission except in the case of brief quotations embodied in critical articles and reviews. Please direct inquiries to:

Editorial Office
Four Way Books
PO Box 535, Village Station
New York, NY 10014
www.fourwaybooks.com

Library of Congress
Catalog Card Number: 01 132488

ISBN 1-884800-40-8

Book Design: Brunel
Cover Art: *Shadow 1.12* by Harry Bernard, mixed media.

This book is manufactured in the United States of America and printed on acid-free paper.

Four Way Books is a division of Friends of Writers, Inc., a Vermont-based not-for-profit organization. We are grateful for the assistance we receive from individual donors and private foundations.

Publication of this book was supported by a generous contribution from The CIRE Fund.

# Table of Contents

| | |
|---|---|
| Preface | / xiii |

### DOUG ANDERSON
| | |
|---|---|
| Xin Loi | / 3 |
| North of Tam Ky, 1967 | / 3 |
| Blues | / 4 |
| Bamboo Bridge | / 5 |
| Night Ambush | / 6 |
| Doc | / 7 |
| Rain | / 7 |
| Itinerary | / 8 |

### SALLY BALL
| | |
|---|---|
| Not Having the Affair | / 9 |
| Disclosures | / 10 |
| Morning Glory | / 10 |
| Went to Bed Without a Blanket | / 11 |
| Absence of Temptation | / 11 |
| Heart Swims Away and Is Lost | / 11 |

### JENNIFER BARBER
| | |
|---|---|
| Hot Morning in the Attic | / 12 |
| San Miguel | / 12 |
| Vendaval | / 13 |
| Nights | / 14 |
| A Village I Love | / 15 |
| In the Bosch Room, Downstairs at the Prado | / 15 |
| Letter | / 16 |
| Oak | / 17 |
| Photograph of My Mother, A Girl in Central Park | / 18 |
| Summer as a Large, Reclining Nude | / 18 |

### ROBERT A. AYRES
| | |
|---|---|
| Alameda Circle | / 19 |
| The Corn Cross | / 24 |
| First Cutting | / 26 |
| The Orchard | / 26 |
| Pilgrimage | / 27 |
| Infested | / 28 |

| | |
|---|---|
| Aubade | / 29 |
| Psalm | / 29 |

## Sarah Gorham
| | |
|---|---|
| River Mild | / 30 |
| Cupped Hands | / 30 |
| Honeymoon, Pleasant Hill | / 31 |
| Shared Cup | / 32 |
| Last Day at the Frost Place | / 33 |
| Interim | / 33 |

## Erin Belieu
| | |
|---|---|
| Watching the Giraffes Run | / 34 |
| Erections | / 35 |
| Tick | / 36 |
| Georgic on Memory | / 37 |
| Prayer for Men | / 38 |
| Another Poem for Mothers | / 38 |
| The Small Sound of Quiet Animals | / 39 |
| The Spring Burials | / 41 |

## Tereze Glück
| | |
|---|---|
| The Coast of Massachusetts | / 42 |

## Brian Kiteley
| | |
|---|---|
| I Know Many Songs, But I Cannot Sing | / 47 |

## Laure-Anne Bosselaar
| | |
|---|---|
| Amen | / 53 |
| The Radiator | / 55 |
| The Hour Between Dog and Wolf | / 56 |
| Hôtel des Touristes | / 58 |
| From My Window, I See Mountains | / 59 |
| Unable to Find the Right Way | / 60 |
| The Cellar | / 60 |
| The Feather at Breendonck | / 61 |
| The Vase | / 62 |

## Kenneth Zamora Damacion
| | |
|---|---|
| The False Angel | / 63 |
| Hieroglyphics | / 65 |
| My Mother's Life | / 66 |
| Gone | / 67 |

| | |
|---|---|
| Last Note Between Heaven and Hell | / 68 |
| Forgive Me | / 70 |

## Sharon Dolin
| | |
|---|---|
| Jacob After Fording the Jabbok | / 71 |
| The Domestic Fascist | / 71 |
| If My Mother | / 72 |
| The Bear | / 74 |
| The Visit | / 74 |
| Spanish Snapshots | / 75 |
| Pomegranates | / 76 |
| Confession | / 77 |

## Patrick Donnelly
| | |
|---|---|
| Finding Paul Monette, Losing Him | / 78 |
| Baba | / 80 |
| I am a virus | / 81 |
| How the Age of Iron Turned to Gold | / 82 |
| After a long time away | / 83 |

## Volodymyr Dibrova
| | |
|---|---|
| Burdyk | / 84 |

## John Donoghue
| | |
|---|---|
| Waiting for the Muse in Lakeview Cemetery | / 92 |
| Sheila's Auras | / 93 |
| Articles of Exploration | / 94 |
| Physical | / 94 |
| Images | / 95 |
| One-Bedroom, Four Floors Up | / 97 |

## Marianne Boruch
| | |
|---|---|
| Then | / 98 |
| The Luxor Baths | / 99 |
| On Sorrow | / 101 |
| Head of an Unknown Saint | / 102 |
| Happiness | / 103 |
| The Hawk | / 103 |
| Tulip Tree | / 104 |

## Pablo Medina
| | |
|---|---|
| Mortality | / 106 |

## Ellen Dudley
- The Bats / 109
- Leaving Lincoln / 109
- The One Thing / 110
- Kilauea / 110
- Night Fishing / 111
- Ojo Caliente Suite
  - The Oranges / 111
  - Recall / 112
  - Corporeal / 112
  - Out of Time / 113
  - Hot Eyes / 113

## Gary Duehr
- All the Little Sorries / 114
- Dog World / 115
- Missing / 116
- Vestige / 116
- Petition: Morning Talk Show / 117
- Ricochet / 117
- Under Total Quality Management / 118

## Linda Dyer
- Hereditary Guess / 119
- Houdini's Daughter / 120
- My Muse: Gravity / 120
- Screen Doors of the 1960s / 121
- Conservation of Momentum / 122

## Michael Klein
- The Play My Father's In / 124

## Terri Ford
- BP Station Employee Restroom, 2 A.M. / 133
- Mister Hymen / 134
- Better Off / 135
- Heartsick / 135
- For the love of an anaconda woman / 136

## Alison Moore
- The Angel of Vermont Street / 136

## Martín Espada
- Colibrí / 145

| | |
|---|---|
| Jorge the Church Janitor Finally Quits | / 146 |
| La Tumba de Buenaventura Roig | / 147 |
| Latin Night at the Pawnshop | / 149 |
| When Songs Become Water | / 149 |
| DSS Dream | / 151 |
| White Birch | / 151 |
| Imagine the Angels of Bread | / 152 |

## Sabra Loomis

| | |
|---|---|
| The Trouble I Have in High Places | / 154 |
| Woman and Donkey | / 155 |
| The Unicorn | / 156 |
| Delia | / 157 |
| Echo | / 158 |
| The Bear He Shot on Their Honeymoon in Montana, That Growled, and Tried to Come into Their Tent. | / 158 |
| Coming-Out Party | / 159 |
| Ziffy-Sternal | / 160 |
| Front Seats | / 160 |

## Dale Neal

| | |
|---|---|
| The Mouse's Father | / 161 |

## Cheryl Baldi

| | |
|---|---|
| Skytop | / 171 |
| First Goodbye | / 171 |
| New Neighbors | / 172 |
| Anima | / 172 |
| Portrait | / 173 |
| Fever | / 174 |
| Prayer for the God Box | / 175 |

## Melissa Hotchkiss

| | |
|---|---|
| Maine | / 176 |
| The Chore | / 177 |
| Temper | / 177 |
| Untitled | / 178 |
| Elizabeth | / 178 |
| The Breakup | / 178 |
| Surgery | / 179 |
| China Lake | / 179 |

## Ha Jin
- Ways of Talking / 180
- A Peach / 181
- Distance / 181
- At Midnight / 182
- In a Moonlit Night / 183
- The Past / 184
- Lilburn, Georgia / 184
- I Sing of an Old Land / 185
- June 1989 / 186

## Faye George
- Amtrak / 188
- The Moon Is in the Eastern Sky / 188
- Norfolk to Boston / 189
- Rain / 190
- Welcome to This House / 191
- What She Looked Out Upon / 191

## Kathleen E. Krause
- Streets / 193
- To / 193
- Train / 193
- Scrape Scrape / 194
- Portrait / 194
- No Dragon / 194
- Foot / 195
- Accident / 195
- Frank and Luna / 196

## Dinty W. Moore
- White Birds / 197

## Frances Richard
- Asparagus Bed / 205
- Now You Are / 205
- Infiltration / 206
- Story About *Yes* / 206
- Reverie/Plus / 207
- The 1950s / 208
- Sign / 208
- Cold Seconds / 209

## Frankie Paino
- Pentecost: Collinwood School Fire, Cleveland, 1908 / 210
- Sometimes the Dead / 212
- The Martyrdom of St. Sebastian / 214
- Each Bone of the Body / 215

## Carl Phillips
- In the Blood, Winnowing / 220
- Undressing for Li Po / 222
- Aubade for Eve Under the Arbor / 223
- As from a Quiver of Arrows / 224
- The Full Acreage of Mourning / 225
- Blue / 226

## Bethany Pray
- In the City / 227
- Conception / 228
- The Nameless / 229
- Tree / 230
- Quartet / 231
- In Dream, in the Eden / 232
- Apparition / 233

## Jeffrey Skinner
- Play Dead / 234
- Come / 234
- Speak / 235
- Fetch / 236
- Stay / 236
- Jocelyn / 237

## Jean Valentine
- Your mouth "appeared to me" / 241
- Mare and Newborn Foal / 241
- Mother, / 241
- The Pen / 242
- October Premonition / 242

Contributors' Notes / 245

Acknowledgments / 252

# Preface

It's all here: the polished candlesticks, wrapped, unused in the silver closet. The skeleton keys, family portraits, and tantrums of childhood. There's a girl learning her times tables, a deer fallen through ice. A hummingbird released through the shutters of a house. There are donkeys and stepfathers and *Dog World* magazine. A virus. An estranged wife. Egrets landing on a lake. A letter unwrites itself. Peaches ripen, then spoil. A woman undresses in the heat of an attic. One poet finds her history in the stiff, curled letters of 1960s aluminum screen doors. Another takes Viet Nam as his subject (or maybe it takes him). There are sunfish and spiders. A feather from Breendonck. At dusk on a hillside, a mother learns to call bats. There are lovesick windows and violets grown up through the asphalt. A woman touching her neck to prevent an affair. In one dream, a man pushes back his own tombstone. In another, a girl splits into twins. There's a subversive scribbler named Burdyk, an adventurer, Carlitos. A woman putting on lipstick in a parked car's side mirror.

Our pleasure as editors of *The Four Way Reader #2* comes as much from rereading these poems and stories as from gathering them together in the first place. These are works of heft and elegance, ricochet and grace—lively voices ranging widely across subject matter and style.

Consider Terri Ford's sexy, alchemical lyrics. Or Jeffrey Skinner's tattered, mostly tongue-in-cheek spirituality. There's precise mystery in Marianne Boruch's poems, and agitated humor in John Donoghue's. For work that tilts between the tragic and the ecstatic, read Frances Richard. Or Frankie Paino, whose poetry of longing and tortured faith shapes its own contrast to Sarah Gorham's, infused with a crisp, pastoral light. Carl Phillips's sleek, indelible poems offset the astonishing, urgent lyrics of Jean Valentine. Alison Moore's storytelling moves with upsweep and surprise, and Tereze Glück's with brisk, telescopic shifts in perception.

*The Four Way Reader #2* collects the work of thirty-seven poets and prose writers. Wherever you enter this gathering, we hope you'll read and read on, knowing that your pleasure is the true destination of our project. As Flannery O'Connor observed, "the act of writing is not complete in itself. It has its end in its audience."

—Carlen Arnett

# the four way reader

# Doug Anderson

## Xin Loi

The man and woman, Vietnamese,
come up the hill,
carry something slung between them on a bamboo mat,
unroll it at my feet:
the child, iron gray, long dead,
flies have made him home.
His wounds are from artillery shrapnel.
The man and the woman look as if they are cast
from the same iron as their dead son,
so rooted are they in the mud.
There is nothing to say,
nothing in my medical bag, nothing in my mind.
A monsoon cloud hangs above,
its belly torn open on a mountain.

## North of Tam Ky, 1967

You were dead when I got there, managed to drag yourself
almost to the treeline across the sandy open place
they planned to kill us in, the clearing I would have to crawl
to get to you, and did, the tracers crossing overhead.
The round caught you dropping to the ground, entering longways
between neck and shoulder, taking the artery, the lung.
I had inside me in those days a circuitbreaker between head
and heart that shut out everything but the clarity of fear.
I felt nothing for you then, rolling you over, looking for
the exit wound, nor when I put my mouth on yours and blew,
hearing the gurgle that told me you had drowned in your own blood.
I knew only the muzzle flashes too close in front, the sniper
cracking on my left and I flipped the switch and went cold,
the same whose wires I tinker with these twenty-three years after,
a filament flickering in the heart and then the blaze of light.

# Blues

Love won't behave. I've tried
all my life to keep it chained up.
Especially after I gave up pleading.
I don't mean the woman,
but the love itself. Truth is,
I don't know where it comes from,
why it comes, or where it goes.
It either leaves me feeling the knife
of my first breath
or hangdog sick
at someone else's unstoppable
and as the blues song says,
can't sit down, stand up, lay down pain.
Right now I want it.
I'm like a country who can't remember the last war.
Well, that's not strictly true.
It's just been too long.
Too long and my heart is like
a house for sale in a lot full of high weeds.
I want to go down to New Orleans
and find the Santeria woman
who will light a whole table full of candles
and moan things, place a cigar
and a shot of whiskey in front of Chango's picture
and kiss the blue dead Jesus on the wall.
I want something.
Used to be I'd get a bottle
and drink until the lights went out
but now I carry my pain around everywhere I go
because I'm afraid
I might put it down somewhere and lose it.
I've grown tender about my mileage.
My teeth are like Stonehenge and my tongue
is like an old druid fallen in a ditch.
A soul is like a shrimper's net they never haul up
and it's full of everything:
A tire. A shark. An old harpoon.
A kid's plastic bucket.
An empty half-pint.
A broken guitar string.
A pair of ballerina's shoes with the ribbons tangled

in an anchor chain.
And the net gets heavier until the boat
starts to go down with it and you say,
*God, what is going on.*
In this condition I say love is a good thing.
I'm ready to capsize.
I can't even see the shoreline.
I haven't seen a seagull in three days.
I'm ready to drink salt water,
go overboard and start swimming.
Suffice it to say I want to get in the bathtub
with the Santeria woman and steam myself pure again.
The priest that blesses the water may be bored.
Hung over. He may not even bless it,
just tell people he did. It doesn't matter.
What the Santeria woman puts on it with her mind
makes it like a holy mirror.
You can float a shrimp boat on it.
The spark that jumps between her mind
and the priest's empty act
is what makes the whole thing light up
like an oilslick on fire against a sunset over Oaxaca.
So if I just step out into it.
If I just step off the high dive over a pool
that may or may not have water in it;
that act is enough
to connect the two poles of something
and make a long blue arc.
I don't have a clue about any of this.
*Come on over here and love me.*
I used to say that drunk.
Now I am stark raving sober
and I say, *Come on over here and love me.*


# Bamboo Bridge

We cross the bridge, quietly.
The bathing girl does not see us
till we've stopped and gaped like fools.
There are no catcalls, whoops,
none of the things that soldiers do;
the most stupid of us is silent, rapt.

She might be fourteen or twenty,
sunk thigh deep in green water,
her woman's pelt a glistening corkscrew,
a wonder, a wonder she is; I forgot.
For a moment we all hold the same thought,
that there is life in life and war is shit.
For a song we'd all go to the mountains,
eat pineapples, drink goat's milk,
find a girl like this, who cares
her teeth are stained with betel nut,
her hands as hard as feet.
If I can live another month it's over,
and so we think a single thought,
a bell's resonance.
And then she turns and sees us there,
sinks in the water, eyes full of hate;
the trance broken.
We move into the village on the other side.

# Night Ambush

We are still, lips swollen with mosquito bites.
A treeline opens out onto paddies
quartered by dikes, a moon in each,
and in the center, the hedged island of a village
floats in its own time, ribboned with smoke.
Someone is cooking fish.
Whispers move across water.
Children and old people. Anyone between
is a target. It is so quiet
you can hear a safety clicked off
all the way on the other side.
Things live in my hair. I do not bathe.
I have thrown away my underwear.
I have forgotten the why of everything.
I sense an indifference larger than anything
I know. All that will remain of us
is rusting metal disappearing in vines.
Above the fog that clots the hill ahead
a red tracer arcs and dims.
A black snake slides off the paddy dike
into the water and makes the moon shiver.

# Doc

*They kill them like flies over there*
he had slurred on the bus full
of drunk marines going back to Las Pulgas.
Like flies. Corpsmen,
he was talking about.
Six months later I was a replacement,
saw coffins being loaded onto transports
on the airstrip coming in.
Lived through the first firefight,
the second; had a little bag
of wisdom to croak out
to the fool who would replace me:
*Break down your medical kit,*
*pack the innards in your pockets;*
*get rid of your pistol,*
*buy a black market shotgun, greasegun,*
*anything to make you look like*
*something other than what you are;*
*and don't walk behind the radioman*
*or the squad leader on patrol;*
*they ambush the center of the column,*
*and by the way,*
*a muzzle pointed your way pops flat,*
*away, it echoes;*
*the round that gets you you won't hear.*


# Rain

1968:
For you, sitting in a barracks in Okinawa,
the war is over. You are quiet,
as if experiencing silence for the first time.
You don't know what to do. Stare at your hands.
From the barracks sergeant you obtain
the name of a place where you can be washed and massaged.
You go there in the rain.
A shy, plain woman hands you a towel,
leads you to a room where you lie on a mat.
She makes you feel like a child lifted from a bassinet.
When you roll over you are hard.

There is a brief haggling to adjust the price.
She turns away from you to do it, facing your feet,
her hair in a tight little bun.
Another woman passes through, smiles at you,
the way women of your childhood bent over your pram.
You think of the lepers you saw bathing in the sea
near Monkey Mountain. When you come,
it is the priming of tears
and as she washes her hands, her back still toward you,
you cry. And the steam. And the water everywhere.
The rain outside. And life comes back.

# Itinerary

In Arizona coming across the border with dope in my tires
and for months tasting the rubber in what I smoked.
With a college degree and a trunk full of the war.
Working in one place long enough to get the money
to stay high for a month and then moving on. Drinking a quart
of whiskey, then getting up, going to work the next day.
A little speed to burn off the hangover. In the afternoon
a few reds to take the edge off the speed and then to the bar.
At the bar, the Madonna in the red mirror. My arm around her
waist and the shared look that said, The World Is Coming Apart,
Let Us Hold One Another Against The Great Noise Of It All.
Waking with her the next morning and seeing her older,
her three-year-old wandering in and staring with a little worm
of confusion in his forehead. The banner on her bedroom wall
that read ACCEPTANCE in large block letters.
At night going out to unpack the war from my trunk.
A seabag full of jungle utilities that stank of rice paddy
silt and blood. To remind myself it happened. Lost them somewhere
between Tucson and Chicago. Days up on a scaffold
working gable-end trim with Mexicans who came through
a hole in the fence the night before. Rednecks who paid
me better than them. Laughing at jokes that weren't funny
to keep the job. At a New Braunfels Octoberfest getting in a fight
with a black army private who wore a button that read,
*Kiss me I'm German.* Don't remember what the fight was about.
Back in Tucson. Up against the patrol car being cuffed
for something I don't remember doing. Leaving the state.
Back with Jill in San Antonio. Finding her in the same bar,

driving her home in her car because she was too drunk.
The flashers on behind me, then the flashlight in my face.
In those gentle days they drove you home. Stealing Jill's car
out of the impoundment lot next morning to avoid the fee.
Later sitting buck-naked across from one another at the breakfast
table wondering who we were. This woman who wanted to live—
with a man who had dreams so bad he would stay awake for days until
the dreams started to bleed through into real time and he had to go back
the other way into sleep to escape them. Who woke with the shakes
before dawn and went to the kitchen for beer. Later walking down
to the barrio slowly, without talking, our hips touching.
The Mexican restaurant, a pink adobe strung with chili pepper
Christmas Lights the year round. Inside, the bullfight calendar
with the matador's corpse laid out on a slab, naked and blue
with a red cloth across his loins and the inevitable grieving virgin
kneeling at his side. The wound in the same place the centurion
euthanized Christ with his spear. Our laughing then not laughing
because laughter and grief are born joined at the hip.
An old Mexican woman fanning herself at the cash register,
her wattles trembling. *Recordar:* to remember, to pass again
through the heart. Corazone. Corragio. Core.

# SALLY BALL

## Not Having the Affair

On the hill, walking to the car, we pass a garden shed
built into the slope and full of orange cones
and flower pots. Peering inside the little window
with your chin above my shoulder, I know
how it would be, the way we'd take each other.

Earlier, on the bench, talking about jobs and books,
I thought, Touch my hair, and tried to listen to you talk;
touch my hair. I took my own hand
and cupped the back of my neck.

## Disclosures

You have your secrets, buried desires, spoken
only in the tiniest motions of the body,
motions you can't detect and suppress.

So do I: and this is what we watch each other for,
more than watch, monitor.
What is he leaning toward?
What started that response in her?

And should we follow?
Might wanting more
exceed receiving more?

We find our mouths to kiss. Then one of us will choose—
foreheads pressed together, or temples—
eye to eye, or the view beyond, the private mind.
We trust our fluent bodies
to each other's arms.


## Morning Glory

The hammock floats above the patio
partway over the day lilies, which in June
you can peer at through the ropes
and see their dust and stamens and veiny petals.

The fence is eight feet high and makes the garden
like a room, the sky all private. Up above, a morning glory
climbs the plum tree, and I wonder if the flower, little trumpet,
is a threat: the leaning plum enlaced

in vine, succumbing to the creeper in its boughs?
I like removing vines, their loosening and tumbling away
from walls and shrubs. I also like the blue and purple flaring
blooms. I need to ask someone if I should worry for my tree.

The morning glory wants to go as high as possible.
It's pretty and resilient. It wants what is has no way
to get. Watching it, you learn its ardent, deepest heart,
which crushes—mirrors—yours.

## Went to Bed Without a Blanket

I wake inside, an utterly black
night swimming in the window,
pushing the lace panels toward the bed
and this breeze: such a full,
shocking touch; my body strains
to be subsumed.

My head has risen
from the pillow—my face I know
gone slack from holy intercourse,
the gods now vanished and my body cooling,
flush and leaning toward their exit.


## Absence of Temptation

The body's wants are paper tables
under the mind's disinterested *thunk!*

As to the primary questions: *honoring my vows:*
I choose them over and over, yet

the memory of bodies hesitating

fluttering in the pre-daring moment, the pre-inquiry, all afire—

even before the vows, that's gone. Love makes itself

differently inside long promises. Leaves you
to theorize about its dawn.


## Heart Swims Away and Is Lost

The sun abandons the neighbors' brick wall,
which is all I can see of their house, massive, supported
by ancient rusted stars that anchor cords,
with painted bits of trim under the eaves,
and all the thousand-colored bricks, a sea, a moving tide,
going flat and hushed at dusk.

Did I say windowless?

Like the sea.

# JENNIFER BARBER

## Hot Morning in the Attic

And I'm taking off my shirt.
It's all right, the neighbors can't see in
though I can hear
their second baby wail.

The air up here,
heavy as a Hudson's Bay
blanket by mid-morning.
I drop my skirt
next to the desk,

then my bra, a fancy thing.
The finches clamor around the tree,
pulling invisible
banners of blue sky.

I'm in the catbird seat
with my heart's tongue and naked skin,
alone. The shrill
monotone of insects tightens like a wire.

## San Miguel

Lying in each other's arms
with too few or too many plans
        for living out the borrowed year

we don't ask what we're doing here,
the first year of our marriage. Here,
        the days are bright, the grass

beyond the washtub gleams
like finely blown strands of glass.
        At night we have no visitors,

no witness but the night, the moon
leaning back against a cloud
        as if she couldn't bear this quietness.

## Vendaval

The brown hen is blown
toward the chopping block
and the red-handled axe.

The sea is rubbed bare in spots,
the sky El Greco blue
between the forking clouds.

The only gods are seasonal:
the holding back, the giving in,
the mistimed caress

against, not with, desire.
The wind dies as abruptly
as it started yesterday.

The day's late light
falls on us, unequally—it
makes a new map

of the blue bedspread,
luring disappointment
from our eyes and mouths,

letting us begin again.

# Nights

No one here dreams louder
than the wind, knocking

at the doors
where Franco's men

conscripted farmers' sons
fifty years ago for war. The wind

blows over strips of farms
no wider than a pony-run

and rivers made of
diphthongs, like the Eo,

and through the greedy
heads of eucalyptus trees,

the bearded, maimed
pines, through villages

whose steeples are crowned
with absurdly large

stork nests, set awry.
After a card game in the bar,

the men scrape back their chairs.
They leave in twos and threes.

Children and grandchildren
have moved away

to cities farther south.
They are all that's left,

a knock at the door
and the wind's long memory

of a bloody mountain pass
elbow-deep in mud.

## A Village I Love

It's stony enough. It's bitter enough.
A boy with a goad in the field
        keeps an ox and plow in line.

Vines cover the window of a shed
like an eye sewn shut by scars.
        Clothespins start clicking

when the wind takes up
whatever the mind won't touch.
        Widows are widows here, they hang

their tears to dry, they have the time.
Magpies on the garden wall
        chase away the smaller birds,

proving they are needle-eyed
masters of all they see.
        They see sudden shifts of light

followed by sudden rain.
Wind mutinies against the plow,
        the boy's dirt-caked shoe as he

takes a rolling step. I let the wind
snatch his breath and blur my eyes
        with his eyes, watching how the field

bends in on itself, his steps
swaying ground and furrow to the grief
        that sees what it holds, holds what it sees.

## In the Bosch Room, Downstairs at the Prado

The days are numbered,
something has to give,
torso or crotch or spindly
trees, and lizards on the bank.

A woman whose nakedness
is seen by giant starlings, whose tears
gouge pools in solid rock until
she too must enter in,
her curtain of hair falling
down her slender back in waves.

Bell-makers, organ builders,
prurient owls, wimpled pigs
all waiting for something
to damn them or release them
from the pale sunlight
which seals their sentences.

Even I, who don't believe
in the pinkish flames
always just out of sight,
can't take the name
Hieronymous in vain, he has
foreseen my standing here
in my dark clothes and dubious century.


# Letter

The letter unwriting itself
like a woman taking down her hair
        would explain to you
                what I am doing here.

The textures of my day, with its loose weave,
the small exchanges that rankle—
        everything would be so clear
    you would have to smile.

The letter would be an opening: it
brings us to a tidal pool
        where mussels fastened
                to green walls barely stir.

I have no letter. All that needs to be said
dissolves as easily as the sea,
                never leaving a wave onshore.
       It is the failure I practice.

## Oak

The oak outside my door
is no joke: one arm
        downed by a winter storm
could shear the second-
        story porch right off,

a higher arm,
like a higher power,
cleave the attic room in half.

Yet I love the oak
the way the German painters did
before the wars:
        they painted it
in snow, or in a summer wood
when being German
        was still good,

before, before,
when dreaming was dreaming,

a young man half-asleep on moss,
        a horn, a cornucopia
held lightly to his lips
        as if that instrument released

the branches' light,
the canopy,
        and summer's breath
in the hatchmarks of the shade,

the Germany to come
still sleeping, unbidden
        in the half-forgotten leaves.

## Photograph of My Mother, A Girl in Central Park

The squirrel is so thin
it must be the Depression.
There you are, feeding him,
wearing a little fur-trimmed coat.

Mother and Father have
made you take your glasses off.
This is the only point
on which they agree.

Unhappy little girl, you smile,
conscious of the camera
as you reach a hand
toward the squirrel on the bench.

Your other hand is clenched.
I have to see, sixty years later,
if you'll open it, if you'll knock,
an orphan at my door.

## Summer as a Large, Reclining Nude

These are the days when summer lies
naked on the lawn, indolent and hot,
careless of the sparrows on her limbs.
In the freckled grass, you hear her yawn
deep within the pleasure of her mass,
giant breasts, belly, thighs and knees,
pockets of moisture soaking in the sun.
Across the street, a radio drones on,
describing the rank and file of two armies
dragging their equipment to the line
though a war seems far-fetched this late
in August. We're sleeping in the fear
of infinitely heavy arms and legs,
weeks defying the measurements of Thoth.
The rose nude yawns, rolls over in the grass,
draws us closer with a gorgeous laugh.

# Robert A. Ayres

## Alameda Circle

*for Vera*

*Houses surrounded us, solid but untrue—and*
*none of them ever knew us.*
        —Rilke

   \*

We raced across the lawn past the statues—
the boy and girl—and up the steps,
ringing our doorbell and catching our breath,
while felt hammers struck the slender chimes,
the decorous rise and fall, those notes
reverberating through the vaulted hall.

   \*

Inside, the doors locked
with a skeleton key, skinny
as a child's finger,
with a worn scrap of ribbon
strung through the socket,
and two crooked teeth.

   \*

In her powder room (every wall
a mirror), its vanity,
its drawer full of matches,
I pried loose a tile—
opening on the labyrinth of house.

I hid a small tobacco pouch inside,
its thin yellow string drawn tight
on the fistful of fireworks.

   \*

Your tantrums.
The tall piece with a marble top.
The right-hand drawer.
The white brush.

The hysterical thrashing.
Hers. Yours.
My silence.

*

No one knew the combination
to the safe. I'd turn the dial
first left, then right,
certain it would open, the tumblers
falling in and out of place.

*

He brought me hundreds of them,
quarters and dimes in canvas bags
from the Alamo National Bank.
I'd sort them for the older, silver coins,
their dull sheen, their worn faces,
faces I'd seen at church, or the country club,
tinkling together like shells
in his hunting vest.

*

No one else could prune
the pittosporums as well as I could, she said.
Nearly inside one, through the thick leaves,
reaching for a place to cut,
I struck a wasp's nest I hadn't seen.

*

My hands reached through the invisible wall,
the place you played with your perfect family.
They tore down the calico curtains;
overturned the tiny table;
broke a tiny chair.
They stripped each doll.
They twisted each Ken on his Barbie.

*

You locked yourself in your own closet.
You were little. You couldn't work the latch.
No one heard you over the din
of the party downstairs, the adults laughing.
We found you hoarse from yelling, scratching

like Lolly-the-gun-shy-bird-dog
tearing the screens from the doors
each Fourth of July.

\*

I spilled them in your hands, cupped
for the lovely oranges, reds and greens
of the *chile tepínes,* then told you
to rub your eyes.

Once with a friend I paid you quarters
to run the hall to my green room,
fall down and lift your skirt so we could see
between your legs, soft pink, your room.

\*

They gave me my own key.
I kept it on a nail out of sight.
I could lock you out.
I could lock myself in.

\*

Solid and pin-striped,
blacks, grays, navy blues,
and rows of belts and leather shoes,
one thick black belt you knew.

You found a hundred dollar bill
in the toe of the buckskin moccasin
you took to show-and-tell,
but they wouldn't let you keep it.
I found a stack of *Playboy*s
on a shelf, in the way back.

\*

He bought me my share of Warner Lambert.
I followed the price—
up a point, down an eighth.
I knew the price/earnings ratio,
the dividend.

\*

Thursdays I laid my jacket, dress blue,
on the bed, removed the insignia
and buttons fastened with safety pins
to polish brass.

*To execute Present Arms,*
*raise your rifle diagonally in front of you*
*with your right hand. Grip the center above the trigger*
*with your left hand . . .*

Unable to open the M-14 without resting the butt on my knee,
I drilled myself in the living room with my 20 gauge
while the bolt bruised my hand gun-barrel blue.

\*

The silver closet:
shelves along each wall
and on all these shelves
in soft cloth bags and tissue,
sealed in plastic,
old urns and chafing dishes,
goblets and bowls,
trays and tea services,
candlesticks, vases.
Never polished.
Never used.
Never sold.

\*

The winter Idella died, I painted her room—
to earn a little money I said—
because I missed her,
felt ashamed of her dingy quarters.

Idella Welch, *Welch like the grape juice,*
working her day around the Soaps, ironing
near the black-and-white TV, where nights
she washed the dishes, angry at the cops
*always a day late and a dollar short.*

Painting, I sang her favorite gospel tune:

*Count the years as months,*
*Count the months as weeks,*
*Count the weeks as days,*
*Any day now, we'll be going home.*

    \*

*In my father's house are many rooms; if it were not so, would I have told you that I go to prepare a place for you? And when I go and prepare a place for you, I will come again and will take you to myself, that where I am you may be also.*

    \*

But this was our mother's house,
and her mother's house.

Behind the glass, in soft light,
our grandmother, Vera Gentry,
one foot on the bottom step, burgundy
covering all but the hardwood
edges of the spiraling stair,
the other foot one step up
creasing the tailored western suit,
her figure slim and sharp;
her hand in a chocolate glove—
polished floor, polished boots, polished face;
painted lips painted nails painted brows;
hair back above her ear, a hint of gray
below the beaver Stetson.

    \*

Mother walked the house at night.
Half-asleep beside my desk she scratched
her hips through the thin gown.
I pretended not to see her dark nipples,
my shrouded nest of twigs.

One night while I worked at calculus,
she fell asleep on my bed, and later woke
and wandered back into the dark house.
She returned with an apple and stood in the doorway,
chewing. I was the pencil about to snap.

On the patio below, I could just make out
the shapes of the statues of the boy and the girl:
the same size; the same distance apart.

*

Down the hollow sounding back stairs,
past the door to the garage and down
to the basement floor, the clink
and heft of a thick white door
swung open on the walk-in locker:
boxes of candles stored like wine
so they wouldn't warp until time
to entertain; cold hooks that held
the carcasses of deer through slits
above the joints of their legs sawn short.
And somewhere, unseen, the motor,
idle, or churning the air to cold
around the carcasses unleashed
from the station wagon's roof, the stiff
tarp folded and put away with the gathered rope,
and hanging from one hook, the delicate saws.

# The Corn Cross

> *The history of religion, right up to our own time,
> is full of dead symbols . . .*
> —Paul Tillich

i.
A woman wrapped in a woven blanket
sits in the shadow that spreads
over chickens, cats, and carburetor parts.
From a basket she picks four ears of corn,
braids the husks to make a circle
in the center of a cross, the kernels—
the colors of *masa* and *sangría*—falling
haphazardly from her hands.

ii.
If the cross seems dry and dusty, bug-eaten even,
is it just our lack of faith, or did its power
diminish as it left the circle of planting and eating?
Would anything change if it hung in tapered light?

iii.
The coffee can, dipped in the barrel of corn,
makes a rusted sound as it's slung under cedar
and agarita. The last bit sings as the can empties
its yellow arc beside the blind. Inside, the cold
creeps through layers of blankets, jeans,
long underwear, woolen socks. The sun arrives
through rectangular cuts, carpeted so the gun
slides silently out. Specks of dust dance in the light
crossing like stars in and out of oblivion.
The squirrels return and the doe arrive, haltingly,
circling the blind, raising their ears,
nuzzling the rocks and grass for corn.
The buck at the edge of the clearing
moves closer, the fine crosshairs quivering
as I squeeze the trigger off. Doves
flutter back to the oaks as the doe, bewildered,
jump the fence and stand watching the buck
kick the matted grass. Once his head has dropped,
I drag his hind legs uphill, a brilliant stream
spilling from the wound in his neck.

iv.
Klomid and sperm counts,
morning's basal temperature, our
couplings scheduled
like conferences, post-
coital exams at the clinic on her
way to work, the pregnancy test—
Peacock Blue! Then
the bleeding again.

v.
How is it now,
when we find time for love,
we pull ourselves apart,
fumble for the diaphragm,
as if to say to joy, *no more!*
*No more!* to pain.

vi.
I take her with me, scatter the corn,
load my grandmother's .257, the last shell in the chamber.
We sit on the tattered sofa, springs creaking anytime we move.

I peel an apple. We take turns eating off the blade.
The sun through uneven slots catches the red in her hair
as it falls across her bare shoulder. An acorn strikes the tin roof,
rouses us, startles the deer, and twenty or more wild turkey.

vii.
Give me the disintegrating cross.
I'll toss it on the compost pile,
tend it there until it's ready to feed
what springs new from the garden,
walking on tender feet,
reaching out with tender hands.

# First Cutting

Because late May the johnsongrass grows tall and thick in the fields;

because the doe prefer to fawn in the cover the fields provide;

because the fawns know never to move: from the heavy bales

delicate legs, bits of dappled hide, protrude.

# The Orchard

I went to the orchard where no one for years has planted or pruned,
Where wild-suckering limbs break under the weight of the crowding fruit,
    and hackberries grow choking the younger trees;
Where the gaps mature trees filled are the gaps between a poor woman's
    teeth,
    and the ground turned by the harrow when moisture was a thing
      remembered
    is the cracked lip of a forgotten child,
And the yellow weeds waist high the hair the dead keep growing.

And though from a distance the leaves dull-green suggested the voices of
    those
    who summers gathered each fruit in its turn—
    the tart plums, the warm peaches, the ruddy pears (remarking
    how unusually sweet this year the grapes sprawling over the fence)—
Up close they crackled, a brush fire spreading from where for days
    it smoldered under the scorched grass.

I went to the one tree which bears every year without fail its pears, the birds
    flapping their hollow bones at my approach.
Through the leaves a small bat uncurled like a wisp of smoke.
And for every pear I gathered there was one too ripe, and one the birds had
    pecked,
    and one full of black weevils, and a dozen the masked raccoon
    knocked to the ground,
Fruit once firm and good, given to the boot's press,
And hornets rising each above a rotten globe.

# Pilgrimage

*after Rumi*

*On the way to Mecca, many dangers.*
At night, in their living room.
She's propped against one arm of the sofa;
He's sunk in the club chair, bare feet on the coffee table—
Caustic postures they've assumed.
*This talk is like stamping coins,*
A counterfeit exchange;
They've set themselves up.
Who could believe the other would fall for such sorry likenesses?
The eye is a weapon.
The soul is digging its own grave.
The mind can manufacture blame at staggering speeds.
He hurls a glass across the room.
Her voice breaks, spills.
The kids wake and come downstairs, crying.
*A lover is always accused of something.*
In the desert, blowing sand.
The eye goes blind;
The mouth, dry as camel's dung.
The wind blows itself stupid,
Laughs out loud.
Night after night the penitents inch through the streets.
By the time they reach the temple,
Their feet are bleeding badly.
*Still, each pilgrim kisses the black stone there.*
Only then do they realize how late it is.
How hungry they've become.

# Infested

    Dark, sleek, onto the scent of rotting potatoes,
their russet translucent wings, stealth squadron
                                        wheeling down
    the linoleum tarmac;
unchallenged
            invaders
    of sprouting tubers' blotched skins,
blackening spots.
              How many,
   how many gathering, gnawing places
in the softening skins;
                each night
    a little fatter, a little slower afoot
inside the back door to her
                        apartment,
    the cardboard box where she put the potatoes
she thought to bake for her suppers,
                        neglected,
    become instead the slow feast
of the brood of cockroaches fucking on her floor.
                                She loathes
    to crack the door to find them
suddenly frozen in the light, antennae
                    casting
    for explanations, for signals as to
which way to run. She
                rushes through
the room, too much to see them,
                    unthinkable
    to take them on—somehow
to get past them another night,
                      the congregation
    she won't see
growing,
        advancing on
    adjoining rooms, making themselves at home
on her sofa, her tabletops, her
                    book-
    shelves. And the smell of rotting potatoes
spreads, and their runny
              shit stains
    her counters, her curtains, her clothes.

How long before they know she's fallen
                              asleep, disregard
      the lights she leaves on? How long
before their bristly
                        legs reach
     her pillow, crawl
into her dreams,
                  lay
      their eggs in smooth ebony cases
in her lush folds?


## Aubade

How much of the comet's icy center boils away
determines this brilliance in the pre-dawn sky.

Mars, tethered to the big pecan;
the great-horned owl in silhouette;
and you, naked beneath the down comforter.

What of the ancestors, peering through the dark
to behold us now? They slip

like night's creatures into live oak crowns
where the finches already are singing.


## Psalm

Cold rain falling, lightest rain
falling in the night, long night,
cold night, the infant year, sleeping.
Hush. Hush. The fog, a cotton field
swallowing sound. Are you okay?
Are you okay? Cover the children,
whisper their kisses lightly—take leave.
Set the table for breakfast, the bowls'
empty mouths asking so much.
Is it asking so much?
Bless the Lord, oh my soul.
And all that is within me . . .
Let go, let go.

# Sarah Gorham

## River Mild

Yesterday, I found a bit of pleasure
in the present, in sycamores kissing the river
with one leaf, in their exposed roots
and hidden pebbles. I believed
in continuance as I sat in the boat
which remembered me and still does
though it hangs dry and upside down.
I had forgotten how to steer
but it came to me, the J-stroke,
out of the deep, through my paddle
to the crook of thumb and forefinger.
I floated under vines, over riffles and swells.
I was measured by the angling shadow clock,
the fox-running-along-the-bank clock,
the clock of hunger and exhaustion.
I passed cows in a chain,
then their owner, his wife, son.
I was measured and found fit. My hand
created a tiny wake. I could remove it
and still grow old.

## Cupped Hands

Knowing then our appetite,
and the table laden with pleasures,
it was by design we were made,

whether left palm over right as in TM
or curved side by side—
human hands are full of leaks. Still,

if we press the fingers close,
by sheer will sealing flesh to flesh,
they will hold something.

—An early disappointment:
a hundred foil-wrapped eggs
in pastel colors. For the taking,

I thought, and began to pluck
from window sills, copper pots,
the dark toes of daddy's socks.

Then the grown-up lesson,
the more I took
the more the eggs resisted

nesting, and capsized, wobbled
away. I ate one tiny handful.
Whether spice drops or wafers

or water carried quickly
over land, we let things slip.
Our hands cupped together

exactly heart-sized;
one hand
alone won't do.

## Honeymoon, Pleasant Hill

Poor sinners, we wandered too far,
lured by those trim Shaker fences
like lace on the good mother's slip.

We slumped in chairs meant to straighten the spine,
ran our fingers over testicle-shaped finials,
our palms down the Trustees railing,

smooth as a woman's thigh.
*Damn* that was good pie, we exclaimed
to the waiter in his Shaker smock.

He cracked a smile (only three survive
in upstate Maine), and kept that
Shaker food coming. Baby

corn, vegetables soaked in lemon oil,
mashed potatoes swollen
around our steak. We tossed and turned the night,

our Shaker beds sheeted too tight—
and woke to labor that zig-zag dance.
First a hum from inside out, then the verse

pitched from brother east to sister west,
against the boards faster, the telltale
thump, heels dug in for good purchase.

Finally, the dousing with an ecstatic shout.
(So sure the Shakers were their Godly Version
would bear the future out.)


# Shared Cup

Chalice in the right hand. Bleached
handkerchief in the left. Still there are those
who never touch the lip. *Dippers* we call them, their wafers
held high like a toe above icy water.
They fear colds or AIDS, are mostly single.
Your clue's in the way they tilt their faces, away.

Or others, shamefully close. A *guzzler*
will lean against your hand, muscle the cup.
Alcoholics are a special case. They
cross their arms over their chest or
when they drink, shake visibly.

Watch out for teenagers who dodge right
then left. Let their parents decide
how much and when. The point
is never to waste a drop, to catch that drop
before it falls into the secretary's starched collar.

And always wipe around the rim,
though it is gesture, though something intangible
still floats in the wine, enters
each version of bent, holy body.

# Last Day at the Frost Place

All sound tucked under glass.
All nature notched down, less eager
to tear apart the sky.

The sparrow who called me
Sam Peabody
(peabody peabody)
moves down the lane. My future
looks bad—always does—
but right now it's deep inside
the brush, like the crow
who scolds something
even deeper in.

Must be the world's aware
the time is past
for poem like a sweat bee,
the lily's twitch and flame
sweet law for my
acquiescent eye.

                They all
let up the pressure: clouds
in presentation over Echo
Lake, but rather heartlessly.
I'm free to go.

# Interim

She loved the subway caught between stations.
A butcher fanning himself with the sports section.
A child's chlorinated hair whorled in a tight nest.
She wanted that face-to-face with a stranger's
boredom, flat and unsmiling.

Or in the late afternoon, the pause
for delicious heat, draped over the city
like a cashmere glove. She eavesdropped,
tuned in housewives for their coping clichés:
*One day at a time. Live and let live—*

like those dream steering wheels
that float in your hands.

Once, she kissed a stranger's ironed sleeve
merely to be outside, to feel his scent replace her own.
With age, she thought, we know ourselves
better, *yes,* our lives rising
around us like a mirrored bowl. What she wanted

was a moment of *unknowing.*
She wanted to be a rose, pressed
between the pages of someone else's story.


# ERIN BELIEU

## Watching the Giraffes Run

> *If the world were only pain and logic
> who would want it?*
> —Mary Oliver

He might. The man next to me,
huge and concerned about his territory,
stands akimbo at the guardrail

challenging all comers to the view
with a pointed, auxiliary eye.
He has hard, red hands,

a General Dynamics T-shirt
rolled up at the sleeves,
and a three-year-old boy hanging

like a camera round his neck.
It is not difficult to imagine him
climbing over the fence

and down through the concrete ravine
which separates the logical from
the other, to picture him lassoing

the smallest giraffe, bending her down
like a wilted sunflower, crawling
on her back, as she buckles

and rears against his weight,
the pressure of his thighs squeezing into
her belly. Then, when she'd been broken,

ridden down to her knees, past the panic,
past rage, past her tight frightened
breathing, if then he stopped

to whisper in her soft ear,
what would he be saying?

# Erections

When first described imperfectly
by my shy mother, I tried to leap

from the moving
car. A response,

I suspect, of not
just terror (although

a kind of terror continues to play
its part), but also a mimetic gesture,

the expression equal
to a body's system of absurd

jokes and dirty stories.
With cockeyed breasts

peculiar as distant cousins,
and already the butt of the body's

frat-boy humor,
I'd begun to pack

a bag, would set off
soon for my separate

country. Now, sometimes,
I admire the surprised engineering:

how a man's body can rise,
squaring off with the weight

of gravity, single-minded,
exposed as the blind

in traffic. It's the body leaping
that I praise, vulnerable

in empty space.
It's mapping the empty

space; a man's life driving
down a foreign road.

# Tick

Remind me of a similar devotion;

how the head, buried
deeply in the brush

and gully of damp flesh,
becomes platonic
in its gratefulness,

a perfect worship.
This is why one body,
fastened to the forest

of another, swells.
This wild dependence

of the host on her guest.

## Georgic on Memory

Make your daily monument the Ego,
use a masochist's epistemology
of shame and dog-eared certainty
that others less exacting might forgo.

If memory's an elephant, then feed
the animal. Resist revision: the stand
of feral raspberry, contraband
fruit the crows stole, ferrying seed

for miles . . . No. It was a broken hedge,
not beautiful, sunlight tacking
its leafy gut in loose sutures. Lacking
imagination, you'll take the pledge

to remember—not the sexy, new
idea of history, each moment
swamped in legend, liable to judgment
and erosion; still, an appealing view,

to draft our lives, a series of vignettes
where endings could be substituted—
your father, unconvoluted
by desire, not grown bonsai in regret,

the bedroom of blue flowers left intact.
The room was nearly dark, the streetlight
a sentinel at the white curtain, its night
face implicated. Do not retract

this. Something did happen. You recall,
can feel a stumbling over wet ground,
the cave the needled branches made around
your body, the creature you couldn't console.

## Prayer for Men

I will not praise your body after sex
naked on the small, white bed

as prayer is sent to gods, and you,
thin-boned and sleeping,

vulnerable to my hands and mouth,
are too humane for ancient games.

If you had come a whirl of smoke, deified
exhausted ire, turned inside me

burning till my tongue learned flames,
then I might praise you.

If you had put on feathers and descended,
pulled me into sky or water, hung me

weightless, pinned inside your beating wing,
then I might praise you.

But you entered the way a man is made to
enter, asked my name, then waited

for an answer the way men do. It's praise
to watch you listen in your sleep, to fit

the curve your body questions; praise enough
to guard you until morning. Then gods will

lie down on mountaintops and dream their human
dreams of prayer, of women, of love.

## Another Poem for Mothers

*Mother, I'm trying*
*to write*
*a poem to you—*

which is how most
poems to mothers must
begin—or, *What I've wanted*

*to say, Mother* . . . but we
as children of mothers,
even when mothers ourselves,

cannot bear our poems
to them. Poems to
mothers make us feel

little again. How to describe
that world that mothers spin
and consume and trap

and love us in, that spreads
for years and men and miles?
Those particular hands that could

smooth anything: butter on bread,
cool sheets or weather. It's
the wonder of them, good or bad,

those mother-hands that pet
and shape and slap,
that sew you together

the pieces of a better house
or life in which you'll try
to live. Mother,

I've done no better
than the others, but for now,
here is your clever failure.

# The Small Sound of Quiet Animals

The night returns humid, sweating through
the damp curtains, then settles at the baseboards,
beginning the pool of evening.

The single expensive vase, its tulip face now
dark, tilts odd-angled on the desk, asks
for the smallest provocation (it's waited

all day to explode). You give it none.
Your cat is sleeping the shape of answers
into the only comfortable chair,

but let him sleep
because he dreams. His haunches shake.
See the smile of his bared teeth?

\*

The man you lived with leaves a note
Scotch-taped to the lampshade. *Gone to Minnesota.*
*Please feed my fish. Here's fifteen dollars . . .*

In bed, you smell his boots, leather and sweat
rising from the dark closet doorway.
You think of Blue Earth, Pemberton, Pipestone

and Mankato, his bike a white spot whistling
up the serpentine highway into Minnesota,
the fat, widowed farmers drinking anisette

in municipal bars. You think of their woman
and daughters, straight-backed, Nordic. How they
lie down like angels, Lutheran as the plains.

\*

Something bangs in the radiator, heavier
than heat, reminds you how all things
speak, how small sounds come even

from quiet animals. A dresser drawer closes
rooms away. Your Jehovah landlord with a key
to the place? The sisters who fight

over men a floor below? You don't fall
into sleep. No splash, no ripple
to disturb the surface. Kneel into the water,

watch the outline of your leg disappear,
then finger, forearm and elbow. Curl yourself
fetal on the empty bed. The shape of a fish.

## The Spring Burials

Violets growing through the asphalt mean
the usual of spring's predicament:

how, busy getting born, still wings and green
will falter, twist, misgrow their management

and die. Violets grow on one curled leg,
a slender prop obliviously crushed,

and newborn birds are falling from their eggs,
still feathered wet and hidden in the brush

when you walk by. They die in spite of us;
in shoebox nests and jelly jars supplied

with best intentions. Bring them in the house,
then fuss, arrange things, feed them. Occupy

yourself with worms and eyedroppers, sunlight
and potting earth. You'll bury them in days,

feel silly in your grief. And still you'll sit
a moment on the blacktop, study ways

to save an unimportant, pretty weed
or bird. You're still a fool—a fool to bend

so sentimentally and fool in deed,
assuming you know better. Spring is kind.

# Tereze Glück

## The Coast of Massachusetts

Some things you never stop thinking about. They get old right along with you. You keep going over them so you won't forget, so you'll get it right. All the while you know that the version you tell, and maybe the version you remember, is changing over the years. Still, some of the things you remember are as hard and stubborn as facts. These get to be your starting points, or the ones you come back to.

When I think about Richard, a man I used to be married to, I always come back to the same things. I come back to the way he paced. He was a mathematician and he paced all the time. His legs were so long I thought he would topple over. He did once, topple over, when he was a baby. When I was a year old, he said, I weighed forty pounds. The weight was all in my head. I couldn't stand up because my legs wouldn't support the weight of my head. Finally I stood up and walked but I toppled right over.
"Brains," I said.

He paced in the living room, a mathematician. He was explaining something about light. Something about photons. This thing about photons had a name. Bell's Inequality was its name. He explained it again and again. Light travels in its beam. Then you hold up a piece of cardboard. Ordinary cardboard would do—the usual thing. You block the light, is the point. Then you make a hole in the card. The light pours through the hole. Then you make a second hole. Now here is the thing. Here is the inequality. His voice rises with excitement. Listening to him I am excited too. It is all at my fingertips. Something is about to be made clear and my heart beats faster as if I am in love, or afraid. Now here is the thing, Richard says. The light makes bars. *The light makes bars!* It breaks into a row of short vertical bars; why should it?

He could not have hoped, could he, for a more rapt audience, a more intent listener. How did the photons know which hole to go through? Do you see? he asked. He had a voice so soft that often I could not hear him and had to say: what? what? But when he was excited his voice would become as shrill as a girl's. He paced just like a mathematician. He would light up a cigarette and pace. His legs were so thin, he was so thin. But his shoulders were broad. He said this was on account of rowing. Rowing takes more strength than any other sport, he said. You have to use the whole body. So although he was so thin that he looked as if he would topple over he was in fact quite strong.

"Do your geranium," I say. "Your geranium thing."

" 'Imitation of a geranium,' " he announces.

And he does it.

He is all arms and legs—there they go. The fact is he really does remind me of a geranium, the way geraniums get so spindly. You could love a man like that, who can do an imitation of a geranium, and does, does do it. What's more the man is a mathematician—imagine. Imagine a man who is a mathematician who does such a thing. The man is full of things and who would know it, you'd never know it.

Once he woke me in the middle of the night to tell me something about prime numbers. "Listen," he said, and then said this thing to me about prime numbers. I was so happy that he woke me. When I told this to people, they said—what? what?

When we moved into a new apartment, after our baby was born, we were unpacking and Richard said: Hang on, wait a minute. He went off and sat in the corner of the room with a calculator. I went on unpacking, unfolding newspaper from glasses, while Richard sat on the floor in the corner of the room, feverishly at work, his long legs stretched out in front of him. Newsprint rubbed off on my hands; I didn't mind.

After a while he finished his calculations and said: I knew it!

Knew what, I said.

Our telephone number is a prime number, he said.

Later when I told this story my friends said: you stood there unpacking while he figured out that the telephone number was a prime number?

But, I said, it wasn't that way at all.

There was a rainy afternoon when I looked out the window.

"What rain!" I said.

He was making something. Maybe it was a computer. He made a little black box once, that had switches and buttons. You turned a switch and a light went on. You pressed a button and the box buzzed. It was just a practice project, he said. He was getting ready for the big project. The big project was going to be a robot that carried drinks down from the summer house to the lake. He was working on the big project with a friend. He was in charge of the electronics and the friend was in charge of the mechanics. He had a laugh over this. The mechanics are really the harder part, he said.

Meanwhile he gave the black box to our baby. This black box was a puny thing but it went over pretty well and our baby played with it for a while, until it ended up somewhere at the back of a closet.

What he was making now looked a little like the inside of a computer. He wrapped colored wires around small bits of metal. I watched him for a while. "Do your geranium," I said.

"In a minute," he said.

I called to our little girl—she wasn't a baby anymore. "Come and see your father do his geranium."

She stood beside me and held my hand. Richard stood up. When he stood up he seemed to unfold himself, unravel. He bent over and hobbled like an old man. Our little girl laughed. He walked like an old man and held his hand out as if he held a cane.

" 'Portrait of a geranium,' " he said.

"Portrait of the mathematician as a young geranium," I said.

"Portrait of the mathematician as an old geranium," he said.

Before our little girl was born we went for drives every weekend and took photographs of wherever it was we went. We kept buying cameras until I thought we had one of every kind. We had the kind of large camera you set up on a tripod. We had an old camera especially designed for taking portraits. You used a black cloth and the picture looked upside down in the big viewfinder, but you got one hell of a portrait.

Richard used the camera with the tripod and photographed houses. I used the camera with the black cloth and photographed Richard.

Everywhere we went we took pictures. Then we'd lock ourselves into the bathroom and Richard would develop the pictures and I'd watch. We spent whole days locked up in our small bathroom, and I got to love the smell of the chemicals. That's how happy we were.

On one excursion, in the autumn, when Richard took hours to photograph a white house, I got him to do his geranium, and I photographed it. I still have the picture—of course I do; pictures are things that people hold on to.

Things that are in pictures are true as hard little facts. They are things you can hang your hat on—real things. But happiness you can invent. You imagine that you are happy. Later you remember yourself as having been happy, and the idea that you were happy just goes along with you in your life, as good as true.

In one version of the facts, I wanted a baby and he didn't. This is the kind of thing that can cause trouble between two people as anybody knows. In this version, I got the baby in a kind of bargain. Richard got himself a green Porsche with a convertible roof and I got pregnant. That was the bargain we made. Richard would say no but I know a bargain when I make one.

Maybe this is the usual story—how the baby needs things from you, and you don't go for long drives anymore on Saturday and Sunday afternoons and take your photographs. Instead you pace around the apartment which has grown too small for all of you, you pace and look out the window and attend to the baby, or maybe you sit in a chair and glower. As for me, I didn't tell the truth—about how I came to hate the weekends, and longed for the weekdays when I could go to the office and have some time to myself. I couldn't say for sure what Richard thought, or admitted, but I can say this—we got bad-tempered, both of us, we were no better than children, either of us.

Somewhere along the line I just started looking around. If you look around long enough you find something, and somewhere along the line I did. What I found wasn't much, but that's just in retrospect. What I found, at the time, was enough. You reach a point in your life when whatever you find is enough—enough to start things unraveling.

If you asked me I would say: everything was my fault. Although at other times I said everything was his fault.

You get to have your versions of things. The business about the bad weekends is one. I said, let's get a sitter and go have some fun. Don't be stupid, he said. That kind of thing goes on for a while and before you know it everything is over.

That's one version.

Other times what I said was, I ran away from home—*I* did it. In this version I remember how I lay on the couch with my hands behind my head, listening to an opera on the phonograph, dreaming of another man.

Sometimes I say that I fell in love with another man although when I say this I always add that I never really loved the other man but at the time I thought I did.

Whatever the version, some things stayed the same. An afternoon in September stayed the same. We are packing for the last weekend at the summer house. We are going to close up the house. I put a pile of clothes down on the bed—I remember this—and say, "Richard, I'm not happy." When I tell the story I always tell how of course I expected him to make up to me the way he always did. But instead he turned around and said, I'm not happy either.

We drove up to the summer house that morning, in the green Porsche that maybe he got in a bargain and maybe he didn't. I cried the whole way and wore dark glasses. Our little girl slept in the back seat. When I tell the story I always add: once a thing starts to unravel there is no stopping it.

We remained friends. We were pleased with ourselves on account of this. Richard came to visit often. Sometimes when he came to visit, I went out, but other times I stayed around and it was nothing unusual to fall into a conversation about this thing or that thing. Sometimes we went to dinner, or to the movies, the three of us, as if we were still the three of us together.

So it was not surprising, not altogether, to find the two of us alone in a car together, driving north. We were going to visit our daughter at summer camp; it was Visiting Weekend. It was a six-hour drive to the camp. Six hours is a long time to be alone with anybody, and six hours in a car is even longer. I remember how in our former life, we had most of our arguments in a car; it was the only place where he couldn't leave the room.

We didn't argue anymore—of course we didn't. But here we had this six hours looming ahead of us, and it seemed odd. I thought about it for days beforehand, and what it might be like, all those hours in the car together. I wasn't worried; just interested.

In fact it was easy, a simple thing. We had our things that we could talk about. We talked a little about our jobs, and then I asked a few questions about cosmology, to get the ball rolling, Heisenberg's Uncertainty Principle, Bell's Inequality, Schroedinger's Cat, the latest in quantum mechanics, that kind of thing. Richard had explained all these things to me many times before and each time, there seemed to be a moment when I thought I was getting it, catching on; but then months would go by and I would forget it all over again, and the next time we would find ourselves in one another's company, I would ask again, and Richard would explain again. It got to be one of our routines—comfortable and comforting.

We talked about those things, and another article I'd read, about fractals, they were called; it had to do with snowflakes and repetitions of patterns, and self-referencing patterns. Something about coastlines, for instance; how if you look at a portion of the coast of Massachusetts, and then look at an even smaller portion of that portion, they would look the same. I didn't understand it but like all of these matters it seemed to be larger than itself. I thought if I could have it explained to me I would see a glimmer of something not just about snowflakes and patterns and coastlines but about everything that happened to you in the world.

So we were comfortable, talking this way, listening to music. We pulled off the road for something to eat, somewhere in the middle of Connecticut. Richard said he knew a place. I expected one of those highway-type places, dim, with canned soups and coffee served in heavy stained white cups. But this place Richard knew wasn't like that at all. It was an old house, with a wooden floor, and uneven floorboards; the uneven floorboards made you believe you'd encountered a place with history—more history than you had yourself.

This was a formal sort of place, and we found ourselves being formal with one another, very polite, very correct. I found myself wishing I'd been this polite back when. We looked like anybody there—any two people just out for dinner together. Everything seemed very slow to me, and strange, as if time had been slowed down for a moment, and the air seemed clear and sharp. I felt like somebody who has his eyes wide open, and they feel cooler than they're used to—as if a cool breeze were blowing.

We spent the day with our daughter, at her summer camp, ushered from one activity to another. At one point our little girl turned to her friends and said, watch what my father can do, and instructed Richard, do your geranium! and he of course obliged. The children gazed at him in what seemed to be amazement, not knowing what to make of him.

But for me it seemed like that September day all over again, the one where I said, Richard I'm not happy, and he said, neither am I, and we drove up to our summer house. I suppose it was that long drive in the car that set off the memory; but since then, I have lived through that day many times, always bewildered, as these children are now.

# BRIAN KITELEY

## I Know Many Songs, But I Cannot Sing

The rare day-long rain fell on the Nile valley north of my wife's parents' country home. During the drive south from Cairo, my daughter Catherine asked me to explain the unusual phenomenon several times. It has rained hard twice in her lifetime. I told her that Europe got all this rain every winter, and because the Europeans were rich and thought they still owned the world, they tried to palm their excess precipitation off on us each year, declaring it part of the IMF package Egypt must accept if we expect to receive more loans. My daughter looked as if she were trying to squeeze this information into her brain. The rain ended in the peasant village a few dozen meters from my in-laws' gate. Their man Ramzi waited for us there, pointing to the clean line of clouds that stopped directly over our heads. Then Ramzi indicated the field of alfalfa to the north, where we could see hard wet rain still falling. "You see," I told my daughter, "the Europeans respect your grandfather. They leave his house dry." The sun was shining on the pool and on the grass in the backyard, slanting from the Libyan Desert like the hand of God. Rain had also fallen on the desert, leaving a great swath of pearl-shaped holes. Two officials from the IMF were listening to my father-in-law describe his plans for new middle-class housing in the desert. My daughter and I sat in deck chairs by the pool, patiently awaiting Grandpa's full attention. The four-year-old girl, always busy at something useful, picked pebbles out of a bowl of dried chickpeas. The IMF officials stood on the grass. My father-in-law watered both sand and lawn from a long twitching hose. We knew, even though we could not hear him, that George was insisting Egyptians could learn to love the desert if only their government built living, breathing communities there instead of sterile apartment blocks. The IMF stood with their arms crossed and their chins thrust out at the awful emptiness of the Sahara.

A few days after my wife threw me out the fourth or fifth time, her father George began to talk nonstop, mostly in a gentle whisper to himself, sometimes without pausing for breath. I had moved in with my in-laws as I always did. I came in very late one night from play rehearsal to find my mother-in-law Hanaa at the base of the round staircase in her nightgown, a candle in her hand, staring up at her husband's study. She described George's mania. I tried to laugh it off, saying we would have more cause to worry if he'd gone silent or if a normally silent man had become suddenly garrulous. She said, "You are absurdly optimistic, Gamal-Leon," sounding for that instant exactly like her daughter. She gave me a parting glance full of some emotional turmoil my shallow mind mistook for sexual longing. When I entered his study, George was talking quietly but dramatically to himself about a set of Nubian villages whose ingeniously energy-efficient architecture might have been a model for all of Egypt had George not stumbled on them a few days before Lake Nasser swallowed them forever—I'd heard the story many times. George appeared to conclude, saying, "Maupassant used to eat at the restaurant in the Eiffel Tower because it was the only place in Paris where he did not risk seeing the Eiffel Tower. You see why I'm talking as I do now?" Then as if to illustrate this point, he added, "In the desert, the temperature is always a great deal lower at night and that cold air remains near the ground during the day if you can keep it in shade. The old Arab towns hoarded this coolness in their narrow streets and alleys. But carve rule-straight boulevards through the old cities, and the wind sucks out the chill. You are left at the mercy of the blazing sun. I have done the same thing to my mind, despite my life's goal of preserving the old Arab ways. I built broad, straight boulevards, when I should have followed the winding path of my thoughts. I have failed, Gamal-Leon." George and I were sitting quietly, his head on my shoulder, when the doctor arrived with my wife.

Sleep was always the enemy when I was growing up. We lived in a noisy, crowded district of Cairo, where the neighbors' arguments were easier to solve than our own. The cafes my brothers and I frequented were open all night. When I was very young, I put my bedding on the wide windowsill to take notes on the Blue Nile coffeehouse. My eldest brother favored this haunt, where joy for life and love of coffee seemed one and the same thing. The nightly celebrations turned to mumbles and yawns only when the sun brushed the sky and the men in the cafe glared at the streaks of gray in their narrow strip of heaven. Ramadan was the happiest time of my year, even though we were Christian and fatherless. Everyone else in the city joined my war against sleep, at least while it was dark. Women and children also stayed up late then, parading through the streets in search of sweets and pancakes and ribbons of delicate dough spun off domes of red hot metal. My wife, years later, stubbornly slept through the night for the month after our baby was born. That first month coincided with Ramadan, and I would sit on the balcony with a small lantern, reading, writing, or taking notes on the neighbors' conversations at parties I could practically touch. The baby would make her tentative gurgles and talk to her thumb, and I would go inside to roll my still-sleeping wife onto her side. I would free her beautiful breasts and bring the baby to its target, both heart-warming affirmation of parenting and erotic torture. But my wife usually surfaced, irritated that her sleep was being sucked from her, angry with the neighbors for their pagan revelry until all hours, and furious with me for enjoying my insomnia. The introduction of American baby formula to our markets allowed my wife to sleep till morning. My father died one night when I was too young to remember. Except I do remember staying up very late with my brothers, enjoying what my young mind mistook for a happy party, finally falling asleep at dawn with the rosy sense that love was something you found only at the end of a long night of wakefulness.

One night before bed I was telling my daughter an old Armenian fairy tale, acting out several parts, and speaking in Armenian. I used props to turn me into different characters: her security blanket, for a mountain lion; the wire mesh waste basket, for the King. With my own Basque beret I became the court jester whose jokes and playlets no one wanted to hear anymore. Catherine, a sigh away from sleep, sat upright at this character. She stretched and, as she yawned, brought three fingers daintily down over her mouth, just as her mother did. "Daddy. You aren't supposed to be in this story. It happened a long time ago. How did you get into the story?" Then she curled up and drifted off to sleep. I continued to whisper the tale, entranced by the unraveling of my imagination. She began to snore, a signal she was feigning sleep and wanted me to leave. But I was debating whether to write this story down, sell it in America, get film rights. The problem was my Armenian tales did not translate well into English or Arabic. They lost their alpine grace and playfulness. I told them in Armenian because my Coptic Egyptian wife refused to learn the language. My daughter understood but did not speak it. I also used Armenian to turn the terrible arguments my wife and I had into funny stories. My pale defense for this practice: I was giving my daughter a leg up if, one day, she married a man as linguistically schizophrenic as myself. I whispered goodnight in French and left the room. A few steps out the door, I heard my daughter's reply, in the Armenian phrase that began all my bedtime stories to her: "I know many songs, but I cannot sing." I ran back to the doorway, but she was asleep. I could tell by her breathing, a delicate whistle, not the pretend snoring she had made earlier.

"*Ayza* some *badi*," she had a habit of saying around the age of two. *Ayza* is the feminine Egyptian colloquial for "I want." *Badi*, pronounced "body," is short for *zabadi*, "yoghurt." We thought this was adorable. She was mixing Arabic and English, but also making a play on words. She meant, early in the morning, that she wanted some yoghurt for breakfast. But she also meant that she wanted *somebody* to play with, some *body* to keep her warm, just a body. She repeated this performance dozens of mornings in a row until it was no longer funny, but it was always funny on its own terms. We made the mistake of mentioning it to Wael Barakat, our good friend, Catherine's godfather, and head of the Euro-American advertising agency in Cairo. Wael decided to use the three words for a television ad campaign, which he happened to be preparing for Nestle, who made the yoghurt rich Egyptians and expatriates were eating. Euro-American Advertising employed blonde Euro-American models to sing—dubbed in—catchy tunes that mixed Arabic and English, sometimes in the same word. My wife fought Wael like a Hollywood agent for the rights to this phrase, which she copyrighted under his nose the day we had the argument with him over it, by mailing off a postcard to ourselves with the sentence written on it, followed by the copyright symbol. There is no such fastidiousness about patented ideas in Egypt, but Wael loved to mimic all sorts of American behavior. We made 10,000 Egyptian pounds. By the time the commercial arrived on television, over a year later, Catherine was speaking in long complex sentences. When she saw the ad, she burst into tears. She said, "I was never that young, Baba. I feel very used." We were alarmed by the last word. We asked if she felt we had exploited her. She knew what "exploited" meant. "No, no, no," she said. "I am not that little girl anymore. She's been used up. She's all gone now. A long time ago, she was used up. I am very old now, you have no idea how old I am."

In a dream my daughter Catherine felt her mother pull one arm and say, "This child is as Egyptian as the sand under the Step Pyramid." Her daddy took the other arm, with a tug, and said, "But this limb feels as Armenian as Arslan, the mountain lion who ate only unbelievers." They held each arm firmly. They pulled. The noise of Catherine coming apart was surprisingly soft, a gentle pop. Now there were two Catherines. But one Catherine awoke hugging herself, very sad she was not twins. She got up and dressed all by herself. It was dark. As she walked down the hall to the dining room she realized her T-shirt was on backwards. Tears welled up in her eyes. She was a girl who liked things in their proper place and threw a fit at the merest hint of chaos. But the feeling of the shirt on backwards was so like being pulled apart that the tears soon dried. The sun was beginning to wake, but like Catherine it had sleep in its eyes, a fog that obscured even the balcony of the building next door, where the big American men laughed too loud and did not clean the dust. Catherine found her parents in the kitchen at the corner of the big metal table Cook chopped chickens on. My wife and I sat on tall stools. We looked funny there, shoulders scrunched up, eyes practically droozed asleep, holding hands! An unschooled observer might assume we were happy ever after. But Catherine knew we were simply too tired to argue anymore about which school to send her to: the German language school (my choice) or the Arabic (my wife's). Catherine left the doorway. It is hard to say whether my wife or I actually saw her. My balcony garden beckoned, my exotic African plants. Catherine stood in the swirl of smells. Deh-deh, our maid, would not arrive for another hour, too long. A plant spoke to her: "Eat me."

"But what if you are poison?" she said.

"You read *Alice in Wonderland* all by yourself and you're only four years old," said the plant. "You know how the story turns out."

We live next door to an American oil exploration company. I sit out on my balcony overlooking the Nile in the morning before the sun rises too high and sip my wife's exquisite Turkish coffee and listen to the general manager of the oil company argue with his partner. I watch them arrive every morning in identical Jeep Cherokees. They live a few blocks from each other in the same suburb, but it never occurs to them to ride together in one vehicle. Both are huge men in the shoulders with skinny legs. One is from Denver, the other from Fort Worth. Denver and Fort Worth disagree over just about everything, but most often about how to treat Egyptians, both at the office and in the field. Denver is no Lawrence of Arabia, but he does speak kindly to his staff and has even made a friend of his chief surveyor, Gaber, a master at computers and a genius at keeping the machines alive despite the fickle currents of Egyptian electricity. Fort Worth calls Egyptians "wops" behind their backs. He rails against their circular thinking and their endless coffee breaks. But he is afraid to be in the building alone with them. One morning Fort Worth was on the phone to Denver, who was home with food poisoning. I was less than five feet from Denver's desk, which Fort Worth appropriates whenever his partner is absent, feeling maybe he is safer in the kinder man's office. Denver also has a balcony, dusty from disuse. It is an easy crawl from my balcony. Our buildings are side by side facing the

Nile. Fort Worth had been alone in the office two hours that day, calling Denver every few minutes with increasingly pathetic and inconsequential questions. Denver hung up on him the last time, but I could tell—don't ask how—Fort Worth kept talking to the dead line. He was confiding to the dead line that the key to prophylaxis in Egypt is to drink an American beer with the juice of one lemon before every meal, even breakfast. I slipped onto his balcony and studied him through the blinds. He had painted half of the black telephone with Wite-Out, the now obsolete correcting fluid. The computer screen at his elbow was flashing the words, NO END IF.

Kimball Johnson of Fort Worth, Texas, was at his office next door to our apartment very early that morning because of an overnight flight from Kuwait. I reconstruct all this from a few laconic sentences he told me. Instead of going home to Ma'adi—Johnson was too keyed up to sleep—he went directly to Zamalek. Then, as he was spreading out a map of a south Sinai oil field, the odor of ambergris wafted in through the window. Johnson does not have an acute sense of smell. That's his wife Leslee's department. In her airtight BMW she can detect a cigarette smoker in the car ahead of them at sixty miles an hour. This is why the scent upset Kimball Johnson: The woman next to him on the plane from Kuwait had shown him a nugget of ambergris during a forgettable conversation. This lump of whale intestinal matter set something off deep in Johnson. Before smelling it, he had been only partly involved in the conversation with the bookseller from London (his mind was also comparing equipment replacement costs using Bombay versus Piraeus suppliers). The instant after a whiff of this powerful, sweet, sexy, rancid odor—like Play-Doh—his attention focused completely on his neighbor. She was not all that pretty. She had a large horsey face, her skin wasn't good, hair thin and wispy, hips too wide for Johnson's taste, which ran, in his private and pathetic fantasies to very young teenage girls. But with an intensity he'd never before experienced—he had not once in his marriage even considered cheating on Leslee—he found himself wounded to the quick by this British woman's beauty and charm and indirectness. Nothing happened. They parted with a tepid handshake, without exchanging names. Then from his partner's office, he smelled the musky ambergris again. Something told him to act. He had never been on the balcony before. For a moment a dust storm on the horizon distracted him. Somewhere nearby was what sounded like a creaking shutter, but there was no wind. Finally he spied on the floor of the balcony next door the twisted, convulsing body of my daughter, vomiting but otherwise strangely quiet. Johnson bounded across the terrifying abyss of twelve floors and scooped up the little girl, grabbed the half-eaten leaf beside her, and thundered into the many-roomed apartment looking for us. His big jeep took the three of us to the American hospital. His connections and intimidating American presence sped us past the bureaucracy of the front desk into the emergency room. Then it was as if it had never happened. My wife and Catherine were asleep in the hospital room, and Kimball Johnson was asking me why he might have smelled ambergris on my daughter. Her clothes were draped over my arm. I lifted her T-shirt, and my little blue plastic container of ambergris fell to the floor. "She must have nicked it from my bathroom this morning," I said. "I used some after shaving last night before we went to a party." Her little body crushed the container when she fell. Opened even a crack, the scent fills the air. Humans can smell one millionth of a part a dozen yards away because it so closely resembles human pheromones. Kimball Johnson was crying. In a hoarse whisper, he said, "You will surely despise me, but I might have left her laying there, had her skirt not shimmied up her bottom when she fell. She was not wearing any undergarments. I would be lying, sir, if I said I jumped onto your balcony only to save her life."

# LAURE-ANNE BOSSELAAR

## Amen

*for Carol Houck Smith*

I'm not allowed to do it, so I hide behind a curtain,
take a last breath through my mouth, slip my thumb
in the space where my front teeth are missing, find
the vacuum between palate and tongue, and suck.
Slowly at first, then in cadence with the panic
in my chest. My parents are packing again, mother
hastily stuffed my suitcase last night: it's already
downstairs. They are leaving on a big boat, I'll
stay on a farm, somewhere in Flanders.

After a month, I get used to living there, with the men,
the woman, the branch whipping the roof. I spend
my days in the hollowed trunk of a willow, watching
Percherons lash at flies with tails thick and swishing
like mother's shawls. One day, the farmer's wife
wakes me before dawn. The black and white cow

had stillborns during the night. She is hemorrhaging,
they must slaughter her before she dies. I must help.
I run barefoot to the barn.

The air swarms with flies, bare-chested men swear
in the dark. One of them hands me a wooden pail,
orders me to empty it in the ditch. It's full with a warm,
black liquid. I run, breathing the stench of moans
and death, pail heavy, warm stuff sloshing and splashing.
I throw it in the ditch, run back; they give me
another one, I hurry to the ditch again.
I want to throw up, but don't—I'm needed—
I'm almost happy.

Day lifts. The cow is butchered. Men carry huge cuts
from the barn to the farmhouse. One of them hands me
something fleshy and gray, I hold it to my chest: finger-like
things stick out of it. It's the udder. I've never seen one
so near before. I go to the willow, hold the udder in my lap.
It's not cold yet, it's not dead. I try to remember my mother
when she's warm, when she's there. I brush my cheek
against the udder, my lips find a nipple, I suck it in,
slowly at first, then find the cadence, the cadence . . .

When I bring the udder to the woman,
she throws it in a basin, adds onions and turnips,
and puts it on the stove. All afternoon I help her
wash the men's clothes in the stone sink;
she sings when she hangs my nightdress on the line.
At night, when she lifts the udder from the basin,
it has shrunk. She draws a cross on it with her knife
to bless it, slices it, puts the slices to fry.
They curl upwards in the sizzling suet.

I watch her patient face, the men's strong hands
as they hold out their plates. I'm hungry, tired,
sucking my thumb. The farmer stoops to stroke
my cheek, his nails are framed with blood.
He pours dark beer on his slice, chooses
the biggest turnip and hands me his plate. My heart
aches with something new, it's terrible, soothing,
I want to feel this forever. At Grace, his hand is a crown
on my hair. He nods at me when he says "Amen."

# The Radiator

Winters in the Ardennes were a monochrome
of brown and gray, as were the huge
wrought iron radiators of the monastery.
I believed the banging North winds came
to die in those pipes. I was eight then,
ugly, awkward and shy.

Nuns slid along granite halls, hands in black
tunnels of serge. Soon, dawn cast its light
through the stained-glass of the chancel.
I longed for that moment, when the hyacinth cape
of the Virgin bloomed, and the cheeks
of Jesus blushed as from a sinful dream.

My uniform itched. Knitted socks stopped
an inch under the knee, flannel skirts
half an inch above. My thighs were chapped
from rubbing on benches and stiff sheets.
At 5:45, we waited at the Chapel doors,
shivering in rows of three.

I was cold, always cold during those endless
Catholic winters. Mother Marguerite was late
that day and the radiator banged next to me.
I lifted my skirt, jumped, and straddled it—
raw thighs against lukewarm metal.
Annabelle pointed: "I'll tell on you!"

Judith whispered: "You'll be punished!"
The door opened—I froze. Like a mad
magpie, Mother Marguerite's cornet
flapped in my face: "Get off there!
*Immediately!*" she croaked. "Forgive me,
Mother Marguerite, but . . . why?"

Her knotted fingers were ice on my wrist.
"It gives *ideas!*" she said. I didn't look
at the virgin's cape that day, or at Jesus blushing.
I couldn't figure out what Mother Marguerite
meant. Years later, in the back of an old Peugeot,
I understood: it was hard, forbidden, warm.

# The Hour Between Dog and Wolf

> "Entre chien et Loup": *time at dusk,*
> *when a wolf can be mistaken for a dog.*
> —Dictionnaire Larousse

*I. The Good Ogre's Beard*

      Home from the nuns once a month, I run
to his shack on the Wool Canal, climb
his belly to bury my face in the stir and curls
of his beard. Sun-bleached seaweed on his chest,
it purls, then stops by the slip in his vest
where he keeps his watch tied to a button
with string. On the left side of his head,
the funnel-shaped gash of a German bullet.
      "That Kraut's blood still shines on my bayonet"
he smiles. I sit on his lap, head warm
between forearms, watch his old fingers crochet
eel nets with green waxed flax, bob on his belly—
a small summer wave, set free on the wheezing
tides of his breath. In every knot he makes
I slip a wish: God, save me from my family, give me
to him, may he live for ever and ever, Amen.

*II. Herman the Bastard*

      He died alone, Herman the Bastard, in Bruges,
during the long winter of '62, felled and frozen
next to his empty rabbit pen. I never learned
whose bastard he was, his name taboo in our family.
He read banned books, was an atheist, and spoke
to Jews: a sinner, father said. But I
      escape to his shack on the Wool Canal,
while my family played canasta, their claret
staining the tablecloth. I run to Herman,
waiting—huge—by a green enameled stove,
drinking beer, obese with stories and life.
"*Ach ja,* child, come, come" he says,
pointing his finger to the ceiling, calling out
ghosts from the mossy tiles of Bruges.
Parading in his stories as in Holy Processions
they enter the shack: the silk-clad Dukes of Burgundy,

the pompous bishops of Spain, Rubens'
peach-hipped women and Emperor Charlemagne.
Bruegel guilds the air with country fairs and wine;
newlyweds wave their blood-stained sheets
from somber windows at dawn. Suddenly,
swords clang, heads roll, it's St. Bartholomew's day,
in the guts of steaming canals, Huguenot bodies
thump against barges filled with linen and lace.
"*Ach ja,* child," he says, "Humanity!"

### III. Feeding the Rabbits

       He wraps his scarf around my neck: "It's time
to feed the rabbits, come." His rabbits
rustle in the straw, the black male chortles,
the gray one scratches the trellis. We kneel
in his narrow vegetable patch, peel leaves
from cabbage, pull carrots, rutabaga, leeks,
both making believe we're not waiting
for the moment I long for, the one I fear the best.
       When the church bells ring, it happens at last:
like a mad, panicked dog, Herman races
through the garden, yelping "No, no . . .
NOO!" punches the air with his fists,
crashes into the rabbit pen: they squeal,
I shriek, he grabs blindly, finds me,
covers my ears with his eel smelling hands:
"The bells are howling, run, run! The catholic
       wolves are hungry again!" He picks me up,
stumbles inside, slams the latch and collapses
into his chair, swearing at the bells, hiding
my head under his beard.
       Later, as we eat raw herring
and bread dripped in beer, Herman shakes
his finger at me: "Remember, child:
don't listen to church bells—that howling
will deafen your soul!"

### IV. The Hour Between Dog and Wolf

       The roofs of Wool Row are charcoal with dusk:
"*Ach* child, look," he says, "it's almost the hour
between dog and wolf: go now, go."

I pull away from his belly, the soft scrolls
of his beard, wave at him hunched
on the threshold of his shack, wave again
before turning the corner, but he looks
away, afraid he'll call me back, afraid
I'll stay. So I run through Bruges,
through dusk and sorrow rising from canals
like black mantillas and when—
from the darkest side of the sky—the vesper bells
        howl: I don't listen, I don't listen.

## Hôtel des Touristes

She had nothing to fire her heart, he had a little
house in the suburbs, so she married him, and tried
to be fond of him. She quietly gave him her days,
the deceptive moans of her nights and raised
his children, one by one, forgetting they were his, also.
Every Sunday she visited her mother
who rented chairs in the Parc du Luxembourg.
She never missed a day in the leather shop,
making men's belts of calf: punch six holes,
sew the buckle, beeswax shine, control sticker three.

It happened around seven one morning in May,
on the way to work. A North-African man
sat next to her in the bus and put his hand
on her thigh. She didn't say a word but felt
as if a sparrow fluttered in her breast.
She got down with him before her stop,
waited on the sidewalk while he paid for a room
at the *Hôtel des Touristes*. There were lilies and leaves
on the walls and ceiling of room fifteen.
She stared at them when he unbuttoned her blouse.

His sweet smell, his dark and grainy skin
reminded her of calf. She touched it gently,
first with the tip of her fingers, then stroked him
with the back of her hand, then the palm, and for hours
begged: *encore, encore, merci*. Once, she cried: *Mon amour!*
The voice startled her, she had never heard it
so loud. It was dark when they came out.

That winter, in bed, her husband smiled, said she bettered
with age. At Christmas, she gave him a book about Morocco
and bought herself a nightdress of black and red silk.

# From My Window, I See Mountains

The morgue man pulls my father out of wall C:
the drawer so heavy he must brace his foot
against another one to pull it open. It jams
half-way, this is how far it will go: one half
available for viewing, the other no.

A voice cries out in the anteroom, then turns
into a wail so unbearable the morgue man leaves.
I'm alone with my father again. This time, I
lift the sheet further than allowed, and look.
This time, it is he who is frozen. And I see his

rage, down there in the dark—like a fist crammed
between his legs. I touch his hands, the huge
Dutch hands that almost killed me, almost killed
my daughter, but once—on a shore in The Hague—
built me a sand castle, the morning after

his mother's funeral. It took him all day,
the deepest terror I remember, watching him
build that castle with the odd tenderness of brutes,
stroking the sand with weightless hands while I
sat at a distance, now knowing what to think,

what to do, Dutch rain sprinkling the sands
like a blessing. When the castle was done, he raised
moats around it, and mountains circling them,
while dusk wrapped us in its cerements, then night.
Not a word was uttered, even when we climbed the dunes

back to his mother's house, where I watched him
rock her wooden shoes in his lap, a hand in each
battered thing, the kitchen stove sighing.
After I buried him next to her, I flew back to this new
country, to this house surrounded by mountains,

with mountains around them. Some days, they seem
so quiet, so immutable I think: shock, fissure, fault;
I think: chasm, quake, wave. But I pray: plant me here
a while longer, plant this in me deep: nothing's perpetual,
eternity only a wood—kind as consolation, but as brief.

# Unable to Find the Right Way

Unable to find the right way to get out of bed
we watch the shades cut dawn
into thin slices, waver awhile, shoulder
to shoulder, then join, lazy.

But love, let's leave this room now: it's given us
all it can, let's go—it's Sunday—have breakfast
out, find a table for two: two eggs, two toast,
two coffees—black. No, nothing plain:

*latte*. We'll read the paper, the story
of a man who rescued the only thing
he wanted from the rubble of his collapsed shack:
his cat—and be moved by it, and like that;

or play hangman on our paper napkins,
find easy words—no double-meanings—day,
night, rivers . . . then send the game
to its fate, crumpled on our empty plates.

Let's step inside a church, sit through a wedding,
a christening, a mass for the dead, but leave before
the last amen. We'll take the long way home,
make plans for summer—winter even.

# The Cellar

I want my father to stop sending me down there
to fetch his daily gin, and potatoes for supper.
But there's no saying no to him, and no more places
to hide: he's found them all. Outside,
by the kitchen window, the cellar's rusted door
stains my hands as I yank it open, scraping

a branch that keeps on whipping back—
and grabbing me like he does.
Six stairs stop by a second door, with a hasp
and a slit between two thick planks. I press my face to it,
whisper to the bottles and potatoes:
"Go away, I'm coming!" But how can they?
We're all prisoners in this big brick house in Antwerp,
and damned: I'm the *Kapo:* I have no choice,
it's them or me. I kneel in the cellar, pray
to St. Anthony: "Guide my hand toward the sick
and dying, don't let me separate families,
don't let me kill a child . . ." I inch toward the shelves,
shut my eyes—reach. Sometimes I think I hear
a moan, a sob, a sigh, but sometimes it's a child's wail
so exactly like mine I think it comes out of me.
So I quickly put the thing back—forgive me, forgive me.
The worst are the potatoes. I know exactly
where they lived before, rooted deep
in the wild, salted Polders, where lapwings
titter between cattails and winds,
and rows of loam run beyond the horizon.
And here they are now, uprooted, cluttered in crates,
pale arms groping for a wedge of light from the door's slit . . .

But then, from up there, comes father's call: weary,
irked, the same every time, with the same pitch
and threat after the last consonant in my name.
Deaf with terror, I grab his gin, a few potatoes,
run out, slam the door, slap the hasp,
holding my offerings to father as far as I can
from my body, throwing them on the Formica
in the escape to my room, where I stand panting,
palms pounding my ears so as not to hear
yet another cry for mercy.


# The Feather at Breendonck

       I am praying again, God—pale God—
here, between white sky and snow, by the larch
I planted last spring, with one branch
broken at the elbow. I pick it up, wave winter

away, I do things like that, call the bluebirds
back, throwing yarn and straw in the meadow,
and they do come, so terribly blue, their strangled *teoo-teoo*
echoing my prayer, *Dieu, Dieu*—

    the same *Dieu* who stained
the feather I found in the barbed fields
of the Breendonck Concentration Camp
near Antwerp in 1952. My father tried to slap it
out of my hand: "It's filthy," but I held on to it—
I knew it was an angel's. "They only killed
a few Jews here," he said, "two, three thousand, maybe."
So I wave their angels away with my feather,

    away from my father, away from the terribly
blue skies over the Breendonck Canal, where barges
loaded bricks for Antwerp, where my father
loaded ships for Rotterdam, Bremerhaven
and Hamburg—as Antwerp grew, and the port
expanded, and his business flourished,
and all the while he kept repeating:
    "That's <u>all</u> we needed: a good war . . ."

# The Vase

    For years, in the old house, it stood
amid books and in the way. It's in the way
again—now on my desk—stopping my gaze
between the page and a daydream.
    I love that. Love the naive
landscape on its belly: trees, meadows, mountains,
a green hollow where a river sings, and lingering
mackerel skies.
    Then there's that tiny silhouette by the water:—
I call it "Art" for Arthur Rimbaud—fishing the same
bend day after day, under the tallest tree,
it's crown cresting up the vase's neck.
    I call him Art, although no one called him
that, not his sister, nor Verlaine, or even his mother
who spat out each letter in his name, using
the formal "vous" instead of "tu."
    But oh, behind the closed shutters

of his musty room, what "tu's" he whispered
to the illustrated pages of magazines,
lavish with Spanish women and laughing Italians!
      But my Art's past those moist offerings;
he's turned his back to the world,
fishing without bait on a vase that stops
my gaze when it attempts to escape.
      Some days, when torpid clouds languish
outside my window as they did in Charleville,
he struggles to his feet, cuts the string, and throws
the carp back to the stream,
      a hook deep in its gill.


# KENNETH ZAMORA DAMACION

## The False Angel

Father, before you moved out into the night
towards the playhouse you patched together
from scraps of wood and sheet rock,
roofed with tarpaper, you paused at the back door
and waited for the kisses from your grandchildren
on your stubbled cheeks. You spent weeks
at the migrant camps picking pears or apricots,
or cutting asparagus with your long-handled spade.
Alone on a dark porch after work
did you close your eyes and conjure up our faces,
did your sore body ache for us?

What gifts do we have for one another?
That playhouse was ours, you took it back
just as you took back your speech, your presence.
Though on winter days when you had no work
you'd drive us to the beach and stoke the driftwood,
the gray smoke swirling up to the gray sky.
Evenings, I'd stand before the window
of my darkened bedroom and talk to the darkened

shed where you slept and imagine what words
you might have said and might they be words
of comfort? The electrical cord you strung
form the house to the shed swung in the night wind,
like an umbilical cord, like a lifeline flung out to a raft.

    \*

Dirty old man, new angel,
I know you were floating above the house
in your newly acquired omniscience,
watching as my wife and I had sex
in my childhood bed while the others
sat around the kitchen table
grieving your death.
You fooled others that day,
superstitious friends from the old country—
votive candles surrounded food you were to eat,
coffee was placed at the space on the bench
where you always sat.

You came back in a dream,
forced back the heavy block of tombstone
and stood by the iron gates of the cemetery.
The plastic flowers remained undisturbed.
The dark trees remained still
though there was wind.
You wore a black suit, black shoes,
a white shirt forever starched and pressed.

Each day I mimic you in life,
climbing the stairs from one floor to the next,
one world to the next,
stepping around the sunlight
on the carpeted floor,
yielding to the gray boundaries,
and mumbling that I'm not ready yet,
who would be dying to see me return?

    \*

Late evening in spring,
my children are playing in the front yard
after dinner and before their bath.
    *You will die soon.*

I know it as I listen to my year-old daughter,
know it as she is walking
over the threadbare lawn
to chide and wag her finger at the baby roses.
    *You will die soon.*
I know it as I listen to my wife's voice,
still with the same youthfulness heard long ago.
In the back of the house,
I'm brooding over poems as if they were epitaphs,
wondering have I said all I wanted to say,
should I have jotted down my love
of the gray clouds floating overhead a moment ago?
    *You will die soon,*
I will breathe deeply the smell of my children's
wet clean bodies as if to breathe
for the first time their sweet smell—
    *You will die soon—*
to throw off
the embalming, encroaching sweetness
of oils and spices, in the urns you carry.


# Hieroglyphics

   *for Amy Thomas*

The angular sharpness of light and shadow
        hurting our eyes;
scorching our skin, blue sky, sun.
Too much of the physical world,
    then a comet trails across the night sky
bestowing us with wonder. My friend is incredulous
    this evening, to how people continue.
She leans against me as we sit on the couch,
my right arm across her shoulders in comfort,
    and she says now she understands
the cave I crawled into after my divorce,
        the shuttered curtains.
    Her husband had died.
        Her voice lately is all whispers.
Her message to me—
    *You know what to do,*
—was to live for our children
    in their ever changing hieroglyphics, and our own.

Has she had the dreams where the dead return. . . .
His death was once.
       Her thousand deaths will be many
as the days and nights continue.

          Even the dead must want a reprieve.
Ask my father whose cheap headstone gets rustier
       with color each year.
The asparagus spears he had once cut in late winter
       he now pushes up to the living.
Ask my young cousin, whose body was left to
       decay in a lake in Northern Carolina.
I remember the large walnut tree
       cradling her when we were young.

Even the living want a reprieve from their deaths,
and the life they thought had a semblance of permanence.

Ask me, sometime, as I watch
       the evening dusk slant up the hill,
the willow's branches across the street cascading down
like the hair of a sad woman,
       and the pines that spear towards the sky wanting
to pierce something, someone.


## My Mother's Life

In steerage, head hanging limp over the railing,
sea sick and morning sick, gulping salt air
between dry heaves, you saw
the fishermen in the port of Oahu,
and craved your mother's fish stew.
Throughout my life, you flaunted your father's
banana plantation and rice fields in The Philippines,
the idle walks in naked feet with your girlfriends.

You bore seven children.
Your knees were darkened brown with calluses
from picking plums off the hard earth.
Was it your daydreaming of a younger life,
or your sickness that made you feel also

the switch that my father tore from a tree
when we worked too slow.
In exacting your frustrations
you too turned on us—my sisters
knelt on kernels of hard rice, the washtub
an altar where they prayed for your forgiveness.
I felt the last of the telephone cord.

We saw you leave one morning in the rain,
Father piled us into the tan Ford coupe,
and drove slowly beside you, pleading
in a language we could not understand.
We sat in the backseat, well-behaved, confused.

Your husband is dead now.
Things resurface.
I still have the urge to remind you
of what you did, waiting for any hints
of recognition and remorse.
The man who loves you now
makes you look coquettish
as he turns you around the dance floor,
and I almost want to forgive you.

# Gone

My daughters and I have a game,
our lips touching each others'
         softly like flower petals,
then we puff, as if into a mouthpiece of a trumpet,
      blow kiss we call it.

In my dream, Chet Baker swan dives from a balcony,
      cleaves his passage through the Amsterdam air,
while prostitutes preen in the show windows
in their undergarments,
      bathed by the pink and red spotlights
before the men gazing at them on the sidewalk.

Perpetuating youth, years ago, against a window
his publicist posed him shirtless,

    while the gaze of a faceless woman
            adored him like a pompadoured Greek god,
a wingless Gabriel,

              and the way he bent a note on his horn,
or shaped the tone of his voice to exact
                melancholic decrescendo
    made me love him too.
In my dream, Chet Baker swan dives from a balcony
and that pleasure of knocking out his front teeth
        should have been mine,
rather than the dealer he owed money to.

                      In my dream
where Chet Baker swan dives from a balcony,
he doesn't owe me a thing,
    but I'm still living, bad note after bad note.

## Last Note Between Heaven and Hell

    *for Andrea Young*

> *The artist has to find something within himself that's universal and which he can put into terms that are communicable to other people. The magic of it is that art can communicate this to a person without his realizing it. Enrichment, that's the function of music.*
>     —Bill Evans

How could Bill Evans's sax player not notice
the last album of his mentor?
    The playing was agile and eloquent,
his hands climbed the ladder of the night sky to the stars.
    On the balcony, I feel
we are alone and we are not.

What if the joy is to lie beside an angel,
        her wings trembling like a frightened bird,
and startled by our humanness and vulnerability,
    the large wings spread open, unlocking our grasp.

Over the phone you complain
    you cannot see the stars as you could

in your West Virginia. I spin a record on the turntable.
                  Connected like two lonely stars
flirting in the night sky,
      I try to listen to your breathing.

           Evans shot heroin
between his fingers because the veins in his arms
were bruised and mottled, you could have drawn a line
from one to another to show constellations of despair.
And what sadness is conveyed by the bassist
or the drummer stroking the snare gently with his brushes,
as they coaxed their friend to live
      or eased him towards his dying?

"Suicide is Painless," "We Will Meet Again,"
      and "You Must Believe In Spring."
Liver bad. His habit of bowing his head
close to the keyboard, listening introspectively
      as he played, wanting to talk to his dead
           brother Harry again,
his feet modulating sound, space
      and thought on the foot pedals.
    I think of you and how someday you'll return
to West Virginia.
           We are alone and we're not.
I'll think of you and how your mouth turned sourly
then sadly when you said the world
      was too cruel for artists.
    Their frailty becomes our music.

I know how I'll exit out:
      the music of Monk, and Coltrane,
maybe Armstrong's "St. James Infirmary"
playing as mirror and a reminder
that the moon bears down upon us,
that we want to lie beside angels,
that we want to be fixed among the stars.
    But the coda
is a shimmering cymbal stricken by the brushes
of the drummer,
and a bassist plucking his instrument
as if it were his own heart, and a pianist
    playing chords and melody

> one last time between Heaven and Hell,
the last note lingering still
> > around the piano bench.

# Forgive Me

Your feet and ankles are like a young girl's.
Forgive me, mother,
> for hiding under your bed after your bath.
Forgive me for stealing the silver coins
> for reeds you could not afford for my school clarinet,
> > for having bought cigarettes from the vending machine.
I waited until you were outside
> hanging wash on the clothesline,
your black purse yawns open for my fingers,

> I wait on the hard bench
of St. Joseph of the Workman, for you to take me home—
> blood and a broken nose,
Blindsided by a girl running around the corner.
Authority files past,
> but no parent is at the door.
Black eyes swollen
> I wait and wait some more.

I'm only ten.

I begin to understand that the world
> is full of hurt and sadness,
it pours gold through the glass panes.
> No one comes.
I ride
> the school bus home.

Forgive me for the scorched circles
> in the high summer grass I lit with a match.
Forgive me for the radio I tried to fix.

I forgive you the names you called me.
I forgive you for the stories told
> of your father's banana plantation in a land far away,
of an aristocracy of mestizos with aquiline noses.

My nose is broad and ugly,
> not even the clothespin would pinch it straight.
I half believed in you because you're sweating
> beneath a hot summer sun picking plums,
your knees are calloused and black.

# SHARON DOLIN

## Jacob After Fording the Jabbok

All night long I
wrestled with an angel—his face
obscured by hair the color
of light—arms, strong thin
swords      we tumbled
on the road as two animals
in the heat of spring—we could not be
parted—bless me, I said—and he touched
my thigh—the hollow of my thigh
and my desires were parted: the upper
from the lower—as in my dream
of angels going up and coming down—
I strove to master desire with
force and I was mastered
by his blessing—as a woman
by the strength of her loving foe—
as a man by the hollow
that divides him from himself.

## The Domestic Fascist

Anger still rises against you
for the time my father

waited, good-humored, downstairs
denied entry

he came, bearing gifts, oblivious
to the engines of hatred churning
above.

Witless I ran up and down—like
messengers passing between ghetto
and death chaperones and compromising
everything.

You would not listen    I brought up
a photo of your mother to intercede
but you were on the bed, paralyzed

by your anger, by your lies, by
the guilt over the Jewish women whose
hairs you had parted.

Nothing breeds hatred like intimacy. You
demanded I soothe you, rub your temples.

When you broke the windows of our house
I had to live within jagged spires

praying you would turn human again. *That*
was the fatal mistake: when kindness goes
it can never be imported.    So you loved

music, teared your face over quartets
of Jewish musicians
while I blundered through the house
of your rage, begging for

a reprieve
and a kiss to call me human.

## If My Mother

were not an emaciated bird
who stands shorn of everything
but her pocketbook
she dangles—empty
save for her lipstick and pounds of change—

the sac worn outside
like the one in which I curled, slept, sucked
my thumb—if there weren't so little left of her
barely keeping herself erect—how could she
ever keep anyone—herself—warm again—

if my mother were not a flamingo that we leave in
the hospital lobby—half-terrified
that her bed—so close to the other patients'
coats—might threaten her—my mother,
who has fought her visions for 45 years
and received no medal—
watched her husband wrench away out of disgust
and grief—if her newest children were not wires
she sees everywhere—sparks
of her life escaping to endanger her . . .

then I could not be brave—
become like
my sister—unshaken who holds me in
the bathroom of some forsaken diner
in New Jersey—after my mother has
cursed the meal, everything, even the rice pudding: *slop,
real slop*—and we have to laugh
at how right she is—
as she gets up
and hobbles out of the diner
to the parking lot—
not knowing where we are taking her
wounded by all the people who
might kill her

except for me and my sister
who glide her
to the hospital emergency
*just let me put on my lipstick*
refusing my compact mirror—an expert
against a parked car's reflecting glass—she
takes up the pink stick and traces—her better
lips—the ones she will purse and hold and
question me with
when she goes to sign herself in—
waiting for me to nod, *yes, it's okay, you can sign*

*no one will keep you here forever—no one will
shock you again—no wires—no one
will do that to you again.*

# The Bear

The bear was there
he was going to help me eat
some meat
but when he'd burrowed his snout
and sniffed me out—
my crotch, my arm—
and held my skin between his teeth,
I thought,
better send him away
and cried out.

Then, at the cemetery party
an ordinary family gathering
I was kneeling over the graves near the headstones
with my sister
my grandmother raving with slashed
earlobes her face deep red
until the mask got torn
away—shredded off into my mother's face
composed and calm: there she was
and I held her hand—held her
soft hand and thought how I'd been missing her
so this was where she'd gone
"life . . . death" I thought to tell
her how all we know is this,
but said nothing, assuming she already knew
and just held on
gazing into the serenity
she'd become.

# The Visit

There will always be this place
inside
where I feel her absence

where I feel the echo of her lost voice—
the one she would have used to call me
back from sadness           as she had to be
called so many times       back from madness.

What would it take to summon her:
Not having an address, just a marker
for where she is not

I can only go and visit
her absence          her remains
which become less and less like her
more and more like the earth and trees,
the sky she continually faces.

I'd rather picture her under the sea
hair waving to the fishes and the brine,
being washed clean by
sharks and plankton

than under those pines by
the stone bench: one more desiccating root
in a garden of bones.

## Spanish Snapshots

Beneath the looming cutout wall—
it's as though all men
and boys were taking their daily exercise
below the prison's multiple black eyes.

A woman breathes under a market
table, a man's head noosed
inside the drapery reads a newspaper.

In the Spanish man I loved: so much sadness
in the cast in one eye I thought,
then, when I held him, I held
Franco's madness.

Is that why I return to these bruised images—
the whores of Mexico with lips
like jutting horns

the boy being beaten each night
then locked in a room, his father bringing
women back from the clubs to where he lay
curled inside a whorled horn.

It took years to learn compassion
entraps the gazer with the gazed—so that the snapshot
his mother gave me

of the gap-toothed boy
by the fountain before she fled
was what I held up to read
his cruelty by—believing he could choose

how deeply the blows would go.

# Pomegranates

To eat a whole one at one sitting
is to descend forever into the winter
                          willingly.

Calling them Chinese Apples
             though they're still from Israel

where I watch a young boy stop
every few minutes in his own sweat
to reach and pluck
             a red globe
             so delicately
then smash it on the ground

in his native way
sucking out only the
             easiest best red part.

So why does young Persephone who grew thirsty
have six seeds imbedded in her name
and how did the juice like wine
intoxicate her—so Hades could carry her off

Was *that* it—made the winter, made the anger
of her mother into winter

As she lay in a cavern with him
his tongue pushing at the
seeds still caught between her teeth

So little juice must have covered
those six seeds when sneaking
with no mirror she
broke her fast

Only enough to stain her teeth
when she smiled at him: *No. I've not
eaten anything.*

# Confession

Yesterday—quickly—I had
three lovers—or rather
allowed myself to enter
be ravished
by three who touched
every part of me:
First, quickly, Monterosso—who was
hot for me midday after a climb
through bamboo and olives and a taste
of wild berries on the hillside.
Next a little beach—whose name
I can't remember—at Portofino
after the lighthouse nodded in
the afternoon sun.
Then, most dangerous—
whipping my hair back in ecstatic
sweepings of *tramonto*
light—while schools of feeding fish
were knocked into and out of
an aquamarine pool—
there, I gave myself (as the mussels
relaxed their doors)
even my fear—which is
the only kind of giving the sea

can know or profit from—
there, to Vernazza, with the washed
butternut campanile chiming the hour
of *ciao* to the sun before the fishermen
would descend, an hour or two later,
with their phosphorescent lures
to keep them wedded to the shore
or else they, too,
would have plunged
into the dark blue pool where all
desires whirl and start.


# PATRICK DONNELLY

## Finding Paul Monette, Losing Him

It's just two days since I read you two days
since your *Elegies for Rog* grabbed me
in the stacks at the Brooklyn branch
grief eating through the binding like dragon blood
dripping through four stone floors
into the charming restaurant in the basement
I check you out and bring you home
so I can love you and pity him
and cry for him and you and myself
I check you out again and again
I think I'll steal you
I don't want to release you back to circulation
I study your picture on the sleeve for signs of sickness
search the flyleaf for year of publication
could you have survived 1987
so long ago dangerous year
to be a sick fag in America
In the cafe at the gay bookstore
I'm afraid to ask Do you know Monette
Did he make it The boys are so young
thumbing through pages of naked men

putting them back dog-eared The boy
behind the counter doesn't read poetry
I'm afraid of hope as I walk
to the back of the store PLEASE BE ALIVE
PLEASE BE among the M's I run my hand
along the spines Maupin McClatchy Melville
until it rests on yours
I tear you open the suspense killing me
please *please* be living with the dogs
in the hills somewhere north of Frisco
writing every day doing well on the new drugs
sleeping like spoons with a guy named
Peter Kenneth Michael or Guastavo
your picture is harder thinner
face lined eyelids sagging
"novelist poet essayist AIDS activist who died"
My face flushes hot
like checking the list of auditioners
who made it into the play
I didn't make it I'm not among them
I'm stunned humiliated
                        You're gone then
At forty-two I made it to the future four years further
who knows if I'll reach your forty-nine
why bother reading your book anymore
what difference do poems make or love
So this is your last face a fox and rabbit kissing
even dead your name earns a "face-out"
guarantees those big sales
who gets the money now
YOU JERK FUCK YOU
ridiculous to die so close to a cure
renders you me us absurd
shameful irresponsible
how quaint to die of this they'll think in 2030
how nostalgically sepia-toned and old-timey
like dying of the flu for godssake or the clap
like talking on a windup telephone or
buying ice for the icebox
                        On the net
I cruise a guy who says he knew you
when you tried to live and love again with Winston
I'm hungry to hear anything about you

but he interrupts with a reflection of his cock
in a hand mirror in a garden of red hibiscus
so for a moment I almost easily
forget my love my love of two days two days
in which you were born loved wrote grieved died
I never loved this way this long this hard
never burned up grief or anger with such verse
never came within two bow-lengths of the paradise
of men's hearts open to one another

Oh God in whom you never for one moment believed
will I still have time

# Baba

Baba feeds me with his own hand.
The night my friend died
he pressed dark chocolate
into a macaroon, popped it
in my mouth. The sweetness
cut the pain. Another time
he shows me how to fry
black mustard seed in ghee,
spoons silky dhal between my lips
with one raised eyebrow:
"Enough salt? Enough cumin?"
The day he gave me his hand
Baba wore a robe the color of mint.
Sometimes he ignores me for weeks,
then comes to me in dreams
riding a tractor or sitting on a deerskin.
Baba has three small moles
on the left side of his face.
When he prays, we see
the bottom of his socks are dirty.
Baba plays a blues lick
on his '66 Fender,
in the dark his glasses glint
and hide his eyes.
Baba says if you're very quiet
you can hear a sound inside
like crickets singing,

then sleeps with his head
in my lap.
Baba shouts at us to stay awake,
says we can sleep when we're dead,
he rocks back and forth when he chants,
sends his wives around
to splash us with rosewater.
Baba gives me his hats
he moves sick people away from me
he drives a red pickup
he gave me five hundred dollars
he gave me a new name.
Baba disappears into a photo booth at the airport,
reappears to give me a small version
of his face.
Baba cut all his hair off, then he grew it again,
he wears no coat when it's cold.
Baba passes me in the coffeehouse, writes
"beh-sin-mim-alif-lam-lam-ha"
at the top of my letter, *Bismillah,* since
Baba does everything in God's name.
When he rolls a smoke
on a picnic table in the moonlight,
watching trains go from Chicago to New Orleans
and back again,
a circle always gathers
to ask the hard questions:
what about abortion, what about gay people,
what happens when you die?
In the silence before he answers
I know the stories about Jesus
are true:

Baba, Baba, I can hardly keep up—
my heart runs after you
with my soul in its hands.

# I am a virus

I am a virus
        probably
I am no plant

    or animal
I am no vegetable
    or mineral
I may not even
    be alive
I do not eat
    or need to eat
I only know
    how to increase
I make your cells
    my brothel
I make your life
    my toilet
I give you time
    if I care to
Or bite your head off
    this very night
I have no king
    or kingdom
I have your life
    and your breath
between my teeth.

# How the Age of Iron Turned to Gold

My death makes her way to me
carrying green leaves.

I hear my prayer coming
behind illness, romantic noise,

urgent telephone messages,
alchemical lab results,

like a brook weaving
through thicket.

Water knows the way,
it isn't lost.

My teacher comes to me
by the western gates,

a sound like a bell
in her eyes,

bending humorously to gather
all her tender puppies by the neck.

## After a long time away

Everything is glad of me.
The radio plays only flutes.
My key fits locks all over town,
turns them over and over.
Plants think up fresh leaves
and even the dust on the shelves
has got a new pair of shoes.
Waxy yellow peppers jump in my pots
and cook cheaply into a thick glee.
Churches open their double doors
and my throat starts singing up and up.
Trucks kindly do not grind my house apart,
and busses watch my movements carefully.
Curly green boys
hide in my old cotton sheets,
and the library has stacked all the books
in my favorite order.
The checks I write
clear quietly and completely
in and out of the twilight,
water-cool vaults
of my blue marble bank.
And death is just a word like doorjamb,
magpie, harmless—
that twirls and worries gently.

# Volodymyr Dibrova

## Burdyk

*A Novel. Foreword, translated by V. Dibrova and Ksenia Kiebuzinsky*

"At the corner of two streets, spreading his wings against May wind, stands my friend Burdyk. A bottle of wine is in his hand. His trusting, untainted eyes eagerly take in the commotion of street arteries. Which of the visible directions, Burdyk thinks, shall I take? Where shall I direct my energies and determination? How and what shall I bequeath to people—a brand new approach to life, the true understanding of nature of things or some original system. Five o'clock. Spring is about to flow into summer. 20 degrees Celsius. Leaves are trembling blissfully. The chestnuts have just burst forth with their tropical candles. The pedestrians are luxuriating in this euphoria, which they can neither grab, squirrel away nor recycle. Damn! It'll eventually go to the dogs."

"That's precisely the way," I say, "I see Burdyk now. Although since that memorable May when he was waiting for me at the intersection of Chervonoarmijs'ka and Saksahans'ka Streets so many years have passed—you go figure it out yourself."

"We understand," they tell me, "but please, go easy on emotions. Our readers want to get the most out of their money. Literature is also a commodity. All they want is a plot bursting with action. As well as a digestible format. The time of voluminous masterpieces is over. Now we're in the fast lane. They'll leaf through a page or two but no more than that! If it attracts their attention—they'll buy it. If they stumble over some boring or obscure description—forget it! They'll close your book and spend their dough somewhere else."

(It was on Monday. Two guys from one of those new magazines approached me. Kids, in their early twenties or even late teens.)

"We," they tell me, "are ready to throw some light on blank spots and forgotten names. To promote the writing of a brand-new, cutting-edge, noncanonical history of the past epoch. Burdyk, we heard, was a figure of subculture."

"Well," I say.

"As we know, you keep his archive."

"Supposing."

"Give us some samples of his literary heritage. We shall publish it alongside with your commentaries and memoirs."

"I'll think about it," I say.

"Till Friday," they say. "We are on a very tight schedule. We are a joint venture. We need to pay the rent. We have to barter."

"At times," I tell them, "when my friend Burdyk lived and created, keeping this archive was punishable by law!"

"Oh! Oh!" they tell me, "We appreciate that. But there is no place for sentiments. The clauses of the contract are strictly defined. Quality and punctuality. The Company takes care of the rest. Paper is not a problem. Everything is computerized. We've got laser printers."

"My," I say, "I mean, our generation took the blow. We are talking tragedy here. How can you understand this! Sure, it's fashionable to criticize now . . . Who doesn't? But tell me, what about all those hotshots? Why haven't they been made to pay for what they've done to us?"

Silence.

"Personally," one of them says, "I am responsible for the literary section, and he—for the sex column. We want our magazine to be the new world. And eventually we plan to go color. Our motto is—Away with Taboos! Annotation in English. Three-sevenths of all subscribers are foreigners. We are backed by a half of the diaspora."

"Burdyk," I tell them, "was a True Intelligent!"

"Super!" they tell me.

"He was a new Hamlet! A victim of the System!" I say. "He refused to be a pawn in their game. His death was an act of ultimate defiance."

"If you can't meet the Friday deadline," they tell me, "then let's say Monday. Not later than 9 A.M. Or, rather, 8:50-ish. Every minute counts. That's why better come on Friday. So that we can send it to the publisher. Otherwise we risk penalties."

"Me, too," I say. "I am no stranger when it comes to the publishing business . . ."

"How nice! Till Friday, then," they say. "It was a pleasure meeting you."

"Well . . ." I say.

They flashed their teeth, squeezed my hand and hurried away to make money.

But where am I supposed to find them "The Burdyk's Works"? What I once had—his letters, his poetic scribblings in notebooks, a draft of a movie script, some weird cartoons—all of it wandered off into dog-eared folders and then, out of despair, during my numerous moves (I had moved six times!)—vanished into thin (thick—? stuggy) air.

Together with the tragedy "A Terrible Death of Ivan the Schmuck" for the theatre of the deaf-and-dumb. And the treatise "Talks of a Part-time Sailor with Oriental Man about the Hidden Meaning of Nothingness." And a sketch for the mural "Get Down from the Tree!" (The grandeur and variety of his talents still dumbfounds me.) And a collection of unerasable last names like Gooditch, Fartoff, Belchenko or Knickerpuke (randomly, I fish them out of memory), or Frigginovsky, or Kanter. Burdyk was never tired of picking or making them up. He dreamt of using them in his prose someday. Where are they now?

However, I did find a draft of his story "In the Lining." Its plot is pretty simple. The protagonist, who also happens to be a narrator, goes home after a day's work in the office.

"I am forty-two," he recalls, "and I am very tired. Why don't I put my hands in my pockets?" In one of the pockets there was a hole. No sooner had he reached in, he fell and tumbled down.

Then he got up, wiped a tear or three away, dusted himself off, sniffed the air and grew accustomed to the dirt and darkness around him.

*What and who,* asks the author, *do I see here?* And he provides a list of common and proper names which now belong to archeology.

For instance:

—Harpo Marx and Groucho Engels (a sample of dangerous political humor),

—"Fisherman Delight"—a brand name of the cheapest canned fish, which contained mainly fish's heads, tails, eyes and soft bones—a symbol of Soviet fat-free diet, stomach-unfriendly but always available,

—"bolshevik" (a bottle of plonk, eight-tenths of a litre, also known as "a bomb," or "bazooka," or simply "the big one"),

—Herm-an-Hesse, rock-and-roll, Zen-and-Tao (symbols of uninhibited spirituality and lust for a "good" life),

—miscellaneous (the old prices of alcohol, details of hard times and pressure, flashes of revelation),

—amateur snapshots of movie extras—Hurs'ky (a conformist and a snitch), Zaremba (Burdyk's school pal), unspecified adults and children, Borovadianka (a reappearing character of female sex) and so on and so forth,

—a couple of explicit Party jokes about the Communist Party's mother-fatherly love and care,

—her blue pullover (a hint of love at first sight. The main character of "In the Lining" was about to flee to the West in a hot air balloon but fell in love and that changed his life forever).

I'm giving this list exactly the way it's written down on that sheet of paper. Although it's not a full text, rather a draft. Of course, without the knowledge of the cultural context it's impossible to see that list as a panoramic insight of the past epoch. Yet with a bit of hard work one *could* turn these ad hoc notes into a solid short story. Or one could leave it as it is but concentrate on an honest and all-embracing commentary.

I'm worried about another thing: Suppose I slave at it and by Friday will whip up an example of Burdyk's literary genius. But suppose they say: We are a legitimate business enterprise, we cater to popular demand which, at the moment, is not interested in this kind of stuff. And, with all due respect, your generation does not run the show any longer. You were given your forty-something years and you haven't created either a pyramid or a tomb. Therefore you must disappear without a bang or a whimper. (Mark my metaphor about a pyramid and a tomb!)

They'll surely say so! And they will be right.

Take, for example, Zaremba. (It's still beyond me why Burdyk made him a character in his story.) In his junior year at secondary school, right in the middle of winter, Zaremba talked Burdyk and me into taking a ride to a faraway suburb of Sviatoshyno to rape a post-woman he knew. However, in his senior year he became a star football player, once even assisting in a goal against Moscow Spartak. After graduation Zaremba moved to Minsk and played for a local team Dynamo for a year and a half. Something went wrong and he was transferred to Odessa Chornomorets on the Black Sea where soon he had a fight with his coach forcing him to leave Odessa for provincial Lutsk with its second league team. But at that time his son came down with asthma. Zaremba groveled to the coach to take him back to Odessa to no avail. Zaremba wrote to the Football Federation, threatened, begged, filed complaints, collected documents and medical records, bribed doctors and was finally caught red-handed. He had to drop everything and run off to Donetsk where he worked as a phys ed teacher in a secondary school.

But then he got divorced and his wife kicked him out of their co-operative apartment. It took him ten years to come back to Kiev and procure a job at the shooting gallery near the Petchesk marketplace. Rumor had it that he became a church-goer. Somebody allegedly saw him near the St. Volodymyr Cathedral giving banknotes away to the panhandlers. Burdyk would never have believed that!

On the other hand, there is Hurs'ky. First the Komsomol, then trade-union and finally the Communist Party boss. He landed a cush job as head of the foreign relations department and went abroad every year. When the Party was dissolved, he laid low for some time to reemerge as president of a private bank.

Last week I was blessed with catching a glimpse of the bastard. I was standing peacefully near the liquor mart right across from a new currency store. When—lo and behold!—a white BMW screeched to a halt and out came our mutual friend and a former University classmate Mr. Hurs'ky, previously known as Comrade Hurs'ky. I guess, on the way home he made up his mind to buy his wife a new fur coat. Something exquisite but tasty. Nothing less than two grand. His hair was receding, which to make up for it while in Rome he bought himself designer gold-rimmed glasses. Although it was windy and chilly, he didn't wear a hat.

That's the way it is now.

The craze. He was also sporting a raincoat with an eye-catching lining; above it—his usual unflinching face. Not a single original feature. A regular Soviet stamped-out product. A man for all seasons.

There are others, however. Those who did not join the Party or take interest in football but rather spent their best years underground. Educating themselves surreptitiously, passing the banned books around to each other, making photocopies behind locked doors, convincing themselves that by doing so they were becoming attuned to the Higher Realms. Now where the hell are these Realms? Still hiding! And doing a very good job.

Oh, what a generation! Compost! I'm telling you! Humus!

"Is this what I dreamt about?" (These are the words of the protagonist from "In the Lining.")

"Is it?" he asks rhetorically. And looking for the way out he brawls with circumstances and lives through a number of adventures.

"Oh, what a cursed time I was born into!" he exclaims at the beginning of a soliloquy.

"Shut your gob!" reply the other characters, circumstances and events. "You've only got yourself to blame. You shouldn't have fallen down in the first place. Why didn't you sew the damn hole? Incidentally, we are unique, too! Don't treat us like we're some riffraff! So cut it short, buddy. Join the club. Push and be pushed."

"I refuse!" he hurls at them. "I am leaving this forsaken lining! I'm going back to the pocket!"

(And with that freedom-loving slogan the draft of the story ends. This is also the key to the whole corpus of Burdyk's works, of which, I have to admit, only this piece remained. That is why it is not quite clear how the protagonist's journey will end.)

It was, however, in real life the following way: At the end of '80s, one sunny afternoon, just as we had agreed before, Burdyk got to the corner of Chervonoarmijs'ka and Saksahans'ka Streets. Something kept me busy and he had to wait awhile, pissed as usual. And not without a good political reason. The Communist Party for twenty previous years had been poisoning us with crappy plonk and prohibited us from fully realizing ourselves. (These snots from that little magazine will never comprehend this!) To open up and show the world the whole scope of our creative potentials—we could never even imagine it! Neither me, nor Burdyk.

That is why he made no bones about his habit of sticking around the liquor store waiting for me.

It was the end of March and unusually warm. Nature was anticipating a new season of flow of sap, release of scents and ripening of fruit. Everything looked the same as fifteen years before. Although where once there used to be plenty of effervescent hope now stretched out layers of weariness. And one could safely draw the conclusion that—yes, it blossomed exuberantly, it smelled sweetly, the bees were buzzing around, as well as nightingales and mosquitoes, but nothing really germinated.

Burdyk nervously paced up and down the street for half an hour. He had just downed a bottle of "Sweet berry brandy" (I have to supply a commentary for the young ones and foreigners who do not know that it is a sort of moonshine, 30 proof, which means Burdyk didn't have enough money for vodka) and he was racking his brain over where to pee.

Suddenly he felt he was being stared at.

He turned back. A couple of feet away from him he saw a woman that in his story "In the Lining" is immortalized as "a blue pullover." Now she had a satisfied air, was well-dressed and still luscious. They used to be in love. Then she married Hurs'ky and hadn't seen Burdyk ever since. Instead of plunging into sweet memories, the former lovers gazed at each other.

We will never learn what was on Burdyk's mind. As for her, she could have become overwhelmed by pity (because Burdyk used to be an Orpheus!), by sorrow, by nostalgic trembling of her heart (as an echo of a nonextinguished desire), by annoyance (a sort of "what-have-they-done-to-you" shock) or even by joy (it's a lot safer to be with Hurs'ky!).

But it's not unlikely that during those few seconds she could have, with her eyes, confessed everything to Burdyk. First of all, that she still loved him (I can't rule this eventuality out). Second, that it was she who betrayed him (by opting for the mediocre over the artist). And thirdly, that she still while sharing a bed with Hurs'ky cannot help imagining it's Burdyk!

"Oh, please, stop torturing me!" she could have begged him with her eyes. "Have mercy! Let it stay the way it is! Don't destroy the Hurs'ky clan! He doesn't bother me, and neither do I. Besides, I'm not ready for a drastic change. The kids are about to finish school. We have to land them in the University. You can't take this away from them! And after all, who would have benefited had I not done my Ph.D.? Or had I divorced Hurs'ky? Or had I not joined the Party? Had I not done this, it would've been Borovadianka and not me who spent six solid months in one of the countries of prosperity and decadence. Didn't you have a craving to if not to set foot there then at least to fly over it someday somehow? Why then are you silent? Why don't you say 'hi' to me? What is behind your stooped posture, which used to be so upright and proud? And what does your puffed face signify? Why is it in a haze? Why doesn't it shine? Why does your body spasm? Is it because of some spiritual or physical need? Is it because at this particular moment you are contemplating the final touches of the ethical doctrine you promised to give people a long time ago? Or are you finishing a seminal novel? Or, perhaps, a drama? But don't tell me it is because you lost interest in me!"

Burdyk could not help shuddering when confronted with these questions. He leaned forward, pulled his knees together and, pressing the soles of his boots to the sidewalk, trudged towards the crosswalk.

Left with no choice, she pretended not to notice him, turned around and headed in the opposite direction.

Why didn't he approach her? Why didn't he want to refresh himself with memories of his amorous youth? Why?

Because (and I claim this because it had already happened to him before) at that moment he felt a warm yellow snake slithering down the left leg of his pants. The snake descended into his boot, licked all his toes, created a puddle and swam into it. Burdyk bent down even more and started to stomp the reptile. But the beast instead of evaporating somewhere, managed to find pits and holes in the terrain and zip-zapped towards the gutter. Burdyk rushed after it, got carried away and jumped into the middle of the street, right under the wheels of a bus.

The witnesses were unanimous in testifying that the victim did it of his own free will and that his head cracked open like a watermelon. The autopsy confirmed that Burdyk was in a state of alcoholic intoxication. The driver was not charged because he had a green light and the pedestrians—red.

But (and these are already my musings) is it worthwhile concentrating on such a death? Is it proper to turn a tragic hero into a laughingstock? By no means!

I showed those dudes the way to the door, locked up my basement apartment and went out to contemplate the plan of action. I reached the corner where Chervonoarmijs'ka Street meets Saksahans'ka and saw a crowd of agitated men there. It meant that the shipment of vodka had just arrived. I took my place in line, dallied for a while and stepped out for a couple of drags. To the very place where we used to meet with Burdyk.

It was April. The temperature, the pressure, the clothes and gloomy faces of the city dwellers—nothing stuck out of the norm. Only Latin letters on the colorful billboards and store signs suggested the early '90s. Under the walls of apartment buildings and between the trash cans there rose little kiosks from which our verminous juveniles were selling foreign humanitarian aid.

I'm not blaming them. Neither these mutants—nor Hurs'ky, although it was he who a long time ago snitched on Burdyk. Because which of us after so many years of rape remained unstained? At least Hurs'ky did not become a waste but chipped off a piece of socialism and melted it down into dollars. For the benefit of his family. Which, I repeat, does not bug me at all.

In the final analysis it all boils down to this: Either everything is shit, or shit is also a form of Grace. And in this case even our life is not without sense. Moreover, if a filthy outmoded city bus snatched from the thirty-eighth circle of life not me but him, who was a lot more gifted, then, perhaps, there was some Design in it! Maybe he, Burdyk, right from the outset was doomed to perish in this bog of ours. Am I, on the contrary, destined to make it? Right now when all the geniuses are dead, when the earth is polluted, exhausted and has a premonition of inevitable changes? Why not?

It's not for nothing that these brats searched me out. What if it is a sign? A signal of the fact that my time has come? All I have to do is to collect his writings, pull myself together and in a week, knock together a story of the illustrious life and labors of the hero of the Tenacious Generation. (My term! Make a note of a subtle echo of semantically distant notions of "tenacity" and "tenderness," which points to the combination of willpower and sensibility.) In other words, by using Burdyk's example I can prove once and for all that we are not some scum or the humus of history!

Because fricking A! We are still alive! While the red banners and mother-kissing Lenins are dead and gone! Yeah! The world should be grateful to us for this! Because we wasted our lives to make it happen! Turning ourselves into cripples while sheltering them from Communism. But everything must change now. The pores must begin to breathe. The wrinkles must disappear. And the miraculously preserved giants must emerge from their subcultural cesspool. To start out a new dignified life.

That is why the first thing I ought to do before embarking on such an endeavor is to make those guys pay me a lavish advance.

I barely had the time to think about these technicalities when a spit away from me I saw a huge rat. He was old, blind and was taking a short cut as if there were neither cars nor bipeds around him. He must have crawled out of the cellar under the store to breathe some fresh air. Or his snarly relatives must have pushed him outside. Or he could have been driven by some primal instinct.

The rat had difficulty dragging his four paws. Some liquid trickled behind him. He reached the edge of the sidewalk and without changing the trajectory dived under the wheels of a shiny "Mercedes." During a couple of minutes of green light the cars and buses turned the victim into a shapeless blot.

## JOHN DONOGHUE

## Waiting for the Muse in Lakeview Cemetery

These two young shirtless guys in cutoffs
don't fit here, they're walking too fast—straight at me—they don't look
at the three-foot lion sitting on Baby O'Donnell's grave, nor at the Hermes
reaching for the knocker on the door to Hades. No, these guys

don't look at shit, unless you count me,
their black T-shirts, leather pants and shaved heads
badly out of place next to the mini-Parthenon mausoleum
and the threadleaf maples, and noway am I some Eurydice

and these two the Orpheus Brothers with rescue
on their minds. And I'm thinking now how *stupid* can you get
to wander an empty, hilly, heavily wooded cemetery alone,
and just where are the grasscutters when you need them, and why

all this Greek-myth stuff when I'm dealing with two guys
in military jackets and those black gloves with the stiff,
funnel-shaped wrist covers, two maniacs
who have now lowered the tinted visors on their helmets

and are revving their Harleys as they weave toward me, crushing
the pachysandra, blowing kisses, calling, "We've got something for you"—
for *me!* who came here *humble,* with a bowed head,
a petitioner to the Muse for *anything*—a fragment of a voice

with a little authority, a feeling, a fragment of an idea,
who wanted only . . . well . . . OK . . .
who maybe lied about the Hermes and the lion,
and yeah, the two guys were the grasscutters, and no,

they didn't come near me, but I lied only because I thought
I was supposed to, that to lie put me on the road to truth,
guided there by Herself, a Greek woman in a white robe
and not two lousy bikers who have now, by the way,

ridden pretty far off, and who, unlike Orpheus,
won't look back, despite my yelling after them, their red

enameled gas tanks flashing in the sun, their exhausts
now just sweet, fading, throaty rumbles.

## Sheila's Auras

In my mother's talks with Christ he's dressed always
in a white gown and sandals, his light brown hair
long and flowing, his young, exposed heart
burning in his chest. That he's there to comfort her
after an "accident," or after a fall as the rich bruise
spreads beneath her skin, is OK with me, and OK too my lies

that 1) yes, I see him, just as 2) I claim to sort of see
my sister Sheila's auras, each of us, she says,
with a personal aurora borealis that I could learn to see
and read—like blood-work on the soul. Sheila worries
mine is dim, a queasy yellow, she says my mooning
for the world to mean more than I make it mean
is laughable, a kind of scientific/mythic schmutz
freezing me within this field of light
buzzing at the surface of my eyes.

And she's right: I'll never see my mother's Christ
or Sheila's brilliant auras; and the red fox
that trotted up out of the cemetery's ravine last week
and stood in the snow and stared at me
will never send a message not of my own making—
always, it seems, *my* hand and fingers up inside
*its* coat, *it* mouthing *my* thoughts, as if its being there was only grist
for my metaphoric mill, its mute
and indifferent B just an accident to serve
my all consuming A, as if that stunning fox
was just a mirror to better see myself.

It left fresh tracks all week, looping,
impossible to follow. (Does it walk the same snow-holes,
coming and going?) Tonight, in her room,
Sheila combs my mother's hair. She tells her she can see
both Christ *and* His aura. My mother, happy, says of course,
she never thought of it, her Christ has always had a halo.
And then they laugh, and Sheila combs her hair: the antique
comb, Sheila's palm against my mother's head, their faces
beaming in the mirror.

## Articles of Exploration

> *That's one small step for man,*
> *one giant leap for mankind.*
> —Neil Armstrong, as he stepped onto the Moon

He sing-songed it to himself as he studied the maps
of the Sea of Tranquillity, he spoke it out loud in the shower—
> *That's one small step for a man,*
> *one giant leap for mankind*
but up there on the Moon
he blew it, he got so caught up with getting down the ladder safely
he left out the rotten little *a*.

*We* knew what he meant, and he knew
we knew it, but he would have slapped his forehead
if he could have, and there was no going back up the ladder.

He doesn't give interviews, doesn't attend celebrations
or go to reunions; maybe in the midst of all that perfection
something in him meant to screw it up. He'll never know:
*Who was Deep Throat? Did Oswald act alone?*

Years later, when Viking landed on Mars, nothing was said:
the camera turned on, a door opened, and the machine
went to work. We could have given it speech, we could have
had it say—flawlessly—
> *That's one small step for a machine,*
> *one giant leap for machinekind*
but words, weighing too much, and with no human
to say them, just aren't worth it.


## Physical

It's *nothing*, he says, a small asymmetry, we'll check it out
when you get back. The worst, is that it's cancer;
the best, is that it's just you.
Is he *crazy*? When I get *back*?—the million-dollar rented beach house
turned to stomach acid?! *Do—it—now!* I shout,

shaking him, let's check it out *yesterday!*, this town
bursting with urologists just sitting on their hands—where they

rest them when they're idle. (Friends,
have physicals in fall, with nothing planned.)

A small asymmetry. A bad sign for one who's been
symmetric all his life—write with the right, throw with the left,
when praised, quick to name a fault.
That's *balance,* he says, not symmetry, and on his pad
he draws a circle. Prostate—the size of a walnut,

pale, firm, partly muscle partly gland, a fist
at the base of the urethra, and *yours,* he says, is slightly
asymmetric—on his circle he draws a bulge
from 12 to 3. You're *fine!* It's *nothing! Relax!*

And what *would* I have him do? Cry out, *Oh, no!*
when he felt me? And he's right, it *is* balance we're after,
not symmetry, not that static, sentimental same-old same-old
across a boundary—one side unable to give
or teach anything to the other—our deep dislike of symmetry
the reason we marry opposites, not clones, the reason one foot

is always larger than the other, one heart, one lopsided stomach,
the reason first there's A, then B, the reason one-fourth of my walnut—
from 12 to 3—stuck out on its own and bulged
into asymmetry. So . . . OK . . . I'll go. It *is* nothing.

I'll put on my Ray•Ban Cats, rub on my #20 Bain de Soleil.
I'll put on my aqua Speedo trunks and my black Rockport thongs.
I'll put on my Spiegel rugby shirt, and my Yankees baseball hat.
I'll carry my red aluminum beach chair and reed mat
under my left arm, and my all-cotton towel and rainbow umbrella

under my right. I'll carry my cooler bag and my book bag
over opposite shoulders, and carefully, it being just myself,
I'll walk my newly strange asymmetric body—feeling now
like a threat—down to the sea.

# Images

Red Riding Hood is having a bad dream: Grandma's house
a hut of boards and corrugated tin, her front door
a closet door, and the forest it sits in has gathered itself

and stares at the house like an animal, its slow,
implacable mind made up.

> *A tube with a screen on its broad face*
> *generates a sequence of 30 still pictures per second.*
> *Through the eye's persistence, the sequence*
> *forms an image that the viewer responds to*
> *as if moving and real.*

Grandma's bed is sour, stained. It sags. Red Riding Hood struggles
up out of it, standing in an image of the window
cast by the moon on the floor. Lines so simple, she reaches into the light
with an image of her own—a dog, barking.

> *Three electron guns, called the red, blue, and green guns,*
> *are mounted at the end of the tube opposite the screen.*
> *The guns generate three electron beams,*
> *and each of the 30 still pictures is created by the beams*
> *scanning across over 500 horizontal lines on the screen,*
> *one line at a time, top to bottom, but first the even numbered*
> *and then the odd numbered lines.*

Encouraged by her dog, Little Hood tries others: a bird
flying, a spider on the pane. But whatever she makes
and withdraws, the moon waits with the window's image,
so she at last lies down on the floor in the image
of the window.

> *As the beams scan each line, they strike thousands of sets*
> *of three phosphor dots—red, blue, and green—placed*
> *along the line. A shadow mask guides each beam*
> *so that the proper beam strikes the proper colored dot*
> *in each set. The intensity of the light emitted by a dot*
> *depends on the intensity of its beam at the moment the dot*
> *is struck by the beam in the progress of a scan.*

It was in the news from South Africa—more than ten years ago—
a video crew recorded a crowd's murder of a child,
seven or eight years old, the daughter of an informer
or a policeman. The girl answered the door to her house
and they struck her with knives and small hatchets.
You could see her face when she realized her fate.
She took the first blows and then ran down a path and fell

with her arms oddly raised. And after she fell, her body took blows
as meat takes blows, and with each blow her hands bobbed
in a graceful, limp way. As she died,
her fingers slowly opened.

> *The electrical video signal that contains the image*
> *continuously changes the intensity of each electron beam*
> *in order to produce the image in light.*
> *Once the beams and dots transform the image into light,*
> *it is said to have become a real image.*
> *The viewer sees the real image by changing the light*
> *back to electrical signals understood by the brain.*

Red Riding Hood lay on the floor in the widow's image
as the woodsman and wolf
pounded at the door. *My father, the sun,* the moon told her,
*warms me and gives me form.* Looking down,
Red Riding Hood saw the window's image on her chest; as the door
flew open she stood up, and with the help of the moon
stepped through the window for a second time.

# One-Bedroom, Four Floors Up

Her life now unmade, the woman in the red robe and slippers
blames years of comfort in her own home for spoiling her,
that's why, she thinks, her heart's not in this,
but *she* is, so she might as well order the mirror
for the entrance hall, and the slender black Pallas lamp
for warmth.

But the lamp's gold paper shade is too dark
in the catalog photograph, the mirror overpriced,
and how, exactly, will its pine frame look, rubbed
with Napoleon Blue?

So if today she cannot make the call, if once again
that rush of purpose has slipped from her as memory
slips from dreams, she can at least ride out the day,
just as, she thinks, the courtyard below
has ridden out the winter: the giant mulberry
now thick with fruit, a perch and feeder for the birds
nested in the ivy on the wall. It was the ivy

and its sound
that drew her to the window, the ivy
in bloom, its thick, sweet scent
drawing bees in under the upturned palms
of its leaves. In the midday light the leaves are supple,
a new and brilliant green, and the bees brush them
with what seems to her a tenderness.

# Marianne Boruch

## Then

Each of us had an angel. I say that now
without doubt. What does one say
to an angel, I thought, I who
never had a thought, going home
the street suddenly unreal
with both of us walking. Ahead, the bigger boys
hurled stones and shouted. Their angels—
how to imagine their beauty
unless it be anger. Embarrassing, this secret,
belief like a boat, like an odd translation
of what one thought
an ordinary word. By Mr. Glimm's crabapple,
I made them out, three
wary creatures standing at an angle,
idly lifting off the small fruits.
I dare not speak. I dare not.
Easier to imagine old men into infants,
sand back into stone. I walked past
the Ingolias' house, Mickey out there
with his big front teeth, a nervous glaring boy—
a suicide, but that was later—kicking grass
down to dirt, into dirty clouds.
Already, late summer. On the roof, his angel
draped himself over the gable, not really a gable,
the roof rising up only a little.

## The Luxor Baths

Before its high red brick,
a street typical of Chicago: rusted cars
and on either side, stores
boarded up, one still selling furniture cheap
and groceries in the back, and the liquor place
too busy, though the men walked past us
slowly and alone, their new bottles
in paper sacks, and singing.
                          I suppose I thought it
a movie set. I was that young.
My friend had brought me, her father
going for decades, cutting deals
on paint in the Russian bath, and even
the hotter Turkish bath, or for the new guys
who couldn't take it, the Finnish bath
with its pure, dry heat.
He was dead three years and I thought of him,
how he must have hated Wednesdays,
Ladies Night. The bored clerk behind the grill
issued us each Ivory soap,
and to wear—a sheet and a towel
for our $1.50
then slid back to her magazine.
                          It was like Riverview, walking in,
it was the fun house, Aladdin's Castle, the narrow stairs,
and that floor, all splinters and dark dust
until a room opened—full light, and in three languages, shouts
then laughter, and rows of lockers that didn't
quite close. This place—a hundred years old,
my friend whispered, more as fact
than devotion. She'd been there, after all; she'd grown up
with someone who called out
every Monday after supper, I'm going—
meaning, the Luxor,
getting in his big car, headed south toward the Loop.
I forgot to say it was snowing. It was
February, so the wet warmth
did something fuzzy to my head.
I mean, I felt faint, not sick
or maybe it was the thought
of taking off my clothes.

                              We undressed quickly,
and hurried the narrow sheet around us, such sheet
there was. But really, I wanted
to look at them, the women. At 19, we were the youngest,
too new, too empty, and hardly worth
the effort of a question
though I feared they'd talk to us—
worried they'd *be polite,* these women
too busy with each other
and the car wreck, and so-and-so's lousy husband,
and the horse's ass of a brother-in-law
who walked out, just like that, and Irene,
what the hell would she do now?
                                        I love my sister, Irene's
sister said, that s.o.b. We were walking
toward the Russian bath, that is, they
were walking. My friend nodded,
and we tagged along. In that webby, steamy room
she and I wore our sheets, the only ones, ten of us
on wooden benches. I wanted more
about Irene. But her sister
kept shaking, *that s.o.b.,*
until a woman got up and dragged the barrel of water
and oak leaves to the center—Snap out of it, Mel!—
flicking a branch over her head, the spray
hitting the benches, the sweating walls
—a million tiny whooshes—
for everyone to laugh.
                        I pretended not to stare
but such bodies, I had never imagined
such bodies—huge breasts and thighs, and pubic hair
in lush spreading mounds, full freckled arms;
thinner women with wonderful bellies,
one had a scar.
*She just let herself go after the baby came:* my mother's
short circuit for anyone
like this. Here, they stood to pour water from the barrel
holding the small bucket overhead, leaning back
suddenly languid, closing their eyes.
                              They set me
dreaming this: I was invisible.
But someone turned to me—Do you want to try it?—handing me
the bucket. They were talking, off the s.o.b. now

and onto the priest
who refused to make a sick call
for someone's uncle. Jesus, the nerve of it.
Do they expect the man to crawl to church? It was hot.
I took off my sheet—
standing there, and walked and stood
and dipped my bucket in.
                         The smell of oak, soaked that way,
vaguely sweet and bitter, nothing
like pine. I wanted
to turn my back to them but didn't, lifted
the thing high
over my head to pour. I thought
of the cold outside, and the snow,
and that long blur
of anything
when it first comes down.

## On Sorrow

The way certain people
run through rain at rest stops, the quiet ones
or the quick shrieking ones,
is the way I want
to think about sadness: brave flash
and the weedy grass too shiny in such light,
say, the middle of September
which is always at a slant, the kids
already school-dogged, hitting
every puddle, that slow motion rush
from the car.

But it's the stranded ones there,
old guys with caps, a woman
with her hood up—I look at them
and hardly think at all.
They stand whistling for their genius dogs, dogs
who half-fly
through the dog walk zone. Two notes
to that whistling, or three.
Each has a rhythm I can't quite get.
They hunch down

into their nylon jackets, shoulders
already dark with rain.
I don't know
what it is—just what you do
if you have a dog, like
it's raining all day, regardless.

Half the time, I sit a few minutes
in my car before
I do anything. One of them is always trying
to light a cigarette
in the rain. Match after soggy match
flung down. This is hope.

# Head of an Unknown Saint

*Most likely used as a home shrine*
—Academy of Arts, Honolulu

He looks addled, or maybe
the paint has simply worn off the iris
of each eye until everything's
gone inward. Poor thing, life-sized
and left here like a puppet. He's wood.
He's full of curious lines where
someone cut then smoothed, then
cut again, some uncle who was best
quiet at things that could be
praised simply. I'd praise that way.
I'd say: if he looks tired, it's the weight
of goodness, not centuries. If he looks
dear somehow, it's because he loved
everything, regardless of its worth
or its chance for eternity. And the rain
at the window—never mind that it rotted
the left side of him or that insects
made a kingdom of his ear. He heard
their buzzing but it was pleasant, the tree
he'd been, the way he kept
mistaking them for wind nuzzling leaf
into leaf, so long ago, before
all this afterlife....

# Happiness

In the old tapestry, how they float
among the flowers, queen and servants both,
all equally. The vast blue
behind lily and rose
is their permanent element, not as sky
or water makes a world, but as
childhood does, wishing the day
would last. An honest-to-god queen
wouldn't like it, really, such weightlessness,
her servants aloft like birds,
obedient birds, just
barely. All this is
dream—ours, when we think about the past.
Or it might be the weavers'
simple ignorance of perspective.
As if ignorance were ever simple.
And happiness? I look
into the faces of the queen and all
her servants, or at how their bodies
take the scented air of centuries.
They're oblivious—to the flowers set skyward
and adrift, to anything but
looking blankly out. The weavers making such eyes
had to drop one thread and let
the endless backdrop blue
leak in. Perhaps it was a sweet thing, emptying
their heads like that. Now each is so light
all rise and rise.
They don't know where they are, what
land, or who
the enemy.

# The Hawk

He was halfway through the grackle
when I got home. From the kitchen I saw
blood, the black feathers scattered
on snow. How the bird bent
to each skein of flesh, his muscles
tacking to the strain and tear.

The fierceness of it, the nonchalance.
Silence took the yard, so usually
restless with every call or quarrel—
titmouse, chickadee, drab
and gorgeous finch, and the sparrow haunted
by her small complete surrender
to a fear of anything. I didn't know
how to look at it. How to stand
or take a breath in the hawk's bite
and pull, his pleasure
so efficient, so *of course, of course,*
the throat triumphant,
rising up. Not
the violence, poor grackle. But the
sparrow, high above us, who
knew exactly.

## Tulip Tree

Some things aren't meant.
Some things aren't plain.
I planted it thinking, just

in case, the giant elms
on either side are riddled old
and ticking, sentinels

thick with shade. It seemed
tiny then. Cars crept by, all
dwarfed it deeper. One brief wind

would rattle it. Some things
aren't meant but we
were careful. The hose lay

cool and coiled and seeped
those nights until the sidewalk
rivered up, or laked.

We thought: in case, in case,
but either side so thick with shade.
Some things aren't meant—its leaf,

half almost square, half some other
shiny figure, lovely to the touch,
exactly as a letter turns, page

by page, read outside
on broken steps. I planted in that spot,
laid the hose so close, good snake

humbled by its ancient fall
from grace. It seeped past night.
Cars crept by but kids

walking liked to take a branch
or twig, thinking to play
at knives, or thinking vastly

not anything at all. It was small.
It lorded over nothing
and gave no shade. But each leaf

kept its distant kingdom
of vein and gloss. Insects never
armied it. And the snake hissed its love

all night sometimes. I forgot
and then remembered it.
We passed it daily coming

from the car. Some things
aren't meant. And even dying elms have
their duty, their everlasting shade

coming down like rain to block
the sun. I chose the spot. I watched
it leaf. One reads outside

on broken steps words dark
and light that drift
into the body and disappear.

It slowly turned away
like that. Kids walking by would
reach and break. It lorded

over nothing. Some things aren't
meant, or seem plain enough.
But I forget, then remember it.

# PABLO MEDINA

## Mortality

Three weeks ago I received a phone call at three in the morning informing me that Carlitos Bodeler had died. I had not seen Carlitos in thirty years, but mention of his name while the waters of my dreams slapped against the sides of my consciousness brought back memories in such profusion that I fell back in bed, overwhelmed by a kind of vertigo. I did not recognize the voice on the line, taut like a sinew, with a strange accent and an upward lilt to the intonation reminiscent of the speech of certain tribes in the desert regions of Chile. Before I could compose myself and ask why I, after such a lapse of time, should be called with this news, the caller was off the line.

    I made myself some coffee and sat by the window to watch yet another snowfall blanketing the city and thought about him whom I had known so many years ago and who was now filling my room with the shadow of his presence. I met him my first day at the taxi stand in Caridad, a large man with an amazing resemblance to Sidney Greenstreet, playing an instrument (I later discovered it was a *bandoneón*) which made the most plaintive and evocative of sounds. I became afraid. I felt like it was my heart he was squeezing, not his instrument. And he called my name before I said it. "Federico!" Just like that: "Federico!" and went on with his song, which I still to this day remember:

> *Perro azul y gato pardo,*
> *esos son mis sentimientos,*
> *hechos tierra con el tiempo*
> *en el desierto de la traición.*

    I nodded to him then. He stared at me through his thick eyebrows, stopped playing, and stretched his hand, which I took in mine and felt an immediate and kindly warmth. By then Carlitos—it was a purposeful irony that led us to attach the diminutive to his name; diminutive he was not—no longer took customers. Instead he sat on his *taburete,* playing for us the tangos and milongas of his native Buenos Aires or else reciting the endless sagas he had learned in Reykjavik, where he had lived for some time. In fact, Carlitos had lived everywhere on this earth, and he spoke with familiarity and fondness of Benin and Saigon, Borneo and the Atacama. His songs, his poems, his commentaries kept me going through the busy times, when I was handling fifteen, twenty rides a day, and through the dead times as well, when time stopped and the midafternoon heat made us all sleep and dream of a prenatal nostalgia for snow.

Carlitos Bodeler was there always, drinking mojito, a tropical drink he much preferred over the heavy Argentinian wine that had made him fat and ruddy, floating comfortably in his lethargy and entertaining us—no, educating us—with his songs, his stories about eating human flesh in a feast of cannibals ("It tastes as only human flesh can taste—divine"), and the poems about Nordic savages and their penchant for death and unbridled rage. Before meeting him I had thought dimly my country and my city to be the center of the universe, but after listening to him, I was convinced.

I had no ambition to drink cow's blood with the Massai or share a repast of blubber with the Eskimos or a breakfast of raw reindeer liver with the Laplanders. It was enough that Carlitos had done these things and told me about them; that he had, for example, fallen in love with a prostitute in Kiev who had not bathed all winter—"Love is not only blind," he liked to say, "It is also odorless"; that he had been both a slave and a slave master in the markets of Tunis; that he had fallen under a spell of a santero in Santiago de Cuba and lost three years of his life; and many other experiences that I would be only too happy to relate were I not bound by my honor and my discretion. Why should I have felt any urge whatsoever to experience these things when Carlitos Bodeler had experienced them for me—absinthe, opium, even incest?

> *Mon enfant, ma souer,*
> *Songe à la douceur*
> *D'aller là-bas vivre ensemble!*
> *Aimer à loisir,*
> *Aimer et mourir*
> *Au pays qui te ressemble!*

he would recite with that far-away look that River Plateans get when thinking of their sisters.

To know Carlitos Bodeler was to know an encyclopedia. No, no, that is not right. His knowledge and experience could never be contained in a limited number of volumes. To know him was to know life. He told me of the devil's barbed penis and of the seven impenetrable veils that covered the Blessed Mother's womb. He sang of the cave of sorrows and the garden of delights. Bullets had entered his body, and he had a scar running from his temple to his chin where a Cossack saber had landed. He had been on the other side of death as well, in the Ardennes, during the war, when he had killed twelve Austrian guards, cutting their throats with a stealth and precision that put him in high demand among the Allied forces in the trenches. "Their blood warmed my hands, and the moans escaping through their wounds turned my heart to ice." After telling that story, he sang a milonga and his *bandoneón* reached the deepest caverns of grief, lingering there for what seemed centuries. I wept with his sorrow. I wept as if I myself had heard the moans of those Austrian boys and spent twelve sleepless nights in hell with their blood burning my hands. Then I did something I had never done before nor would ever do again: I drank mojitos with Carlitos and became copiously drunk. Despite the fact that it was my busiest day of the week and I had many rides waiting for me, including several regular customers who were generous tippers; despite the risk of losing them to the other cabbies who roamed around my customers like sharks, I stayed with Carlitos that day weeping and drinking and singing, too, my shy squeaky voice barely audible over the registers of his baritone and of his *bandoneón*, which, at that moment, gave off the attar of God.

Then the vertigo came, a maelstrom of emotion, intellect and sense that sucked me to a place where everything whirled and collided and finally blended into blackness. I was not then nor have ever been since a drinker. Lights popped under my eyelids and my body turned inside out, then outside in, then inside out again. I remembered nothing and I remembered everything. I woke at night with my cheek to the pavement and an ache in my head like a stone must feel when it cracks. Manolo the constable was poking me with his stick, his flashlight square on my face.

"Hey, you, Federico!" he said. "Are you dead or alive?"

"Worse," I said, speaking the truth.

I raised myself off the ground with great difficulty and went home. I do not remember how I got there, but I fell in my bed and slept deeply through the night. The next day I did not feel any better but I was at the taxi stand promptly at my usual hour. Carlitos did not show up that day, but he was there the following one, drinking a coffee someone had bought for him. I avoided him from that time on. I did my job, driving people where they needed to go, and came home at night too tired to want anything else but sleep. When things got tough and the good money dried up, I left my country and came to this city where it is always cold and always dark.

Thirty years is a long time and much has happened. I could tell Carlitos a story or two and he would listen. To be honest, there wasn't a day that I did not think about that man and relive his songs and his poems. I don't know why I was called. The phone call seemed an intrusion on my memories. Perhaps he was fonder of me than I thought and he wrote my name down somewhere where it could be found. That anonymous voice could have announced his death to me as it did to ten thousand others, and all of us may have felt the same sense of displacement, the same vertigo. I had known Carlitos Bodeler in life. Now I knew his death. As the last snowflake fell and the sky grew light, I felt revived and at peace, and I heard him calling my name. Carlitos was here. Carlitos was everywhere. Time stopped altogether and I came to understand what it was he waited thirty years to give me.

# ELLEN DUDLEY

## The Bats

Just at dusk, when the man I lived with
had set about his drinking, wineglass polished,
ashtray on the couch arm, book in hand—
my daughter and I walked the quarter mile
to the dirt road, and at the top of the hill,
sun falling between the mountains in front of us,
she taught me how to call the bats, clicking
high-pitched in our throats.      And as the sky
gathered itself into a dark blue and Venus
winked like a plane's starboard wing tip, they came.
And whirring softly, they dived through our hair,
leaving us laughing with their wind on our scalps.
We stayed in the road until full-dark
when we picked our way back to the house,
which, lighted and open, looked like a refuge.

## Leaving Lincoln

Stopping on my way out of town for gas, the late wind
blowing the poplars till their tops touched the ground,
tornadoes threatening from the south, I waited, hipsprung,
at the counter. In front of me stood a man who wore no shirt

and the dust of a day's work lined his smooth back
just above his jeans. And below his left ear three gray hairs
nestled in the black. Fresh from the library
where I'd held the dead man's poems,
I was streaked with graphite from the page
where he'd left his thumbprint and my fingers shook a little.
And what I wanted to do then, as the wind
rattled the roof, was to put my top incisors
on that peak of shoulder, let my tongue out to taste
each grain of salt, to feel the water molecules
laid on by the Nebraska afternoon.

# The One Thing

Then I waited on a park bench in Athens,
outside the agora, for a man in cotton pants,
black haired and beautiful. And there in the rain
under the garden Priapus, I opened my coat
to give breasts, belly, thighs to a loving tongue.
Now it's another April light, and cold,
and I'm putting this on the table for you.
And with every hiss and thump of consonant,
every mouthful of vowel—even though there are
no statues here, no plane trees muttering *Never
be importunate, ephebe*—I open my coat.
*Here*, I say, *Taste.*

# Kilauea

In the crevices of the new flow, green lichen
thrives on what would kill us.
Upslope, the eucalyptus are roman candles
and down here along the cliffs
we line up to watch the earth move.

Toward sunset you can hear the clicks and whirs
of cameras, and down below lava snaps and pops
as it hits the ocean in a red stream that floats
yards out to sea, then solidifies and sinks.

We crank the film out, as if what we take home
will let the others know: *We were there; we saw this.*

A Japanese tourist in pressed blue jeans elbows forward
to put his back to the flow and sea, just so.

And his wife, perfect white tennis shoes slipping
on the lava clinkers, stands to take this study in perspective.
We talk about our cameras. We wait for dark.
We are carving our names on the cliffs; drawing
on the walls of caves.

# Night Fishing

A bilious moon skewered on the end of the jetty
and bass jumping shiny as dimes are what he leans toward,
these nights he can't sleep. As he rocks, casting
into the surf, his old tennis shoes
suck and drag, and as his shorts slide
along his thighs, the shrapnel furrows are bled white
and harmless in the moonlight. I want to put my lips
on them, my wet fingers. But what I do is take the hooks
from the fish, too small this July to be keepers.
I slide the barbs out for him, holding the hook up
so he can see it in the moon's path,
and then I let them go, and they pour themselves
out of my hands, slowly, back to their own element.

# <u>Ojo Caliente Suite</u>

# The Oranges

It's been days since I sat with you
as you pulled the little dagger
from your pocket and cut around the fruit until
it gave off its rind in spirals, and I'm still
full of the smell of you, your heady slipstream—
full of the sight of you sinking into me.
You sliced right through the navel and juice poured
out over the blade and even now I want to draw its edge
across my tongue.
                Here at my kitchen sink, I jam

my thumb in by the stem, pull the peel
in clumps, and with the liquid running down
my wrists and chin, the whole room reeks
of blood orange, tangelo, mineola
and I see in my reflection at the kitchen window
that the three small bruises on my neck—
where you held on as I bore down—
have faded to a smudge.

## Recall

To keep myself from this lover, to shut the door,
I clean the bathtub. Stinking of chlorine,

I close the curtain, a varicolored
children's map, and there under my left hand

is home to him, time zones away—so
I drive the fire truck because I know

the concentration it will take. And wheeling
the big Reo diesel through the back roads,

the fields green enough this spring
to set your teeth on edge, I try to find the place

low range kicks in, the torque just right.
Shifting on the curves, the muscle memory is back,

the gears come easy now and I know
forgetting is the last thing the body does.

## Corporeal

This morning, I found I could say your name clearly,
without sound, in the back of my throat—
no labials in that one syllable,
but a secret I could keep—over and over
as he moved on me, against me;
when I put my arms around him I took your name
in my mouth, in quiet, the way

prisoners learn to come silently in the cell,
the bunk barely moving, the air
undisturbed around them while the earthquake
takes place in the throat, the gut,
the dry heart.

## Out of Time

Let me tell you what I love:

To fish—whistling the line to the middle of the stream—
and time to think before the strike,

The curve of my own lip

Oysters

Any song by Hugo Wolfe and Goethe

The tide slapping a freighter westbound through the Golden Gate

Wind from the southeast—

and rain on your mouth.

## Hot Eyes

As you lifted off, I drove, windows open,
deep into the Sangre de Christo.
While you changed planes in Denver, I came over
the top of the pass into Colorado and for a minute
we were in the same state again.

A town called Angel Fire to the east,
west the hostile teeth of the Rockies,
and my hands sliding on the wheel wafted
the scent of the night's semen. The red dirt
pinged in my wheel wells—Colorado,
red in Spanish, that sweet redolent tongue—
red, the color I left last night
on your rented bed.

Now you're sleek over the Marin Headlands,
the Pacific booming, beckoning you.
I'm heading east, your gaze still on me like a hand.
Seventeen time zones and I still believe
we could wake to bananas and passionfruit,
that my brown skin will wear a sheen of sweat
and when you touch me you will shake fire
from your fingers. In the humid room,
under the net at night, you will slide
your palm up my slick thigh and my mouth will
groan *no* and my body rise to you.

# Gary Duehr

## All the Little Sorries

The one who cries out longest from an open
Window is rarely serious.
Police know this. The detective sets

His coffee down and climbs the five flights
Like each footstep's squeezing
His breath out. Below, firefighters relax

The net. The jumper's screaming for everyone
To listen to her, just
Listen, but the crowd noise drowns

Her out. She vanishes. Then a swirl
Of blue lights, camera
Whirs, bears her away. Waking the next

Morning, in the hospital, she's not
Confused, doesn't think
She's dead or in heaven or anything. She wants

What anyone would: to get
Up, brush her teeth, fill
An ordinary glass of tap water. Between

Sips, she says it was all because
Of her boyfriend. And
Her one great sorrow takes its place

Beside all the other little sorries.

# Dog World

Because you must, you sit and read through *Dog World*
Cover to cover, among all the other men
        Sitting and reading. The pink
Afternoon light is hitting the library's pale
        Columns. You never think
Of hair dryers, chrome cages, or how to train
Your dog by monks on videotape. The whole

Point of this, as far as you can tell, is how
Far apart everyone's grown. The curl
        Of a newspaper or a plastic binder
Hides most faces. In the library frieze,
        Horses rear up on their
Hind legs, reined in by grooms whose togas unfurl
Sideways. You've never felt such sorrow about

Nothing you can pin it on. "Put Your Puppies
On TV," "Maximize Your Pet's Potential."
        Some teens in hoods erupt
In laughter, snorting. The other kids, just out
        Of school, too, sit and input
Y or N when asked in *Search* under *File*.
The books in their stacks, the clean, straight aisles.

# Missing

The world is full of missing persons.
In small moments, between what's taken
Back and what's not, they go
Away to become shadows, former
People in a rainy landscape.
We may see them driving past

A corner, or they may live another
Lifetime away. The person they were
Has ceased—it's as if the soul has left
Its body empty, hollow as a slight
Smudge of cloud. It's their numbers

That stay. We use them to count
Their absences around a small black
Table through a rupture in cigarette
Smoke, or while reading under a lone
Telephone pole at dusk.

You can understand how it happens.
Someone loses touch, moves
Away, and details fade—loves,
Deaths, weddings. And then it's then.


# Vestige

This time you come back a woman
With a furry and unmistakable mustache crowning
Your upper lip. You live out of a grocery cart
On the street, a hallucination
Ghosting in store windows. At every commuter's
Face that sweeps past, your line of thought
Disperses: a plume of smoke across a vast plain.

How can you explain how you once moved
Among them, that your mustache carries the last vestige
Of a past life—carriages, black boots? And that you were once
A corporal who was betrayed, tried, then

Condemned to the cell of his own garrison.

# Petition: Morning Talk Show

For the father whose fall down the stairs, while shielding
His one-year-old, bruised his spine,
So that his speech emerges clotted, halting;

For the patient who fears her transplanted heart may betray her
At any moment, while driving the car
Or reaching for the top shelf in the grocery store;

For the mother who lost track of her two small boys
For five years while straightening
Herself out, in order to pare her effects down to their cause;

For all these, let them surpass their Surprise Fashion
Makeovers, that they may re-enter their lives as nonfiction.

# Ricochet

*And now, I am on the mirror's other
Side,* he thought, *after having passed
Seamlessly through its glass.* The way a kiss

Transfers from one mouth's small dark
To another's like a note, a flame. But this
Feeling was new to him. Waiting in the car
For school to let out, in a rain

Whose rivulets on the windshield cast
Everything as tremulous, even his old place
Around the corner seemed unfamiliar.
*On the other side:* last night, again,

He couldn't shake the dream in which a
Camera, as the shutter's closing, falls apart
In his hands—not a bad or good
Feeling, just different. He could see that the area

Around his life had cleared some, as if through grace,
As if the constant ricochet of hurt
Had paused. And now, he was on the other side.

# Under Total Quality Management

Once the problem was heart: how
        To have enough,
Or at least squeeze it toward

The right place at precisely the prompt
        Moment: just as
Hannibal understood mass is merely

Appearance, direction forcefully applied
        As he outflanked
Rome's legions and shut the gate

Disastrously on them. Or how
        Waiters bitch
The second they swing the kitchen door

Closed, then reassume their public
        Face as they
Approach holding a tray aloft.

In a way, every part of existence
        Is theatre, deception
Meant to conserve scarce resources.

Now the problem is trying to define
        The problem, which is
Taxing on each of us as we nurse

Our beers. Meanwhile, you keep one eye
        On the bar's TV
Through decorative latticework: it's been

A bad news cycle—lost
        Kids, found
Bodies, fires inexplicably begun

That smolder far into the night.
        Or the problem
Might be trying to get across

Slivers of information in the middle
> Of all this
Life going on around us. Who

Could blame anyone? Even frustrated
> Postal workers
Depend on codes to tell them when

To break, talk, eat. The problem
> As they see it
Isn't appearance, but taut control

Of quality: hovering now near ninety-
> Seven percent
And promising a steady, gradual improvement.

# LINDA DYER

## Hereditary Guess

I come from a long line of drunkards and cheats. My mother
touched the oil paintings in museums explaining symbol to
us, explaining style. My father pocketed artifacts from
the Petrified Forest when mounted guards surveyed the
valley in another direction. My cousin draws police
sketches, composites of criminals, all made to look like
his father. My brother lights candles without dropping
coins in the box. Me? I steal my own memories so they
can't be used for profit or loss. My sister, in her diary,
asks God to show her a sign, rearrange the ashes in the
fireplace. How do I know? I read the secrets in diaries,
an averted glance, a furtive reaching for something concealed
in the hand.

## Houdini's Daughter

Too loose.
My physical therapist tells me I'm
lucky my parents didn't sell me to
the circus, haha, if I had been born
in China I certainly would have been, oh, if.
If only I would have gone the way of the circus,
telescoped myself into the teeming clown car,
splayed like a lozenge on the lion's tongue,
a feeder for the flea circus, I extend
my arm for the bites and resulting itch.
I am large and small and every minute I wriggle
away and stand next to my padlock, my cage, my
underwater death in a straightjacket.
Houdini's lost daughter, subluxing one shoulder,
I nearly lived before myself,
stepping through my arms.


## My Muse: Gravity

I was conceived between
one argument and another
drunken destruction of property.
Philadelphia, 1960, most likely
April. Dish me up,
the one with the dent in her
head, a bowl my mother could
drink from when she was drunk
and tired from the new turns:
three babies, the philandering husband,
new job, the coming home, chicken
pox, her own philandering. Who
wouldn't drink from her baby's head
and forget to nurse?

My mother now white haired,
toothless, dentureless even,
chuckling to herself over my letters,
over the dried out geranium,
crashing empty bottles down into
the alley, her old therapy of noise

and splinter. We are each other's
subject matter: follicle, scrap,
fragment of a dish, some clamoring
explanation and address.

## Screen Doors of the 1960s

Of all the houses in the years
we moved so often, someone else's
family initial, in script,
greeted visitors, "S" or "T" or "W"
amidst the curling aluminum,
maybe so we stayed anonymous
when the lawn grew higher
than the hedges. Or, like a sermon
I heard about believers sprinkling blood
on their door frames so that God
would pass over their house without
extending one curse or another
as to the unbelievers.

And we were spared absolute
destruction, though not some
of the lesser curses (fire,
robbery, eviction),
especially under W,
but we expected some
trouble and figured with our
borrowed initial we might be
getting someone else's share—
maybe less than what we deserved.
Another barrier between us
and whatever threatened
our relative safety:

deadbolt, front door, screen door, initial;
which left us to save our own
for the next life.

# Conservation of Momentum

1.
After the first month
of moments (kiss,
embrace, sweaty wrestle,
a moon gone through
its phases),
*something* compels a
look to the end,
and what might
signal it (collisions
or explosions conserve
momentum identically):
the warm morning when
nothing, not one dream,
argues you awake
too early;
not one thing has
gone wrong
or remains unsaid.


2.
Then the sharing of night secrets:
untranslatable phrases, repeated,
somnambulant leaving and returning.
And he has begun to say "It's all right,
no one is here," so the vision
of known strangers may recede
until tomorrow night.
The lone snore and a willingness
to be coaxed awake—
a private moment made public:
morning urination,
paper as it curls into flame,
chair scraping along the breakfast
floor. The lighthouse keeper
adopts a cat to share
a loneliness compounded
by vast external space—
ships, entire cities, a moon,
presumed in the fog.

3.
A solar system is being formed
under confirmation of the new
mighty telescopes—an empty
sphere around a star, likely site
for stellar companions. It's mostly
a race among men—the kind of men
Whitman predicted in his
celebrations, who will name
new planetary masses after
themselves, followed by a number
(#57, #58) to allow for additional bodies
he may discover or properly document.
The eye trained to a telescope hour after hour
will give him a headache, but his pulse
will pound, he'll hardly be able
to contain an outburst when he discerns
an unrecognized mass or a steady
light moving toward the red
of the spectrum.

4.
The moon wakes me again
startled and guilty for not doing
some required thing—
a corpse in the living room
which eventually one night is a corpse
in my bed. Did I forget to feed it,
comfort it? The smell is what
rouses me as it stretches its length
against me like a dog
while the moon fades
like an accusation.

5.
I am an uneasy prediction
for a man in love with numbers.
After sex, his limbs are sprawled
and motionless as if he'd been
dropped from a great height—
maybe pushed backwards
over a moonlit balcony—
but happy.

# Michael Klein

## The Play My Father's In

After the broken one, matched to the summer of 1949 (when policemen roped off the entrance to 7 Park Avenue because her mother's flowered nightgown got caught, stopped her a torn minute, and then let her almost finished body go the whole way down—out the window and through the sky she jumped from), my mother grew two smaller hearts. In Washington, D.C., five years later: twin boys, in the second chamber of summer—August, 1954.

Max and Rex. Four minutes apart. They sang before they talked.

On August 18th, after floating with her babies into motherhood, Kathryn Jacqueline went back to having one heart, scarcely remembering it. When they were old enough, she strolled her new ones into the shade of a pink umbrella in a D.C. park, to nap, while she sold hot dogs.

To curious passers-by who asked, *Are they twins?* my mother replied, *No, they're chicken pot pies!*

I rose in front of Rex, so my mother tells me. So it says somewhere on a piece of important paper in a building that got burned down. Rex came through the shadow of me. Speedboat racing from a cave.

I'm Max: listener like the grass.

Rex is a talker: like the rain.

We're still alive.

On August 19th, 1990-something, Rex is talking into the outgoing tape of an answering machine in Boston-soliloquies modeled after Ruth Draper or Anna Russell—monologist women who've mastered the sound of life without men in their trembling, high-pitched voices. Rex loves people, but doesn't have a life of many of them. He's alone most of the time in the provincial city. He spends time reading and writing. He sees people at the movies. Seeing people is enough of people. Rex doesn't long for people, he remembers them.

Of course, my brother knows he is a person, but he doesn't know it in a group of persons. In a group of people, my brother feels unique—*terminally unique,* as they say. So, he can't learn a lot from them. He can't teach them. How can he love them?

Rex and I used to listen to Draper and Russell in a New York closet. We were twelve or thirteen. We hid behind a door so our parents wouldn't see us sitting by the little record player like it was a little fire. With Draper and Russell in the air, we found an early way of not being known to our parents. Physical reality didn't entice the brothers. Trees didn't interest them nearly as much as whatever it was shivering in those leaves. Was it something specific to trees?

Mostly, we huddled behind the closed door because my mother had married again. We knew she would have encouraged us to listen to Draper and Russell or the original cast album of *Mame* for that matter—they were *her* women, too—but the stepfather was a dark horse. What would he have made of a couple of tow-headed boys listening to divas (we didn't know the word, but that's what they were) on a toy phonograph in the middle of the afternoon?

We didn't want to know. News from the stepfather was already difficult, edgy and short. I don't think my stepfather could ever settle down with my mother. He was restless, which gave him habits he couldn't break—biting his nails, twirling a place in his hair until he went bald there.

Floating above his already darkness was another cloud Rex and I could see. We knew that he didn't like women—the way only a male can know another male doesn't like women. The answer about disliking them went far back, I think—the eerie fact that when Robert Martin Burger was born (his mother, Mae, used to joke about it)—the doctor delivered him with the umbilical cord around his neck. *A disaster of my love,* she told her first-born son. And Rex and me, the first time we met her.

Mae Burger was, obviously, the kind of woman who could say the wrong thing at the wrong time, and she seemed to thrive in the discomfort that sailed badly to the other person. She interrupted people, pointed out misfortune, made sure that when she gave something away she made you know how much it cost.

One of the strangest things Mae ever did was marry her own stepfather. It didn't last very long. She married a total of three times, I think, and lives today (very shrunken, my sister tells me) in Florida. She's outlived practically everyone she ever had in her life and apparently doesn't utter a word now.

After I laugh at the characters on Rex's answering machine, I always want to shake my head in regret. I know the tape is so far out of range because Rex knows no one will be calling except me or our birth father, who lives far away, in Germany—transplanted there since 1970-something. My father and I are allies in this one and only sense—we let life go by in sweeping measures of no music before we answer Rex. Rex is our key, in a way, of any music we have. Rex is how my father and I have come to know each other, and it's a strange configuration. The temperature has changed. I'm colder from that version of love, less love, no love.

Sometimes, I can be colder to Rex than I am to anyone else in my life. Not only because of my father, but also because of Rex himself. On his own. Rex can't talk specifically about the way he feels which is what I've really needed from people, lately. My father is cold, too, but he loves Rex through the chill. In a story I imagine him writing with his mind, my father loves Rex more than Max. Rex and my father share alcohol, and skipping some tracks of life.

They share something invisible, too, which is dream country to me. I don't know what it is that draws them toward each other. I don't know what ensures them the comfort of the draw. My friend R. says that fathers who spent a lot of time in a war love their sons in a way that makes it seem like they know better than the child could possibly know what's good for him. My father loves Rex like that.

Once, when Rex was between gigs, my father told him to go and join the Air Force. Rex did. He went to Biloxi, Mississippi. He fell asleep with a cigarette which started a mattress on fire. He flunked basic training and they put him in a psychiatric ward. My father and Rex never talked about Biloxi. My father wasn't mad about the fire or happy that Rex hadn't succumbed to it. He was between feelings.

My father must have a secret life sometimes. There must be a kind of person my father is that no one really knows. In his secret life he isn't responsible to anyone but secret people. In the life I see him living, my father can't relate to people who've been through situations in which they've been saved. *How did they get into a situation like that to begin with?* my father says, when someone poses the question—a question involving the saved.

Then again, sometimes I think my father is sitting in a theater and watching a play about Rex and Max, two twin boys he once held, when there was only romance in the world. During the play, my father keeps going to the lobby to smoke a cigarette, make a phone call. He misses important scenes and when he gets back to his seat he makes up what he's missed without checking it with the person sitting next to him to see if it's right. My father isn't the kind of person who wants to know if he wasn't the first to catch it.

He was in the Air Force himself, once—part of a generation of men who didn't question what the government said they should do next. In his case, he had a mother and father who were very vague. If his parents did have a dream for him, they never dreamed it. They barely spoke to each other. They got divorced. They sent their son to Yale, which was around the corner. He took up a plane. They forgot about him.

In the '50s, anyone who didn't trust the government didn't have much moral support. All that's kaput. Now we know. Too much, my father thinks. We know what we once suspected . . . that none of it works.

The way my father loves me is the way he loves the government. He goes on the mission they give him, but doesn't know if he'll come back in one piece. He has to go, it's his job. My father knows I'm there, which makes him think about love—*knowing someone's really there*—but he's just fixing his mind on a place on a map. Duty, not desire.

He takes off his hat and places it on the map, like a change of heart the Chairman of the Board is having during a business meeting. My father drops the hat like a toy soldier tied to a handkerchief parachute over the place between Fatherland and Homosexuality. When the soldier lands on the map, my father thinks: *People live there. Why do people live there?*

My father calls from far away and insults Rex's outgoing message into the incoming message. If only they could overlap. If only my father could interrupt Rex's Draper or Rex's Russell. But he can't. Technology has made it so that he can't overlap or interrupt. My father gets one chance to hear the sound of Rex being out of range. My father's one chance is a variance of: *Rex, get a real life.* Or, a variance of: *Rex, it's time to get your shit together.*

My father is a string of variances, like those thin leaves of see-through color I watch curl away from the heat of spotlights in an auditorium on 11th Street, where we are living in New York. We have to interrupt the rehearsal of *Oliver!* so Mr. Kreitzburg can climb the ladder and change the gels.

The auditorium is in the wood-lined heart of a school called P.S. 41, and the most important day will be when these two things happen: in the morning, a group of teenage girls will strip me and throw me out into the street. And, later, that afternoon in a rehearsal with a pianist, I will discover that I want to make acting and singing my life. When I am naked in public and singing or acting, I don't remember my life, which is what I want. With singing, it can happen with a chord. One chord, and I disappear.

But when I'm naked in front of the school, away from its wood-lined heart and deeper into the world of citizenship—the feeling of not remembering my life is not as joyful as the one chord. In the street, it's like looking into a fire. You look, and time feels stacked—not on the line of *this happens next* that it usually is.

I am standing in the middle of 11th Street without any clothes because of those girls, thinking of what it is that makes me *me* and falling instead on everything other than what I know I am. In this otherness, I am poor and parentless. But, I still have a brother named Rex. Rex is the hinge of the gate of what I know about myself without thinking.

The girls find me in the lunchroom and tell me they have something to show me, etc. I know they are bad. They dress like they're bad—haphazard, no color. I know they have done other things to other classmates—twisting their arms and challenging them to fights. They are one of the *something*(s) about the school. After the stairs and my shirt and pants and underwear and shoes and socks that float through the landings and bump off the red banisters on the way down, real life comes back in the form of a rehearsal. I walk through the auditorium—naked—before anybody gets there and find my costume backstage. I wear a pair of pants that don't make it to the floor of the stage, and an old T-shirt.

Rex and I are the best actors in the school, which makes the teachers love us and the students hate us. I'm playing Oliver and Rex is playing Fagin. Oliver is looking for his mother and for love. Fagin is looking for money. Actually, they are looking for the same thing.

Oliver is the softer role, which feels closer to who I really am. It is the role of a lifetime. It is a role written around wonder and empathy and a certain naivete about men and women. Aside from the fact that Oliver is an orphan, I would like to be everything else that he is. He can sing.

Fagin is tougher—older, bathed in blue. But, I can still sense his heart, and Rex plays him (I suppose), the way I would play him—cranky, but with a sense of play. Rex and I share an aesthetic already. We like the same things, but we have different spins, different approaches. In the play, for instance, I improvise, while Rex rests his arm on the banister of knowing his lines. He likes to know where he's supposed to be standing by the time he's finished singing a song called "Reviewing the Situation."

When I'm finished with the song "Who Will Buy?", I might as well be floating in the clouds. I never remember exactly where I'm supposed to be standing, but the director doesn't seem to mind. She always seems transfixed directing twins—she's never worked with them before. She doesn't know that most of the time, I can pretend I'm singing from a cloud.

Rex is structured differently inside, which complements our coupling. There's a staircase, well built and sturdy, that rises up in him. Or, at least that's what it would seem like if I could see into him. Me, I'm just dandelions there. It *feels* like dandelions, but I don't know what it *looks* like.

There's a scene in the play where I've been adopted by the mean undertaker and don't want to live with him. I escape from his house and have to go through a window into the backstage. During that climb in staged time, between leaving the stage and entering what's behind it—the backstage of heavy curtains, cables, painted sets, and the glow of E-X-I-T— I feel the moment has an indelible aspect to it. There's a life behind my life.

In *Oliver!* my big song is "Where Is Love?" It's a plea, with more than one object. It's abstract, but I don't know that yet, the way I didn't know then that Oliver and Fagin are both looking for the same thing.

I think singing will bring people to me. I think I will be discovered singing.

Rex gets to sing "You've Got to Pick a Pocket or Two."

I switch roles with Rex in a dream it has taken years to build. We spend our childhood switching roles, switching classes, switching boyfriends and girlfriends. In the dream, in the latest version—I'm Fagin—an old man, living in a den of beaming male youth—a loft in Brooklyn, who sends his graffiti artists out along the rail-lines to mark up their city. I take the boys from their mothers because I love them more than any woman does. I know what they need, which isn't just physical. I tell them that my love will turn into money, if they want it hard enough. Like money.

In *Oliver!* I make asking for more sound like singing. Rex makes the song "You've Got to Pick a Pocket or Two" sound like an anthem, a march. We are good little actors. Singers. Troopers. On stage, off stage, school, on the way home. Home.

We're discontent.

That was the first day I found out anything about anonymity—a life billowing behind a life. It was a secret way of feeling. Later, I will be anonymous in different ways. I will join groups without telling other members things that don't have to do with the group directly. In this way, I will be part of the group not as *myself,* but as a *member* of the group. In one group, nobody knows how I get money. In another group, nobody knows how I move through sex or relationships, and so on. It isn't as if I'm not getting help by not revealing anything. I get the whole picture in a group. But mostly, and fervently, I get the sense of my own insignificance, which makes me right-sized.

The feeling of anonymity is an abiding spirit, in a way. But it can also be a culprit. Sex can make anonymity a culprit or anonymity makes sex a culprit.

There was no birth father then, in back of that day of spotlights, the way there is what's left of him now. My mother divorced him the same year I was singing "Where Is Love?" My father shifted his '62 Triumph convertible into neutral and put it on a boat headed for Germany because there was nothing left for him in America. I'm guessing there was nothing left. I may be wrong. He may, very well, have buried a dream somewhere, right under our lives.

At the beginning of being gone, my father sent Rex and me birthday cards. He told us that he couldn't tell what was going on in America. He'd lost touch, especially by the end of the '60s. There was no German equivalent to the Woodstock music festival, which I wrote him about. In the letter, I told him that Rex and I were tripping our tits off on acid, and that we'd run into a kindly mid-westener who gave us some Thorozine to bring us back to earth.

I didn't understand anything about my father moving to another country, another wife, and having to find the language to put that in. My father was good at languages—a trait he couldn't pass on to me. I'm musical, but I have no sense of translation—of turning meaning into more meaning. The way I hear it first is the way it is.

My father can speak Vietnamese and Russian. He once told me he was a spy, but I don't think he was, really. I don't think my father could stay interested long enough in a person to be a spy.

It's given me a little shame, having only one language. English doesn't have all the words, I know that. I know when I'm speaking it, that English doesn't have all the words.

Rex and I had a language, but we lost it.

Rollo May came to study us before we lost it. He told my parents it was common for twins to have their own language, which made them stop worrying about us. We spoke our own language until we had something to say to my mother and father. But it could have been a song we said first to our parents: "Angels Watching Over Me."

Sometimes, (I remember thinking), singing kept you alive better than talking did.

Sometimes, instead of birthday cards, my father sends us photographs of the tranquil Rhine river he is living on. The river is shining in the margin. In one particularly busy photo, there's a flea market going on and I can see a shirt shining—green velvet—through the trees. It's him, but I can't see my father fully. Most of him is standing behind the third wife, who is beautiful in a hard way—like the Rhine itself. Or beautiful, in the same way a victory is.

My father's wife is named Bridgit, and by the time Rex meets her, she will drink a bottle of pink champagne and make a pass at him while my father is away on business. Bridgit will flirt with me, too, but I won't accept her. I will be drunk in a way that makes me stuck in the past where my lover is. My longing will drift out the window, like a perfume, over the Rhine, and back to America, without picking up anything about the present.

I amuse Bridgit, mostly. She can only imagine my life, I think, when she says she doesn't understand homosexuality. I don't answer in real time. But on my mind's list of things to do, I write down Genet, Baldwin and Ginsburg. I will lend her my favorite books if she will teach me German.

German is a very hard language for me to learn, like any language. It keeps sinking with a flourish to the bottom of a lake. My mouth can't find its way around German. I can't feel German teeth. I can't copy German with my mind. I last a week with Bridgit, the tutor, and comfort myself by remembering that most of the people around know English, even though they don't like to use it. I can't tell what the German gay men really think of me, the American, when I ask them to speak English and they tell me that they can't.

They *won't*.

When I visited my father, we drank and took his car into little towns. We learned how to walk around Germany through the dark. It should have all felt like a ride—a new place in the breezy dark—but with my father, it felt like a drill. He was teaching managers how to manage in a conference room at an old hotel in Ludwigshafen and I picked up a boy who shared his hashish with me.

In the morning, as we were leaving the elevator and walking through the lobby, we ran into my father. I introduced the boy, Geoff, to him. My father was completely kind and charming, in the beginning-of-a-party kind of way.

Geoff kept calling me after I got back to America, but to me he represented such a specific moment that I couldn't call him back. I wouldn't know what to say. He was so far away now that he had become an idea.

It was Christmastime then, in Germany, and my mother—my father's first wife—had died that past summer, in the closing door of July. When he wasn't driving for his job, my father stayed home and wrote letters to drum up more business. Then we'd usually go out somewhere after dinner and get drunk together.

Sometimes my father would get too tired and leave me at the bar. He'd leave me at the bar in the middle of a sentence in German that just got spoken to the bartender. All the bartenders knew my father because he was such a good tipper and he was blond and lived in America once. They all liked him because he'd defected. They liked him because he was funny in their language, which made him seem German. He'd translated.

When my father left me there at the bar, I had to get home alone, which meant taking a cab. Like I said, I'm not good at languages and I had to re-pronounce the name of my father's street over and over again until the driver could figure out where I was going. I had to vary the sound of the street name ever so slightly until the right key fit in the lock. Click. Home.

My room had a long ultraviolet ceiling unit that hung over the bed like some kind of detector—a *sober yet?* detector?—and I would put on goggles sometimes and swim along the purple light. I'd lie in bed for a few minutes for a brief dose of some German inventor's sunlight, and it made me feel like a patient in a room, cut off from the rest of the hospital, which reminded me of how I was cut off from my family.

When I wasn't getting a tan at night, I climbed out the window and sat in the grass, looking at the Rhine and the lights of Dusseldorf, shining brighter than most of the stars. I was in a kind of backstage now, in the bigger world, and it was there, right under his nose, that I'd make up my father's life. He had to leave America because he couldn't figure out what to do with the kids. He had to drive a silver Mercedes now, up and down the autobahn looking for managers—hitch-hikers who needed him more than his own children did.

I thought that the trip to my father in the '70s would make up for lost time. That I would meet and love a man who had, for so many years, been an enigma. I was thinking on the plane over there (dressed in leather and nursing a black eye sustained in a horrible mugging in Times Square the week before), that what I wanted most was to hear my father's voice again.

I hadn't forgotten so much what he looked like, but I couldn't remember his voice or how he put sentences together. I couldn't remember his mind. I was still sad about my mother's death. It was a big death because of its string connecting to people, of course, but also to ideas. My mother had been the center of so many different universes:

| | |
|---|---|
| Public death | She'd written a letter to Jacqueline Kennedy after the assassination and got a personal letter back |
| The dining room table | Daiquiris and Joan Baez records after school |
| Movies | Saturday |
| Light streaming under a door all night | Guardian angel that couldn't sleep |

Nobody's love could quite hold her in the world because she had a different version of it in her heart, which never fit into anyone else's. An orphan heart. Like Oliver's heart. No home. And so, she died. And when she died, I wrote my father a letter. He sent me a plane ticket. I buried my mother in the rain and got on a plane to Germany. That was twenty years ago.

I remember my mother less and less now—the specific form of being in her body is hard to see. But I remember her voice, and especially her mind, and how it lit up the room when she was putting Rex and me to sleep with a story she made up about the city or the country. *They're very different places, you know,* she would always say. The country was the place where all the animals lived and in the city there were all the people. In my mother's mind, they didn't live together. She sang the story about the animals and talked the story about the people.

My mother had two minds.

My father's voice gets left inside my phone machine sometimes—in short messages all in half-voice—cancer took the other half. Once, my father called to wish me a happy birthday and was startled that someone had actually picked up the phone. He was confused into having to finish the song. His mistake. He thought he was calling Rex. The only reason my father will call me, nowadays, is to find the other son. Rex has a phone, but there are long periods when it doesn't ring because he doesn't pay the bill.

Because I know the game my father is playing, I tell him I'm tired of having that kind of relationship—the one that involves me having to face the fact that he cares more for Rex than he cares for me. I'm tired of having to know that, of walking up and down the city, the stairs that lead to the sea and away from the sea, the earth—knowing that I will never reach my father's heart. It isn't so much that I need my father to love me. It's too late for that. I've loved already, without having been loved by him. I made it up. I found a way. I figured it out.

I wrote a letter about three years ago and told my father that I didn't like how I was being used to get to Rex. But my father never answered me. Then, last year, he called to say he was going to send a letter—that actually, he owed me a letter. My father keeps thinking that he'll get to say in a letter what he can't tell me over the phone, so he never sends it. My father is the kind of a person that will put the fire out on an idea to keep it from happening.

Sometimes I see him in a dream in the middle of a tunnel in Central Park, huddling over a little fire like homeless men do—the way movies roll them out, a little idiotically. I'm an actor in a play, telling my father from the Delacourt Theater stage to *send the letter*. It's a pseudo-Shakespeare play.

Rex always appears towards the end of the dream, riding on a horse through the tunnel, dressed in a wedding dress, galloping past me and our father. I don't know where my mother is exactly, but I feel the pressure of it, suddenly—not knowing where she is exactly. Then, like a breeze off the lake near the Belvedere Castle that rises out of the park, like a myth, I feel my mother in the colors of the dream—like her being, what makes her herself, is what the colors are: the choice.

When I ask my brother who he's getting married to, he says with the confidence and blind faith of someone getting married: *the world*. And I'm thinking—or do I say this in the dream: Do you propose to the world first, or just do it?

*I do*, you say to the world.
*I did*, the world calls back.


# TERRI FORD

## BP Station Employee Restroom, 2 A.M.

Here's the diagram. Here's
what a sawed-off shotgun
looks like. Here's

a Derringer, here's
a Colt. *Here are some words
we used for drunk: Smashed. Trashed,
and bombed.* Do not keep
any large bills on hand
after midnight. *Here are some words
we use for kill: Hit. Taken out. Elimination.
Snuffed. Offed. Knocked off.* Keep the lot
lights up, as well as

inside. *Here are some words
we use toward love: Crush. Flame.
Arrow. Torch. Fallen. I

fell.* Maintain eye
contact with each incoming

person. Greet them. Hi.
Hello, chief. Buenos
noches. Hey, buddy. *Nobody
move.* Hello.

## Mister Hymen

*Relent,* says he with his cigarillos, his
splintered windshield. You fain think
he's neat, is boss, is mustang,

yup. When he covers your north
with kisses,   oho the hymen
hies, bucolic        inland you're tossing

edelweiss, unmown and springing. This thump
and wag hath no repose     & when, how soon, he's

dying (says)   — So you, as
foreordained, give      in. What he broke's
not glass, but a low grief, volcanic
and inactive years. See him run. All

of the villagers run
from heat, and you spread,
spread.

# Better Off

When I let him go, I will rise from the earth
and be borne up, balloon
my shoes, balloon
my tooth, balloon

haiku. When resentment lifts, fireflies
shall alight in my skirt and beep with me, high over
the lawn and the globular
peonies, this aggressive

riffing air. When the yearning
stops, if it ever stops, I will dance

the most strenuous hula, and mine own
cabana boys will candle me back down, signal

the all-clear, and I will
come home, safely in slow mo
drifting on down.

# Heartsick

In the bang shock section of the gag
catalog, you can purchase bang gum, bang wallet,
bang cigarette, bang toilet seat, bang

sex report, and an exploding pen. In the fourteen
stages of ballistic, how long until he talks

to me? How long can he keep
this mad, keep turned away? Bang

the bell, the bone, bang the stones
in the forcing pot, the silence

of reports. In the dark his fear
comes near me still: cry
of the peacock, the bugling
elks. Oh, the space between us

leaking, full, never
empty, never
closed.

# For the love of an anaconda woman

To be with her, as many as ten men
anacondas will wrestle with her and each other
for weeks in a slow breeding ball. They look
like a moving circle of bike tires, adjusting
their claims. They look like a bad dream

of embrace, this global
grip woo, although (come on, fellas) her strength
is the mother of strong. Still they writhe
with her, licking
the air, so legion and so
single-minded: can these perps

be far from us? Their mouths
full of needles, wide
as bejesus, sleeping

in the hyacinth marsh. Somewhere I hope
there is one with my name, tetchy
and muscular, seething off
toward the cormorants, loved,
overloved, loaded
with small triggers.

# ALISON MOORE

# The Angel of Vermont Street

For as long as she lives and probably longer she will never forget his face. And if memory truly lasted beyond earthly life, then she knew he took something of her with him when he closed his eyes and died—the memory of her face—an angel that had at long last shown herself and come to gather him home. She wondered if he even knew she was the one who hit him. The bicycle lay on its side, one wheel crumpled—no more substantial than a child's pinwheel beneath the car, the other wheel still spinning crazily as if it only wanted to free itself from the frame and roll safely away. He made no sound as she leaned over him. But his eyes were luminous, clear. When she moved her head so that the street light directly above them cast its full illumination, his pupils failed to respond, leaving him wide open to the reach of light and the shape of her moving slowly above him. When he closed his eyes she moved her head again. Her shadow passed across his face like the shadow of earth shielding the moon from the full force of the sun.

Later she would learn that he was partially crippled to begin with, that the bicycle moved him through the world, that his hands held the handlebars only by some sheer miracle of faith. The newspaper had said, quoting someone who knew him from the men's shelter where he lived, "He was an accident waiting to happen." But he had happened to her, come out of nowhere on the switchbacks of Vermont Street. He'd lost his balance, surely. She had not—she was almost certain of this—run into him. He had run into her, or at least fallen precisely in her path. Had he planned it? Was this a botched attempt at collecting insurance, a lawsuit to live on for the rest of his life? Or had he meant to go further—all the way beneath the wheels?

His body. Breaking. That was what she heard. Solid and heavy against the thin steel of her foreign car. A sound she still hears repeatedly. There was no scream, no cry, just the body taking it, that final rendezvous with a faster thing.

She had just come from John's house. She had told him she couldn't see him anymore. Isn't that the way it went? Or was it him saying that to her? Wasn't he the one who had gone too far one night, his hands on her neck losing their caressing innocence by degrees as they tightened and would not, despite her frantic struggling, let go? He said she was imagining things, and always had. Maybe the feeling of suffocation was emotional rather than visceral and she had conjured the image as a warning to herself—cut and run before it's too late. John, she believed, was someone capable of going too far, even if he hadn't actually done anything. But as she stood there on Vermont Street in the aftermath of the accident, when the nameless man was taken away in the unhurried ambulance because he was beyond resuscitation, after the police had gotten her statement, after the fire truck had come to hose down the blood—after it was all over she returned, shaking, to her car to wait for John. It was his name and number that had been in her address book under "In Case of Emergency" and this, finally, was one. She had only been in San Francisco a few months—there was really no one else she knew well enough to call.

After he got there he led her to his car—"Don't try to drive yours—we can come back tomorrow for it," he said, taking her in hand. She turned to him in the dark, in the green cockpit glow of the dashboard lights and the square of solid red for the unreleased brake. She wanted to say, "Take it back, what you said two hours ago. Don't say you can't continue. Don't let me get into my car. Don't let me hit that man because I'm running scared from you." But she said nothing because she could not remember what he'd said or even the sound of his voice saying it. Shock had made her memory unreliable. She couldn't even count on herself anymore.

In his living room she wrenched off her clothes. The spots of blood on the sleeves were not her own. She drew him to her there on the floor because she couldn't wait any longer, because she believed he still might be capable of tenderness in the wake of an emergency. What she wanted was shelter, the certainty of his weight riding above her. But what it felt like was impact, all her bones bent to breaking beneath him, the breath driven from her lungs, her heart seized with a sickening fear that the next beat could be the next to the last. "Stop!" she said, terrified, but it was too late. He'd already come inside her.

In the morning she left before he woke, took her keys once and for all. She never saw him again.

The officer in charge of the case told her the next day that the man had been identified. He had been living as a permanent resident of an independent living project in a hotel that had once been marked for demolition. The residents were doing the renovation themselves. She got the number of the hotel and spoke to a Father Alvarado, who had sponsored him, and who helped supervise the construction. He said Eduardo León was the man's name, that he had come from El Salvador. "How much do you want to know?" Father Alvarado asked. "All you can tell me," she said, but then immediately felt afraid. Hearing his name had been hard enough. Father Alvarado told her that Eduardo had been spirited into Arizona, then California, by the Sanctuary Movement. In the hotel, he had laid tile in the bathrooms, though he was far too slow by commercial standards. His right hand had been broken by government soldiers, or at least that's the story he told about himself, and who could make a thing like that up? They broke his hand, a finger at a time, to give him time to think, an incentive to tell all, to not hold anything back. They wanted the details—who he knew, where the guerrillas met, what was said. They believed he was lying when he said he knew nothing. "They worked very hard to make him remember," Father Alvarado said.

She arranged to meet Father Alvarado at the hotel. Claire wanted to see Eduardo's room, to at least look through its window. She hadn't thought this through, not really. In a way, she felt like an adopted child searching for clues that signified who he was. She wanted to know exactly who she'd killed.

She hadn't counted on feeling so dangerous beneath the stares of his coworkers and friends. "So you're the one," their faces seemed to say, as if she'd taken a gun and shot him point-blank. But eventually she moved past them, down a long hallway thick with a mist of plaster dust and a vapor of paint fumes to the room where Father Alvarado was hanging Sheetrock. He was a young priest in blue jeans and a black shirt, a dark beard curling over his white clerical collar. He had a crucifix around his neck and a massive ring of keys clipped to his belt loop next to a retractable tape measure. Safety glasses shielded his eyes. He seemed to know who she was immediately. She thought he could probably sense a confession coming a mile away; she hoped her face would not betray her. She had come to look, not to tell.

He lifted his safety glasses. He looked like an aviator getting out of a biplane, his vision trying to rapidly adjust from cloud to ground. She had told him on the phone she wanted to see Eduardo's room but he seemed puzzled by her presence and she did not want to repeat this request to his face—it was hard enough to ask the first time. He wiped his hands on his jeans, leaving a white, dusty smudge like flour on his thighs. He simply placed his left hand on her right shoulder and guided her toward the stairs.

On the second floor they walked down a long hallway of numbered rooms. He stopped in front of number eight and frowned. The door was partly open. He stepped cautiously into the room while Claire watched from the hallway. Bureau drawers had been wrenched from their wooden frame and were empty. The closet was bare. Only a pair of boots remained—one heel stacked at least an inch higher than the right—useless for the even-legged man who had taken Eduardo's clothes. Father Alvarado gave a long sigh. "I wish they would have waited a little longer." He motioned Claire into the room. She tiptoed in. Somehow it seemed proper to do so.

Her eyes went immediately to the wall above the bed—a foot-high crucifix displayed its human decoration—an emaciated, bleeding Christ carved of wood, but instead of his head hanging, resigned and forsaken, he looked up, as if in the act of asking a question. He was, not anguished like all the images of Christ she'd seen, but surprised, as though he couldn't believe the way things had turned out.

"He carved that himself," Father Alvarado said.

She nodded. She knew.

There was a picture on the dresser in a wooden frame. Two figures. She approached it slowly as if the people there would suddenly avert their faces from the directness of her gaze. One of them was Eduardo. She would know him anywhere. And the woman—she could only be his mother. He is grinning—he knows what the camera is, but his mother looks instead at him. Or maybe she did know and wanted the picture to record that look so that he could always feel her gaze upon him from afar. The photograph was proof—he had been alive, he had been born of a woman who clearly loved him. It felt suddenly to Claire that the building rolled beneath her feet. She wished it was an earthquake that made her grab for the wall. She jerked her head around to see if Father Alvarado had felt it, too, was bracing himself in the door for the aftershock. But it was only her own body, seismic with guilt and dread. Father Alvarado looked at her, concerned.

"Please—I'd like to be alone for a moment here—you understand."

His head slowly moved in affirmation. He was, after all, in the business of understanding. "I'll be downstairs if you need me."

She closed the door when his footsteps died away. She turned again to the bed. She balanced on her right foot and slipped off her left shoe. She slipped off her right, nearly losing her balance as she did so. She steadied herself, walked barefoot across the naked wood floor leaving dark sweaty footprints in the dusty surface. She sank slowly into the mattress. She stared at the ceiling, at the once-true squares now curling at the corners. It looked a lot like the linoleum in her mother's kitchen and for a moment she felt turned upside down, as if she lay on the ceiling and was staring down at the floor.

Beneath her she felt the shape his body had eroded into the mattress. She tilted her head back, took in first the feet nailed to the cross, the long lean legs flowing upward toward the arching ribcage, she spread arms, the neck thrusting the head upward—the whole body a white slender flame straining to stay lit, the word "why" the wick that kept him burning against the indifferent gusting breath of God.

She made herself memorize it—the last thing Eduardo saw each and every night in America, the first thing he saw in the morning. Something to superimpose on the image of his face, as if seeing what he saw could return him to his own bed once and for all, that she could then rise up, return to her own bed and finally sleep.

She took an emergency leave of absence from her job as a counselor at the community college. She told her supervisor there'd been a death in the family. She didn't offer any details and he didn't ask for any. "Take as long as you need," he said.

She had lost the rhythm of her life, her habits fading from her like words on a page left too long in the sun. Sleep stopped coming altogether, leaving her stranded, a passenger waiting for a train that has been shunted onto another track. And she felt a huge loss—she had always loved to sleep, had enjoyed vivid dreams of weightlessness or flying, or erotic sex. But she began to have a waking dream, or a memory, she didn't know which. An image arose from the night of the accident that she had forgotten. Moments afterward a porch light went on at the nearest house. Someone stood silhouetted in the open doorway, a hall light on behind. Claire had shouted to call an ambulance. The person closed the door and disappeared inside. The moment after Eduardo had closed his eyes for the last time Claire ran toward the house. But before she reached its steep stairs, a woman appeared—out of the trees, out of the fog itself?—a woman who came and put her arms around her and—did she imagine this part?—rocked her, saying over and over *"Ay Dios mío, pobrecita, Ay Dios mío,"* a soothing incantation. Then she heard the ambulance in the distance. "Who are you?" Claire finally asked when she pulled back from the soft press of the woman's arms and the scent of woodsmoke mixed with gardenia perfume in her clothes. "Lupita," she said. But Claire knew that angels always had aliases. She'd sat through two showings, back to back, of *Wings of Desire,* which confirmed what she'd always suspected, that angels were ambivalent, torn by the world they presided over, pulled by passions and concerns they could not always keep safe distances from. Lupita vanished when the police came. Whoever she was, she didn't want to be identified as a witness. She had only come to comfort and disappear.

Eduardo's mother had been contacted. Claire waited for the phone to ring, for an anguished, accusing voice in Spanish, but no call ever came. Claire's insurance company reported that all his mother wanted was his body brought back to his country for burial. The insurance company, only too relieved to comply, had gotten off easy with such a modest request. So Eduardo was prepared and boxed and shipped south to his family, his country that probably he had every good reason in the world to leave but now he was returned, like a soldier from a senseless, undeclared war.

Then it was like the accident never happened, except that it still continued to change everything. Claire chose to see this as an omen. She waited for another sign. She wished she could open a fortune cookie that contained a clear itinerary. Go here. Do this. She would be glad for such direction. She thought of a pelican she had seen once as she drove the interstate in southern Arizona. It had been standing on the shoulder of the highway, lifting its feet one at a time from the burning pavement in a heart-wrenching dance. How could it let itself get so far away from water? Why was it just standing there, why in the world didn't it save itself and fly away?

The car stayed on Vermont Street where she'd left it, collecting a sheaf of tickets that fluttered from their windshield-wiper binding. One day she watched a city tow truck take it. She felt strangely satisfied that the real culprit had finally been shackled and led away.

She walked down Vermont Street often. For several weeks the skid marks remained—a black hieroglyphic whose meaning was clear only to her. And to the angel, Lupita, if she was still around to see it. Claire found herself looking for Lupita, searching the windows of houses up and down the steep hills.

One day she followed a woman who looked like Lupita to a

laundromat on 18th Street. Claire watched through the window. This woman settled into one of the orange plastic chairs to watch the television that was chained to a shelf. A hand-lettered sign hung from it saying DO NOT CHANGE CHANNELS OR VOLUME THANK YOU THE MANAGEMENT. The woman didn't seem to have any laundry—the machines were all silent. Claire's vision telescoped. Through a window, she was watching the woman who was watching a program on a TV screen and on the screen was a woman looking at a smaller TV screen on which a woman could be seen climbing out a window. For Claire, time stopped. There was only this endless repetition of women and windows into infinitesimally smaller screens.

The sun emerged briefly from the swirl of incoming fog, throwing Claire's shadow on the linoleum floor right at the woman's feet. The woman slowly turned her head to see who was behind her. Claire held her breath. She waited to be recognized. But it was not Lupita, at least she didn't think so. She wore her hair young—long and loose, but the face the dark hair framed seemed at least middle-aged, and she sat with her hands on her widespread knees, reigning over the substantial territory of her lap like a Maori queen. She motioned Claire to come in but Claire froze, as if she had been caught and was about to be reprimanded. She walked quickly away from the window, turned the corner, and headed down the hill, her heart racing. She knew she needed to go back—after all, the woman had summoned her. But she needed to bring some laundry with her—she couldn't just go in empty-handed. Bringing laundry would give her something to do in the event that she had mistaken the woman's gesture.

When she came back the woman was still there. Claire glanced at her as she put a load of sheets into a machine, but the woman was intent on the television. Claire shut the lid on the roar of water and she sat down at the opposite end of the row of chairs.

Claire hated TV, the whole blaring catalog of things for sale spliced with lean bits of entertainment, preferred the sheltered calm of public radio. This woman seemed transfixed by it. At 4:00, the worst began—people bearing their private horrors, weeping, terrifyingly vulnerable in front of live audiences who seemed ready to have their minds changed by whichever side told the best story. The woman was rapt while a father of four told how he'd found his wife in bed with his own father. His wife calmly explained to the camera that she regarded what she did as an act of mercy, that her father-in-law had been impotent and alone ever since his wife died and she believed if she did not intervene with that kind of tenderness he would have killed himself in complete despair.

"Lord have mercy," the woman cried, clearly angry, not with the wife but with the jeering audience.

Claire wondered if the wife's story made her an opportunist or a victim. It was hard to say.

On the next show, a woman reluctantly talked about her bulimia. Her husband, a therapist, seemed to be leading her through this public ordeal, as if disclosure was part of his prescription for her recovery.

As Claire listened to story after story, stopping only once to transfer the sheets to the dryer, she was struck by the nakedness of these confessions, the mesmerized witnessing by the audience, elevating the whole experience to some kind of religious ceremony. These TV programs could replace the Catholic Church—people, it seemed, could be absolved or damned right there on camera. She imagined herself in such a situation, sitting there and saying into a microphone for all the world to hear, "I killed someone—it was an accident." Would they jeer or weep? What part of the story would be true? How much would she have to fill in, make up, to keep their interest and sympathy? In what way could she make it a better story?

Claire broke out in a cold sweat, felt her stomach clench and heave. She leaned forward and put her head between her knees.

"It's a terrible tragedy," the woman said, touching Claire's shoulder, mistaking her reaction as a response to the man on a commercial preview for *Rescue 911*. He was crying, said he'd accidentally shot his son coming through a window at night, thinking it was a burglar. The son had forgotten his keys.

"Sometimes," the woman said, her hand on Claire's back, "these stories seem far away, like they could never happen to you, but they're so close, but for God's grace you could be up there, telling it all, too."

Claire looked up, turned her whitened face toward her. "Those stories—do you think they're true?"

The woman shrugged. "True enough." She looked over at Claire's dryer, which had just stopped spinning. She got up and headed toward it. She opened the door and took out the sheets, clutching them tightly to her chest as she crossed the aisle to the counter. She set them down and began to fold.

"Wait—you don't have to do that!" Claire said, rushing over.

"This is what I do."

"For money—I mean, do you work here?"

"No, not money. I just like to do it, watch the television, talk to the people." She smoothed her large palm across a yellow pillowcase. "The clothes are warm. They're clean again. It's nice."

She took out one of the sheets, then tucked it beneath her chin. "You are not married," she said.

"How do you know?" Claire was feeling naked now, all her laundry spread out, being read like so many tea leaves.

"Single sheets—one set," the woman said, tucking the fitted sheet's gathered corners expertly together. "You may have sheets but you don't sleep," the woman said, looking at Claire sympathetically.

"You can tell that from the sheets?"

"No," the woman said, "I tell that from your eyes."

Claire's hand went involuntarily to her face, where the signs of sleeplessness were as telltale as a scar. She let her arm drop.

The words came out of her brain directly, without passing through the filter of her mind, more calmly than she would have thought possible. "I killed someone," she said. She fully expected the woman to say, "I know" as if this fact of her life too was in the sheets, in the features of her face.

The woman gasped, took a half-step back.

"Your husband?" she whispered.

Claire shook her head. The woman seemed to assume that murder was too intimate for complete strangers.

"Your lover?"

Claire considered this, looked away from her, let her gaze turn toward the window for a second, as if some vision might be reflected to guide her, but she saw only her own bewildered face. Should she lie, should she tell a different story? It would be appallingly easy. What if Eduardo had been her lover? She had, after all, been in his bed beneath the mystified Jesus. From there it was only a small stretch of the imagination to see herself helping him with his shirt buttons because his hands were more hurried than his affliction would allow. But she couldn't go any further. Why? Because it was someone else's story? She was stuck there in his little room, unable to go forward, to consummate such an improbable love, or return to the fact of her life in a laundromat at that moment having said only a single sentence which could lead anywhere, and a woman waiting breathless, for the rest.

The woman's voice brought her back from the dark comfort of Eduardo's small room to the neon-lit laundromat. "Did he hurt you?" the woman asked, leaning in slightly, as if the terrible beauty of a story of self-defense only needed coaxing.

"Yes," Claire said, shocked and oddly excited by what she was suddenly capable of.

"A gun—a knife?" The woman did not ask this eagerly. They were into the details now, the things that make it all too real, that can be held up in a court of law as concrete evidence.

A lover. Who had hurt her. His touch too brutal? His touch nonexistent and therefore just as cruel? It was an old, old story.

Claire looked at the woman, knowing the next cue would come from her face. Claire would leave and never see this woman again. She could say anything, anything at all and still walk away free, maybe freer than when she came.

Another lost image surfaced from that night—the moment before the angel Lupita came to her. Eduardo León closed his eyes. Claire could feel him slipping away. Frantic, she bent closer, listened for his heart, then brought her mouth to his and breathed, finding the rhythm, her deep breath a loud whisper that reached all the way inside to call him back. She felt him take his own first breath as if she had been the one who taught him to live. She pulled away slightly, and then he opened his eyes. That's what she couldn't forget, the way he'd looked at her then. Like a lover.

"He died in my arms," she said, urged on by the beginning shine of the woman's tears that had been summoned to the corners of her eyes and waited only to fall.

She continued, emboldened now, so close to an unplanned revelation whose meaning she dared not reach too quickly to fully understand. "I wanted him to know I was the one. I wanted him to see my face, *mine*, and remember it. Always."

The woman reached for her hand. Claire hesitated, then held out her hand, palm open, to receive her.

She felt herself drifting into the night and the broken glass and the rain to look once more. This time, when she looked at Eduardo she felt herself fall slowly, face first, until she completely slipped inside him. She felt the excruciating pressure as she turned herself carefully around inside a body that was seconds away from death. She looked with him, at the shape of herself bending close. A face he might have created, a face that had waited in wood for him to release its true human expression, tender and astonished, exactly like his own.

# MARTÍN ESPADA

## Colibrí

*for Katherine, one year later*

In Jayuya,
the lizards scatter
like a fleet of green canoes
before the invader.
The Spanish conquered
with iron and words:
"Indio Taíno" for the people
who took life

from the rain
that rushed through trees
like evaporating arrows,
who left the rock carvings
of eyes and mouths
in perfect circles of amazement.

So the hummingbird
was christened "colibrí."
Now the colibrí
darts and bangs
between the white walls
of the hacienda,
a racing Taíno heart
frantic as if hearing
the bellowing god of gunpowder
for the first time.

The colibrí
becomes pure stillness,
seized in the paralysis
of the prey,
when your hands
cup the bird
and lift him
through the red shutters
of the window,
where he disappears
into a paradise of sky,
a nightfall of singing frogs.

If only history
were like your hands.

# Jorge the Church Janitor Finally Quits

*Cambridge, Massachusetts 1989*

No one asks
where I am from,
I must be
from the country of janitors,

I have always mopped this floor.
Honduras, you are a squatter's camp
outside the city
of their understanding.

No one can speak
my name,
I host the fiesta
of the bathroom,
stirring the toilet
like a punchbowl.
The Spanish music of my name
is lost
when the guests complain
about toilet paper.

What they say
must be true:
I am smart,
but I have a bad attitude.

No one knows
that I quit tonight,
maybe the mop
will push on without me,
sniffing along the floor
like a crazy squid
with stringy gray tentacles.
They will call it Jorge.

# La Tumba de Buenaventura Roig

*for my great-grandfather, died 1941*

Beunaventura Roig,
once peasants in the thousands
streamed down hillsides
to witness the great eclipse
of your funeral.
Now your bones have drifted
with the tide of steep grass,
sunken in the chaos of weeds

bent and suffering
like canecutters in the sun.
The drunken caretaker
cannot find the grave,
squinting at your name,
spitting as he stumbles
between the white Christs
with hands raised
sowing their field
of white crosses.

Buenaventura Roig,
in Utuado you built the stone bridge
crushed years later by a river
raving like a forgotten god;
here sweat streaked your face
with the soil of coffee,
the ground where your nephew slept
while rain ruined the family crop,
and his blood flowered like flamboyán
on the white suit of his suicide.

Buenaventura Roig,
in the town plaza where you were mayor,
where there once was a bench
with the family name,
you shouted subversion
against occupation armies and sugarcane-patrones
to the jíbaros who swayed
in their bristling dry thicket of straw hats,
who knew bundles and sacks
loaded on the fly-bitten beast
of a man's back.

Buenaventura Roig,
not enough money for a white Christ,
lost now even to the oldest gravedigger,
the one with an English name
descended from the pirates of the coast,
who grabs for a shirt-pocket cigarette
as he remembers your funeral,
a caravan trailing in the distance
of the many years
that cracked the skin around his eyes.

Buenaventura Roig,
we are small among mountains,
and we listen for your voice
in the peasant chorus of five centuries,
waiting for the cloudburst of wild sacred song,
pouring over the crypt-wreckage of graveyard,
over the plaza and the church
where the statue of San Miguel
still chokes the devil with a chain.

## Latin Night at the Pawnshop

*Chelsea, Massachusetts*
*Christmas, 1987*

The apparition of a salsa band
gleaming in the Liberty Loan
pawnshop window:

Golden trumpet,
silver trombone,
congas, maracas, tambourine,
all with price tags dangling
like the city morgue ticket
on a dead man's toe.

## When Songs Become Water

*for Diario Latino*
*El Salvador, 1991*

Where dubbed commercials
sell the tobacco and alcohol
of a far winter metropolis,
where the lungs of night
cough artillery shots
into the ears of sleep,
where strikers with howls
stiff on their faces
and warnings pinned to their shirts
are harvested from garbage heaps,

where olive uniforms keep watch
over the plaza
from a nest of rifle eyes and sandbags,
where the government party
campaigns chanting through loudspeakers
that this country
will be the common grave of the reds,
there the newsprint of mutiny
is as medicine
on the fingertips,
and the beat of the press printing mutiny
is like the pounding of tortillas in the hands.

When the beat of the press
is like the pounding of tortillas,
and the newsprint is medicine
on the fingertips,
come the men with faces
wiped away by the hood,
who smother the mouth of witness night,
shaking the gasoline can across the floor,
then scattering in a dark orange eruption
of windows,
leaving the paper to wrinkle gray in the heat.

Where the faces wiped away by the hood
are known by the breath of gasoline
on their clothes,
and paper wrinkles gray as the skin
of incarcerated talkers,
another Army helicopter plunges from the sky
with blades burning
like the wings of a gargoyle,
the tortilla and medicine words
are smuggled in shawls,
the newspapers are hoarded
like bundles of letters from the missing,
the poems become songs
and the songs become water
streaming through the arteries
of the earth, where others at the well
will cool the sweat in their hair
and begin to think.

# DSS Dream

I dreamed
the Department of Social Services
came to the door and said:
"We understand
you have a baby,
a goat, and a pig living here
in a two-room apartment.
This is illegal.
We have to take the baby away,
unless you eat the goat."

"The pig's okay?" I asked.
"The pig's okay," they said.


# White Birch

*for Katherine, December 28, 1991*

Two decades ago rye whiskey
scalded your father's throat,
stinking from the mouth
as he stamped his shoe
in the groove between your hips,
dizzy flailing cartwheel down the stairs.
The tail of your spine split,
became a scraping hook.
For twenty years a fire raced
across the boughs of your bones,
his drunken mouth a movie
flashing with every stabbed gesture.

Now the white room of birth is throbbing:
the numbers palpitating red on the screen of machinery
tentacled to your arm; the oxygen mask wedged
in a wheeze on your face; the numbing medication
injected through the spine.
The boy was snagged on that spiraling bone.
Medical fingers prodded your raw pink center

while you stared at a horizon of water
no one else could see, creatures leaping silver
with tails that slashed the air
like your agonized tongue.

You were born in the river valley,
hard green checkerboard of farms,
a town of white birches
and a churchyard from the workhorse time,
weathered headstones naming women
drained of blood with infants coiled inside
the caging hips, hymns swaying
as if lanterns over the mounded earth.

Then the white birch of your bones,
resilient and yielding, yielded again,
root snapped as the boy spilled out of you
into hands burst open by beckoning
and voices pouring praise like water,
two beings tangled in exhaustion,
blood-painted, but full of breath.

After a generation of burning
the hook unfurled in your body,
the crack in your bone dissolved:
One day you stood, expected again
the branch of nerves
fanning across your back to flame,
and felt only the grace of birches.

# Imagine the Angels of Bread

This is the year that squatters evict landlords,
gazing like admirals from the rail
of the roofdeck
or levitating hands in praise
of steam in the shower;
this is the year
that shawled refugees deport judges
who stare at the floor

and their swollen feet
as files are stamped
with their destination;
this is the year that police revolvers,
stove-hot, blister the fingers
of raging cops,
and nightsticks splinter
in their palms;
this is the year
that darkskinned men
lynched a century ago
return to sip coffee quietly
with the apologizing descendants
of their executioners.

This is the year that those
who swim the border's undertow
and shiver in boxcars
are greeted with trumpets and drums
at the first railroad crossing
on the other side;
this is the year that the hands
pulling tomatoes from the vine
uproot the deed to the earth that sprouts the vine,
the hands canning tomatoes
are named in the will
that owns the bedlam of the cannery;
this is the year that the eyes
stinging from the poison that purifies toilets
awaken at last to the sight
of a rooster-loud hillside,
pilgrimage of immigrant birth;
this is the year that cockroaches
become extinct, that no doctor
finds a roach embedded
in the ear of an infant;
this is the year that the food stamps
of adolescent mothers
are auctioned like gold doubloons,
and no coin is given to buy machetes
for the next bouquet of severed heads
in coffee plantation country.

If the abolition of slave-manacles
began as a vision of hands without manacles,
then this is the year;
if the shutdown of extermination camps
began as imagination of a land
without barbed wire or the crematorium,
then this is the year;
if every rebellion begins with the idea
that conquerors on horseback
are not many-legged gods, that they too drown
if plunged in the river,
then this is the year.

So may every humiliated mouth,
teeth like desecrated headstones,
fill with the angels of bread.

# SABRA LOOMIS

## The Trouble I Have in High Places

It could kick back, the gun—
it needed to be taught a lesson,
to stand in the closet with its back to us.
It had its own harsh moods
and drawbacks, like a rebellious daughter.

I was not to be counted on, was the lesson
I was learning; not normal. My words were bad,
and harmful to the natural sympathies of the world.
And I could be straightened out by a man, he said,
but who would do it, who would take me on?

I wouldn't say cheese, or have my cake and eat it too.
Mother stayed out of the discussion, in these cases.
What does it have to do with *now*, with the courage
to walk into high and dangerous places?

When as kids, he took us to the high places, windy and tall—
outside of buildings, up masts and the tallest trees;
was he teaching us to be like the masts of ships, to be like men,
or break our necks trying? Would it be foolish and womanly of me,
would it be normal, to look down and fall?

# Woman and Donkey

The donkey refuses
to carry these rocks any farther.
On the saddle of land between Slievemore
and Dooagh, with a Hee-Haw he stops.
Then up again, with wooden climbing
under clouds up a stairway of rocks.

She wants to open this mountain
and plunge in, to tear apart
fields, wade in among the clouds.
She wants to tear apart the white grammar of clouds.

The cattle lie like buttresses
along a hillside. She has her high wall of echoes,
protected: back from the road behind a gate.

She has her chill walk of echoes,
going with firm step
up a side-path, through the weeds and nettles.

She fears, she imagines,
she fingers the wooden gates.

She wants to open the still-dying gates of the fields
to the blue gentian of a mountain;
with low-bursting clouds, with clouds flying—
wants to open the water fields to the fringes of death.

Her donkey sits down.
He has his wall of pebbles,
his plate of time. The donkey sits.
His plate is full; it is tossed
with white crumbs: the lonely clouds.

# The Unicorn

*for Ellen Farnsworth Loomis*

He came stepping down on the flowered carpet
at the center of the living room—
and was reflected in silver doorknobs,
in the hand mirror (an heirloom!) their grandmother raised.

He looked into the room
with upturned eyes, and with a daily eagerness
of hope. His eyes registered everything:

the way rooms were divided,
how the living room longed (the living room hedged
and grew complicated, it threw obstacles in their way
and it threw proud scenes). The gold ropes
of the curtains held them back as in a theater,
and the living room breathed in a fiery essence.

The unicorn rested
on cleanly divided sofas,
or the ottoman of a white chair
pulled up by the living room fire.

He remembered the aunts and uncles,
their initials, the details
of hunting parties, births and marriages.
He rested here and there,
and listened to the beehive of their talk.

The living room grew proud and resentful.
It threw away the children's best accomplishments,
their best things! Hid personal belongings
under window seats and behind sofa cushions.

As the curtains held, the children drew apart—
it threw away their best accomplishments!

The pictures on the walls were copying themselves endlessly.
They were dark, as curtains rose,
they were dark Madonnas. Like the children,

who gazed past their grandmother's profile,
into the empty theater of the hall. They were looking past Life!

The unicorn trembled, as he walked
through an army of tables, the ornate armchair
with a hunting scene of courtiers around a lake.

He remembered to leave a light trace of himself,
like a breath, or a visitor's card,
in the silver tray on the front hall table.

The unicorn walked with their grandmother
into the open enchantment of the hall—those opera spaces!
as she sat reading her book beside the living room fire;
as she rested, candidly or courteously, in the white chair.

# Delia

When the child sat at the piano,
squeezing on the pedals, splashing,
Delia loved to sing!

Delia liked to see the windows
opening sky-blue, cranked by a slow,
elbow-bending effort.

      "O believe me if all those endearing young charms . . ."

She sang lustily,
she waltzed loud and breezy
in the forgotten room—

      O believe me!

The windows sat, calm and window-seated.

The delightful windows were engaged.
They were opening like bouquets, white wedding bouquets—
Invitations! for those endearing young charms.

The windows sat peacefully, window-eyed.

And suddenly there was a voice,
the room was a rustle of chords,
and there was a crowd of lovesick windows, opening!

# Echo

He forced their mother, many years ago,
to submit to the honeymoon conditions.
She had to climb mountains in the daytime,
he held her over a cliff—

he dangled her,
making her swear she wasn't frightened,
that she was a woman and she trusted him.

If she combed her long, honey-blonde hair,
she had to climb the high mountains with him,
be dangled over cliffs—
with a Valentine waistline and heavy-lidded eyes.

(she must despise him now)
No, she must depend on him now,
like a voice and its echo.

She trusted him night and morning
and had managed to walk
across the high, narrow footbridge of his life
away from the grief, and the utterance
of her own life.

And so,
so,
she must depend on him now.

# The Bear He Shot on Their Honeymoon in Montana, That Growled, and Tried to Come into Their Tent.

This was home, and love and country:
him helping himself to another martini,

lighting the fire with a Cape Cod lighter,
with briquettes, with anything—
a pinecone, a rolled-up newspaper.

Each day he sang a new
honeymoon song of praise.
He tried helpfully growling,
he tried to come into the children's tents.
Without saying anything, without saying "briquettes"—
but whatever came into his head, he'd say it.

In the thickness of coat-closets,
the hat-racks, the gun-racks.

Sitting down to dinner,
he reserved the choicest morsels
for himself. Look, look who he speared!
He was rearranging the food on their plates,
making them look away, tricking them for their dinners.
And look at all the white meat he speared!

# Coming-Out Party

He wanted to go to a dance long ago,
but decided to show up in his bedroom slippers.
The hostess was the debutante Brenda Frazier.
It was best to dress up, but he went there
showing off his broken-down bedroom slippers
and she was shocked. She had thought
he wanted to dance with her
but he was laughing    laughing

He had to run away then and there
to prove how forcefulness could win a war,
how he could set the styles, just like that!
He came out and ran the whole thing himself.

As he sang, and bragged about it,
it was warm. It was a warm summer night.
That sense of being in a cocoon:
a lazy, breezy, by-the-ocean feeling.

## Ziffy-Sternal

When the stepfather made a motion
of guiding his knuckles in their direction,
the children ran to hide
behind the living room sofa.

But he reached in after them,
like God reaching after Adam in the depths of Time,
because he needed the strength
that came to him from child-flesh,
and sinking his knuckles in the quick-breathing bodies.

He'd grind his knuckles
into their waists,
called it a "ziffy-sternal."

He needed to touch the children with whatever fear was,
and bring his knuckles into the silence again.
He pushed through the blue-eyed fear of the child,
out the other side,—like going through a field
of new wheat or barley—into what light of a new world?

The children understood
their wilderness had been trampled on,
their childhood home left far behind
(at the meeting of two rivers), and they would never
in this world ever again reach home,
or the kindliness, the quiet handling they had known before.


## Front Seats

He wanted to keep himself a gate
between them and the world,
wanted the manhood of his son
to be dependent on him.

He was their conductor on summer trips,
could get them through customs
in first class, to front seats at the bullfight.

He took the passports,
put them in his pocket

and strode up to the customs desk.
Then he told them to sign a paper
saying he would not be responsible.

He gave love-signs to his daughters,
kept the letter-of-conduct for his son.

What his daughter thought of it:
when at night she came out of hiding,
(it was when she was nineteen)
she went around and around the world
in silent orbit, like the moon.

He said, what a shadow you are.


# DALE NEAL

# The Mouse's Father

—He's not home, she says.

*I know.* I nod in the dark.

—George? Her sharp elbow in my ribs.

—I know, I say out loud. The illuminated face of the alarm on the dresser shows two o'clock. I have to get up in four hours.

We lie in bed, two middle-aged adults waiting on our child to come in from the night or worse yet, waiting for the phone to ring, Bad news, terrible news—Mr. Lewis, you need to come down. Your son's here.

I nod off. Marie elbows me again. Someone's at the door. The doorknob rattles.

—You locked it? I whisper.

—I left the light on. She whimpers.

The key finally fits: the door opens. No lights come on, but footsteps sound down the hall. Is it our boy or a burglar? A shoulder bangs against the wall. Too noisy for a thief. Then sounds echo from the bathroom, the obscenely loud stream of urine in the toilet, five minutes to clear the bladder, a sigh, a flush. The door to his bedroom slams shut. Thank you, Mr. Considerate.

—George, you need to speak to him.
—In his condition? Tomorrow, Marie, tomorrow.

When I look back, it's probably all my fault. That's the deal with parenting: guilt. I remember once when Mickey had a cough that wouldn't quit. Marie wanted to take the lad back to the doctor, another twenty dollars. I proposed a home remedy. At the liquor store, I bought a bottle of Four Roses. I mixed it at the kitchen sink, a tablespoon with hot water and sugar. I remember taking a whiff from the bottle, wrinkling my nose. I've never had a taste for the stuff, not even a beer. Give me coffee or ice tea.

—Drink this, Mickey, you'll feel better.

I sat on the corner of his bed. Looking down from the walls of his room were all the Disney characters—Mickey, Goofy, Pluto and Donald Duck—their cartoon eyes watching me about to give a toddler his first toddy.

—No, swallow. I know it tastes bad, but it'll do you good.

He screwed up his face, but he kept it down. Mickey slept sound that night, and so did Marie and I. There was no hacking through the wee hours, the house finally quiet.

I'd forgotten all about the Four Roses, I'm sure I never used it again, but screwed on the cap and stuck it in the back of the bathroom closet, behind the old towels. Years later, looking for a hot water bag, I found that same bottle, empty, with only a sticky amber ring at the bottom.

I've never considered myself good with kids. After college, I tried teaching high school math. Kids were better behaved then. The worst you had to deal with was girls smacking gum or giggling, or a jock napping in the back row. I'd march a theorem of x's and y's across the chalkboard, factoring in, factoring out, white dust flying in my face, then I'd turn and see their empty eyes. I might as well have been speaking High Martian to them. So I gave them all C's, even the jock who should have flunked, then quit myself. I took a job at Western Electric, dealing with figures instead of blank faces.

But kids meant everything to Marie. We'd tried for a while: nothing happened. I could have gotten along fine without, but Marie moped. So we went to the Children's Home, and started the paperwork. There wasn't as much in those days.

When the matron came down the hall, leading Mickey by the hand, half pulling him, bashful and small for his age with those dark blazing eyes, well, I felt my own eyes well up. Marie knelt down and gave him a hug, then she looked up at me.

—Meet your son.

We stared hard at each other, sizing each other up I think even then. I reached out and manfully shook the little guy's hand.

Once at the beach, he would have been about eight or nine, Mickey buried me alive. Marie had bought him a pail and shovel, but when we came trooping over the dunes, he threw them down, proclaimed them babyish, after he'd sized up the customers constructing sand castles.

Burying me in the sand seemed a good alternative. Actually it felt good. Him scooping the cold gray sand over my arms and legs.

He tapped my chest. —Why you got that hole there?

He was referring to my sunken chest. All the Lewis men have it, which probably explains our family's failure to produce outstanding athletes or war heroes or even decent ditchdiggers. The impression in my sternum looks funny, like I'd been punched in the chest and never caught my breath.

—Runs in the family. Got it from my dad.

He looked at his own skinny chest, tapped the fine bone there.

—Why don't I got one?

Had he forgotten the Children's Home, that he was a Lewis only legally and not from my loins?

—Look. I brought my arm out of the sand and squeezed my fist into my chest. —It's where you stole my heart.

I opened my hand out to him, palm up, nothing. —See. It's gone. But I've got your nose, mister.

An old baby game we used to play. I would pinch the tip of his nose. He'd clap his hand to his face and I'd show him the fleshy tip caught between my fingers that he and I knew was actually my thumb and not really his nose. It used to make him laugh, but he wasn't buying that today.

—I'm not a baby.

—No, you're not.

The sand lay heavy on my body, pressing the breath out of my thin chest.

—Help me up, Mickey. I'm stuck.

He considered me with narrowed eyes. Perhaps a shovelful of sand in my mouth, he could finish me off.

—I'm stuck. Help. Help! I waved my arms, wiggled my toes.

He barked out a laugh and bolted for the surf. I came up out of the cold sand, chasing after him.

The years washed by. I moved into computers at work, traded my slide rule for a computer keyboard, learned Fortran and Cobol. Marie kept house and made sure Mickey got off to school. She's much closer to the boy than I've ever been. Mothers and sons have different stories than dads and their heirs.

We kept waiting for the Mouse to sprout, but he stayed small through grade school and junior high. His features grew darker, sharper, his teeth more pointed, the tip of his nose, even his chin. Something feral, rodentlike, became ingrained in my mind.

In the suburbs where we moved, there were block parties. We carried picnic tables out to the street, filled them with fried chicken, pies and strange gelatin desserts. Someone usually got out a football, suggested a game of touch with fathers and sons.

It was a friendly competition. Every father and son took turns calling the next play. The Gillettes came up with a double reverse that gained no ground. The Phelpses went for a long post pattern down the sideline. The Joneses tried an option that went nowhere but into the sideline, scattering the moms clustered over the chicken salad. It was our turn.

—What's our call, Mickey?

—The bomb.

—Sure you can throw it that far, son?

—Just go deep.

I lined up on the far left and bent down to tie my shoe. When the ball was hiked, Mickey dropped back, looking for a receiver over the six-foot heads of the opposing papas.

—Mickey, over here! I waved my arms, wide open with daylight down to the apple tree that marked our goal line.

Mickey stared in my direction then took off the other way. They tagged him about ten yards downfield.

Back in the huddle, I tapped his shoulder. —I was open. Why didn't you throw it to me?

Mickey had his head down, hands on his knees, huffing. He spat on the ground. —You'd drop it like always.

All the fathers looked away, nervously coughed like something was caught in their throats.

I did what all fathers did: held a job, worked hard, saved money for Mickey's college fund as well as retirement so he wouldn't have to worry about his old man.

We bought him toys, a camouflaged tommy gun that spat out a few seconds of carnage when you pulled the trigger, and when that mercifully broke, he still mouthed sound effects for his imaginary firefights full of ricochets, flying shrapnel, screaming victims.

Later we tried Scouts, thinking he'd like the uniforms, the snappy three-finger salutes. But he chafed under the neckerchief, the knots unknotted him, he never ranked higher than Second Class. Too goody-two-shoes for him, I suppose, although I suspect he was teased about his size. He took a latrine shovel to one kid, and the Scoutmaster asked him not to come back.

After that, he pestered me into buying him some dumbbells. I could hear him grunting and clanking the weights on the carpet behind the always closed door of his room.

He kept his hair short, wore jungle boots and fatigue jackets from the Army-Navy surplus store. He acted like he was training for Nam, which was, thank God, winding down despite Nixon's secret plan. He saluted me, an insolent cock of the hand to the brow. I think Mickey loved authority, so long as it did not belong to me.

I suppose I could have told him about the Nike missile I was helping program at work, but it was top secret and I'd been warned not to talk about the project at home. Loose lips would sink continents, not just ships, in the Cold War. Maybe I would have seen his eyes light up just once at what the old man was doing.

He hung out in the woods that shrank each summer as more lots were cleared, new houses raised. I used to know who his friends were, but soon there were so many new kids moved into the neighborhood, who could keep track?

One night, I'd come home tired, my eyes blurred from staring at the computer screen all day, checking the command strings against the green printouts in my lap. Marie had dinner on the table, but Mickey wasn't home yet. She wanted me to call him.

I went out into our yard and stood at the edge of the darkening woods, calling my son's name. There was no answer. Dry twigs and dead leaves crunched under the soles of my wingtips. I found their hideout, but no boys. A fire ring marked the clearing, littered with cigarette butts and soda cans. I brushed against something dangling from a shrub, then stepped back. It was a dead cat, a noose about its neck. Claws lashed the air in a frozen panic. The fur was matted and starting to stink.

Back at the house, I mumbled I couldn't find him. When Mickey came home after dark, Marie shot me hard glances to say something.

I took my seat at the head of the table. We'd already eaten an hour before. Mickey was slumped in his chair, stirring his plate of cold food. I stared at his face, trying to see what kind of person he was becoming.

*Who are you?* I wanted to ask, but that's not what I said.

—Look, there's rules around here, and we don't make the rules just for you to break them.

He stuffed his mouth with cold mashed potatoes, grimaced.

—You don't come home, your food gets cold.

He had a bad habit of jiggling his knee under the table. The whole house shook with that vibration of excess energy.

—We get mad, okay Mickey?

—Mick. My name is Mick.

—Okay Mick, you hear me?

—Yeah, sure, I hear you. But he didn't. He never had.

There were other ugly discoveries along the way: the time we found the rolled plastic bag of dope in his drawer, the beer cans in his closet, the morning I found him passed out behind the wheel of the car, the evening the cops called after he'd been picked up for trying to set fire to an abandoned house. There were conferences at school, teachers who shook their heads, clicked their tongues, made you feel like such a failure. I wanted to say, he's not mine. He's adopted. That would explain everything.

Marie and I used to lie awake in bed, cowering under the sheets, waiting for his footsteps.

—You have to speak to him. He's out of control.

I hadn't spanked him in years, the hairbrush unused in the top dresser drawer. I had lost my hair, my nerve. What could I say to my wife, his mother, that I was scared of our boy?

—Did you hear that?

—What?

—I think it was a car.

We waited. The clock marched toward three.

—George, you better go check.

I went to the front door, but thought better of turning on the light. In the dark, I could see his car parked under the spreading oak. I walked across the yard in my bare feet, acorns bruising my heels.

—Mickey!

No answer.

As I came closer, I could make out his silhouette by the cigarette's glow.

—It's late. You coming in?

—I'm listening to the radio.

I could hear a soft ballad coming from the car, not the heavy metal he usually played, but a sad song about love. I thought I heard him crying in the dark, a wet snuffling like when he was a little boy, but I couldn't see his face.

—It's late. Your mother can't sleep when you're out.

He flicked the cigarette, a fast meteor that landed in the grass. My yard, the yard I had to mow because my son was too lazy or too hungover to do it.

—Come on in now, it's late.

He drank from a can he was holding in his lap. I gathered it wasn't a soda.

—Look, I haven't got all night. Are you coming in or not?

—Man, can't you leave me alone?

—It's my job. I'm the guy who's responsible.

—It's not like you're my real father, you know.

I went to the car and stuck my head in, got right in his face. I could smell his breath, hot and fermented with beer.

—You don't give a damn, do you?

—What? He was surprised.

—You heard me, mister. I was surprised too at what I'd said. I'm not a man given to language like that.

I pulled my head back as he opened the door and stumbled out of the car. It was his turn to get in my face. He was my height but wider, bulked with muscles from hours of weightlifting.

—You're right. I don't give a damn. You ought to teach me a lesson, you know. You ought to kick my ass up and down the yard. I would, if I were you. Go ahead. Make me give a damn.

He grabbed my wrist. I tried to pull it back, but he wouldn't let go. I gritted my teeth. We struggled. He held my hand immobile in the small space between us. Suddenly I gave up, relaxed my biceps. My fist flew into his mouth.

—Oww! I was the one who cried out. He let go.

I popped my knuckle in my mouth and tasted blood. He was rubbing his lip. I guess he was bleeding, too.

—Lesson's over. You happy? I said.

With what pride I could muster in the middle of the night in my boxer shorts and T-shirt, I marched back to the house, stopping only to pick up that cigarette in my yard.

The greatest day of a father's life: not when his delinquent son slouches across the stage for his high school diploma, camouflage fatigues and combat boots visible beneath the black gown. No, it's when he enlists in the God almighty Marine Corps. The Mouse was just tall enough to make the minimum height requirement. If the Marines hadn't taken him, he'd probably have turned into a serial killer. I already had my alibi, in my worst daydreams, when the TV crews came after all the bodies had been dug up. I'd stand before the house of the infamous murderer, and shrug my feeble father's shoulders—He was adopted, what could I say?

Mick wanted to ride the bus to Parris Island, but Marie insisted that I drive him. It would be our last chance together. I could impart a father's wisdom to a son, have that heart-to-heart, man-to-man talk we'd been avoiding the past decade.

We rode in the silence we were comfortable with, exchanging pleasantries on the hour.

—Flat, I commented on the landscape by the interstate.

—Flat, he agreed.

—McDonald's, I pointed to the golden arches.

—Sure, he agreed.

We munched our burgers in the car and kept going.

I drove him to the gates. He insisted on walking in by himself. I wanted to strike a manful attitude here at our parting, show there were no hard feelings.

—Well, I guess that drill sergeant won't be so tough compared to me.

—Yeah, right.

We were locked into our roles, our banter that never took the other seriously. I got his duffel bag from the trunk.

—Well, this is it. An idiot's grin spread on my face.

He kept glancing toward the gate.

—Mickey, Mick.

—What?

I drew myself up straight and gave him a good soldier's salute, crisply snapping my hand to my side.

—Jeez. He slung the bag over his shoulder, started walking.

I smiled, got in the car and drove home.

I'd done my job. Now, the U.S. taxpayer would be footing the bill for his room and board. The Marines needed a few good men like the Mouse, a born killer. He loved boot camp. With his crewcut and a new tattoo, he was a jarhead, a leatherneck, the hero of his own comic book, ready to kick ass for the good of his country.

For the first time in years, I slept sound through the nights, woke refreshed in the mornings. None of that pit-of-the-stomach stuff, I feasted on bacon and eggs and kissed my wife goodbye each A.M., knowing I would come home to peace and quiet each evening. I knew what faced me.

I even felt a little frisky toward my wife, if you know what I mean, something I hadn't really felt in years, worrying about an eye through the keyhole or listening for his bedsprings to squeak with the *Penthouse* under his pillow.

Wouldn't you know Marie and I were in the middle of things, when the phone call came after all these years? I stand by the dresser, staring at myself in the mirror, the receiver screwed to my ear. I can't believe what I'm hearing. I watch myself nod in the mirror. —Uh-huh, uh-huh, I see.

I hang up, and turn to tell Marie. She's sitting up in bed, her breasts sagging under the nightgown, the strap twisted on her round shoulder. Her mouth and eyes agape, waiting for the worst I can give her. How old she looks in this light, and I realize the toll the years have taken. I can feel my shoulders sag, the weariness in my voice.

What we knew all along would happen has happened.

Later I would read through the MP's report twice. Neatly typed. Very thorough, like the sergeant himself. —I'm truly sorry, sir, but the little guys are the biggest trouble.

Tell me about it.

He was drinking, of course, off base with some buddies at a topless bar. One of the girls was trying to go home after shaking her tits in front of boobs all night. She was in her car, but my son wouldn't let her go. He was trying to be sweet, but things got ugly. She pulled from the parking lot. He was running alongside, kicking at the car door, yelling how he loved the bitch. He threw himself on the hood.

Imagine his face through the glass, screaming obscenities. The car accelerates, fishtails, brakes. Mick flies off, a windshield wiper in one hand. He sails through the drizzle and lands in a heap on the street, the crumpled body of my son caught in the headlights shining into the night.

We drive through the remainder of the same night, rehearsing our roles, what we'd done, how we could have prevented it, if only we'd been tougher, if I'd spoken up. We pull into the hospital parking deck at dawn.

Marie and I walk hand in hand down the corridors. Nurses in white drag themselves along at the end of their shifts. Our shoes click along the shiny tile, pools of light glowing under fluorescent fixtures. We hurry toward a terrible appointment. Somehow I keep thinking that a nurse will come down the end of the hall, with a little boy in tow, our son again from the start.

Instead at the end of the last hushed hall, we come to the glass window and our reflection, two small people caught suddenly off guard, no matter how many years we had prepared ourselves for this moment. Behind the glass and our ghastly faces is what we've come to, like an exhibit in a museum of nightmares. They should paste a placard here: WHAT CAN HAPPEN: AN EXAMPLE.

He is where I never could quite picture him: lying in a white bed, a white gown, white bandages swaddling his head, a fogged respirator mask taped over his mouth and nose.

We wait outside until the doctor comes with the news. Out of danger for now. But the prognosis is not good. Paralysis and brain damage. Time will tell. The months and years ahead will mean feeding him, changing his diapers, teaching him to walk and talk. This is the best we can hope for.

The doctor is very thorough, but kind enough to ask if we have any questions.

—*Why?* I want to ask. *Why why why why why why.* But I bite my lower lip and keep quiet.

—Can he hear us? Marie asks. Sweet Marie.

The doctor shrugs. —Act as if he can.

We go inside the room full of softly beeping monitors, their soft hum and beeps keeping our boy alive. I'm afraid to touch him, but I bend over the bed. His eyelashes are long and soft. With my thumb I push back the hooded eyelid, searching for my son in there.

—Mick?

His eye dilates against the light. I can see myself, a tiny man reflected in the full-blown pupil.

—Hey, Mickey, hey Mouse. I whisper, afraid to wake him.

One night when he was still new to us, I stole into his bedroom and shook his shoulder. —Hey Mickey, wake up. Come on, little Mouse, there's something to see.

His dark eyes flicked open. He knew me right off the bat.

I stood him on the bed and pushed his arms into his little coat. I put my finger to my lips. —Shhhh, this is a surprise.

Hand in hand, we snuck down the hall, out the front door. We went around to the side of the house where I had left the ladder cleaning the gutters last weekend. Mickey was wiry for a four-year-old. When Marie hadn't been watching, he'd scampered up the rungs and tugged on my trousers leg, wanting to play with his new daddy.

—Upsy-daisy.

We climbed together, my belly against his back, my hands making sure his held on, boosting his behind with my knee when he needed it.

—Okay, hang on.

I lifted him from the ladder onto the roof, hanging onto his coattail, while I got myself up the last rung. Marie would never forgive me if I were to drop our child off the roof.

I held his hand and we stood, one foot on either side of the slope. I walked him over to the chimney. —Christmas, Santa Claus will be dropping down here. You know about Santa, don't you?

Mickey nodded. He was so quick, you could almost see the thoughts flashing by in his eyes.

I sat, leaning against the rough brick of the chimney and held him in my lap. The world looked strange from up here. Every stalk of grass in the neighborhood cast a shadow. I could have read a newspaper by the full moon. I glanced at my watch. Almost time.

—Mickey, look! Look at Mr. Moon! Oh no! What's happening?

The moon was suddenly shrinking. A slow nibble then a curved bite came out of the circumference, the advancing shadow of the earth we perched on, me and my boy.

I looked down into my son's eyes, dark and wide and unfathomable to me. He blinked at the cosmic spectacle overhead, until he eyes slowly closed and did not open.

I had so much to teach him. I could tell him how far the moon is from the earth. I could multiply out the planets for him. I could slide-rule the universe. But I couldn't measure what I felt for him then, in my arms, asleep. I sat on the roof with my new son, until the moon came out of the shadows, still shining on the other side.

# Cheryl Baldi

## Skytop

I tell myself there's no chance
a deer will fall through the ice as one did
last season. In these sub-zero winds
the mass is frozen 12" thick,
dusted with snow. We've been sledding
all afternoon down the slope,
out across nearly the width of the lake,
finding it dangerous walking back,
our rubber-soled boots slick
against the fixed glassy surface
that in this cold cracks and heaves beneath our feet.
I imagine the deer, the jagged break in the ice—
Why didn't it know to stay along the bank with the others?
And why are we here, my children and I,
my husband who falls behind
dragging the sled to the lake's center
where we wait in this open, unforgiving world?

## First Goodbye

Her blond braids tied with ribbon,
my sister slumped in the backseat,

her duffel bag packed on the floor below.
She was on her way to camp,

and as the screen door banged, and the engine
turned over, I waved from the sandbox

where the day before we'd carved a village,
sand houses shaved with popsicle sticks

that doubled as fences
for the gardens we planted with moss.

There, we imagined whole families,
a church picnic at the local pond—

white-stuccoed town that I watered
that day and every other

though I doubt now it lasted a week.
Who knows? Time then made no sense—

one day drifting into the next: my father
packed and left; the new kitten died;

my sister called to say she'd cut her hair.

## New Neighbors

Finally, they've fenced in the pool—
last spring's picnic
coming to a terrible grief
when pulled too close to the edge
their child drowned. Now, it's spring again,
and while I've kept away, most mornings
I strain to see through the trees
over our lawn to theirs.

I never met the child,
and though it's useless, I invent her:
sun flashing its signature where she slips
through a yellow tube, her tiny, careless hand
waving as she slides into the water.
It's not idleness on the pool's surface
I see, but calm swirls, not a child cradled
on the bottom but diving
down for pennies or a hoop to swim through,
a child not indifferent but feverish,
not cool, not colorless,
not weighted like stone.

## Anima

Late in the day the dog curls against my daughter's feet
listening as she practices the piano—
chromatic scales, chord progressions—
her thin child-fingers curved and firm on the keys.

Each time she pauses, he wags his tail
as if to say, *Come on, play,*
*the Kuhlau Sonatina, the Clementi.*
Who's to know what he longs for, waiting
for his dinner, drawn to the worn spot on this rug
in this room where repeating rhythms echo
off a soundboard warped with age.

I know he dreams. Last night,
running in his sleep, he whimpered aloud
as if stumbling over a log or against a sharp rock.
But quick to forgive he chased on
fetching a rabbit or a mole
the cat, in her lust, had abandoned.
All the while his joints seemed to ache—
his stiffened right hip—
but on and on he ran, never wearying
of some earthly joy; a rush of wind,
the stream's cold crevices.

# Portrait

Today we hang the photograph—
a black and white of our daughters,
16 x 20, taken at such close range

I can count the freckles on one. You say
you expect the other to speak,
can feel her breath on your lips,

and I know by the tautness of your mouth
you are thinking of the third child,
perhaps wondering

how tall she might have been
or how she would have fit in this frame,
its design so tight, the cropping

so close. Should we have left room
to imagine her now
kneeling on a stool behind the others,

her hair lit up as she smiles at one of your jokes?
How much we joke, not knowing
what else to do. Some days,

like today, it's as if at any moment
she'll run through the door,
angry, having been tripped by the dog,

her jacket torn, her face
scratched and proud
even as she turns away.

# Fever

*Can she hear my whispers*
*cross her window in the rain?*
*Can she feel my hand*
*brush back the hair from her cheek?*

Tonight, in another city, my child lies sick,
and though it's just a virus it recalls
the summer she was born, those days of heat
blurred finally into an indistinguishable landscape.

Whatever relief the nights held I remember
only her newborn flesh
and the flutter of a luna moth against the screen
where we rocked long past midnight.

That she stopped nursing was the first sign
of illness, and later, at the hospital
a scream that spiraled like a siren
as the doctor twice pierced her spine for a drop of fluid.

For two days she looked half-dead—her arms
dangling across the white sheet
through the crib's metal bars,
the way her eyes glazed over but never closed.

In that time I learned to pump my breasts and to be alone
with the knowledge that death is imminent.

Most days this ache subsides
as she learns her times tables—the 7's, the 8's.

But not long ago I woke from sleep to find
I'd been crying. So foolish, pretending
all these years to bear this pain.

## Prayer for the God Box

My daughter's first love no longer
speaks to her, and at night, trying to sleep
she calls his name from the dark,
from the pillow she's crumpled,

lonely for someone to hold her
the way I no longer can—
stroking the crease in her neck—
as she'd stroked the cat's the week he grew jaundiced.

With him now on the porch,
she sleeps unsettled
by the sudden emptiness in her life,
her face skewed as if in prayer.

*Help her,* I breathe, my own prayers
reduced to small words, a plea
for this grief to pass,
though I don't believe it will, really

knowing loss clings
like lint to this worn sweater I wear to garden
cleaning leaf rot, cutting
the first thin sprigs of mint.

Soon she'll wake and call to me,
her voice rising and falling
in the morning's stillness,

*Don't leave, don't leave*

words struck with fatigue and hope,
words, finally, I place in the god box,
having whispered them all my life.

# Melissa Hotchkiss

## Maine

White with soap
Each arm looking bleached, parched
In the sun
You chose
Only to lather the tops
(Not the pale undersides)
Also, just the fronts of your legs
I stood in the cabin
Wondering
You looked so peculiar
Half done

With bits of light falling onto gray rock
Your shadow stretching
You dove down
Straight
Deep into black water
Soft flurry of bubbles
Leaving an oval, visual caviar
On the floating surface

Your body submerged without light
Quickly, I reached
The door opened into air smelling cool, pine

Folding over in water
Your movements unforced, unrehearsed
The easy sound of your breathing
Creating creases in my skin

# The Chore

She sent her
To gather mint
For tea

From the kitchen,
Watching her daughter
Floating, cartwheels

Toward water
Where leaves soft green
Grow wild

Small hands
Then, into the cool dark brook
Pulling stalks

The mother
Needing a moment
Lets rising steam
Layer the window


# Temper

Ripping down from their pillows
That morning he decided
To be dramatic

White small feathers
Floating
Softly, with no breeze

Deliberately, the kind of kiss
He gave to her, earlier

Biting, needing
So much to damage

# Untitled

I dream the final wave

Spotting it from shore

Each roll of water

This one, no, that one

By my side, someone saying

"Why do you pretend it is visible?"

# Elizabeth

My niece has this way
Of holding her face tightly between her hands
Rubbing her fingers across her eyes

I noticed it after her father started stabbing
The dead chicken frying in a pan

Oil foaming circles on the stove
My sister was crying

# The Breakup

It was walking into the sprinkler
I remember most clearly

Not because of thick water slapping my face
Or the way my dress stuck to my body

But because I was blaming you
My voice was louder than your voice
And I was blaming you

# Surgery

Waiting for the evening breeze
  to move in slowly
  through the screens
  onto the porch, into my chair

Lift me towards the ceiling
  above the light green carpet with its almost invisible yellow lines
  I'll float for hours

From room to room
  following my sisters, their steps quiet when they brush
  their long hair, pulling knots with small dark combs

These scars across my stomach—
  one summer night
The smell of horse manure, cut grass
Running into the fence, in the humid dark
  there were so many bright lights, the doctor's black string
  threading itself, with that sudden sharpness

I understand why air won't search for a body
  or fill the lungs during a hot spell so long even the artichoke plants are
    dying
  my hand stops the sun
My hands rip my skin, as I choose to float
  and separate


# China Lake

I see my grandfather
Standing in water, carrying the lake to his face,
  back and forth, over and over
  rubbing his hands

I am on the shore, parts of my body
  touching metal of the green canvas chair

I keep watching him, unable to block
  the sounding waves, or clawing sun

One more thing happens:
  he points towards his feet, signaling

Round golden sunfish nibble his toes
  I know this, he lets them touch him
They tickle, he says, which I never believe
  because I cannot see how this biting doesn't tear—

How he can stand there, letting it happen, wanting it to happen,
Why blood doesn't flood from his feet as he leaves the lake.


# HA JIN

## Ways of Talking

We used to like talking about grief.
Our journals and letters were packed
with losses, complaints, and sorrows.
Even if there was no grief
we wouldn't stop lamenting
as though longing for the charm
of a distressed face.

Then we couldn't help expressing grief.
So many things descended without warning:
labor wasted, loves lost, houses gone,
marriages broken, friends estranged,
ambitions worn away by immediate needs.
Words lined up in our throats
for a good whining.
Grief seemed like an endless river—
the only immortal flow of life.

After losing a land and then giving up a tongue,
we stopped talking of grief.
Smiles began to brighten our faces.
We laugh a lot, at our own mess.

Things become beautiful,
even hailstones in the strawberry fields.

## A Peach

Father, do you remember the peach tree
before our home in the Russian barracks?

It bloomed by the purple paling,
its leaves opened like scissors
in the breeze ringing with bees.

I was three, in a green bib,
eager to pick the peach as big
as a Ping-Pong ball, the only one
I saw on the tree.

You were weeding with my little spade.
You told me to wait.
"In two months it'll be juicy
and sweet," you assured me.

Every weekend back from the kindergarten
I'd watch my peach. It turned
pink like a bashful face,
bigger and rounder week by week.

Then, one morning I found my peach
half eaten by worms or birds.
A valley was gouged in its belly,
the rotten wound gaping at me.
I didn't cry or say a word.

Father, have you forgotten the peach?
It was my first fruit on a branch.

## Distance

Your voice is so young
it led me to a younger generation.

Yesterday I played many times
your nameless message
thinking of all the young women
who might have my phone number.
None of them had the childlike voice,
so familiar, yet out of reach.
I don't know this girl, I thought
and didn't call you back.

This morning I woke with your voice
ringing in my head, mingled
with the cuckoo in the birch woods where
we walked together fifteen years ago.
It was in Harbin, in that windy spring.

Suddenly I felt old, tired of
wandering alone in this land.
I called San Francisco
but you had left
with the delegation
of your country.

## At Midnight

Suddenly ducks and geese were clamoring.
On the lake the shadows of a street lamp
were shattered by wings exploding.
Startled, she went
to drop the window curtain.
"My God, so many of them," a man cried.
He was feeding them, his dog barking.

She stopped to watch
the water swashing and sparkling.

Her cat jumped into her arms.

## In a Moonlit Night

Tonight heavy dew disabled mosquitoes
that have landed with drenched wings.
Lying on a deck chair on the grass
I watch stars flickering—a luxury,
which I forget I can easily afford.

Fireflies are flitting on the treetops,
katydids chirring in a shaky voice.
A nut or a fruit drops now and then
capering through leaves and twigs.
In the dark a raccoon is lingering,
whose footfalls are timid but never stop.

So large and white is the moon
it reminds me of a huge cake
awaited by hundreds of children
week after week till finally
the Moon Festival came.
Grapes, melons, cherries, crab apples,
nuts, so much food piled on tables.
Every year we skipped lunch in secret
to save our stomachs for the night feast—
eating while watching the harvest moon
and listening to the legends of astral creatures.
Some boys, overstuffed,
would throw up in the small hours.

In Massachusetts tonight
I'm thinking of an old man
who had a bony face and a degree from MIT,
a man we paraded through the streets
and forced to kneel on a platform
because he claimed the American moon
was larger and brighter than the Chinese moon.
How amazed I am to see he was not wrong.
But he couldn't make us believe
there were two moons in the world.
He was silly to use the hated words.
Perhaps he should have explained:
the air here is fresher

and the sky more transparent,
so the moon looks larger and brighter.

No, that won't do.
The implications are still enormous.
He couldn't avoid eating a cowpat.

## The Past

I have supposed my past is a part of myself.
As my shadow appears whenever I'm in the sun
the past cannot be thrown off and its weight
must be borne, or I will become another man.

But I saw someone wall his past into a garden
whose produce is always in fashion.
If you enter his property without permission
he will welcome you with a watchdog or a gun.

I saw someone set up his past as a harbor.
Wherever it sails, his boat is safe—
if a storm comes, he can always head for home.
His voyage is the adventure of a kite.

I saw someone drop his past like trash.
He buried it and shed it altogether.
He has shown me that without the past
one can also move ahead and get somewhere.

Like a shroud my past surrounds me,
but I will cut it and stitch it,
to make good shoes with it,
shoes that fit my feet.

## Lilburn, Georgia

I broke some large stones
and with a hand truck shipped them home.
Along the edge of the lake in my yard
I piled them piece by piece
to make the soil stay.

My joy in the labor evoked Tu Fu's line:
"The river flows but stones remain."
I saw him stand on a cliff
lamenting the disappearance of things man-made—
fleets, palaces, cities, empires, fame.
Above, geese are passing,
below, the Yangtze lapping sand.

Time and again
his voice rings among my stones.

# I Sing of an Old Land

I sing of an old land
where the gods have taken shelter underground,
where the human idols eat human sacrifice,
where hatred runs the business of philanthropy,
where blazing dragons eclipse the wronged ghosts,
where silence and smiles are the trace of wisdom,
where words imitate spears and swords,
where truth is always a bloody legend.

I speak of the old land not
out of love or wonderment.
Like my ancestors who were scattered into the smoky winds,
who scrambled to leave home
or rushed towards the approaching enemies,
I join those who fled and returned,
      who disappeared in other lands
bearing no hope but persistence, no honor but the story,
      no fortune but parents and children,
singing a timeless curse,
a curse that has bound us together
and rooted us deep in the wreck
      of our homeland.
I touch the land at night—
My hands trace the map on the wall,
from mountains to villages and to rivers,
from plains to cities and to seashores.
I see the green fields of the South,
the dark soil and birch woods of the North,
and snow swirling in summer.

I dream of myself in that land,
not for happiness or harvest.
I dream of suffering together with my people,
of being understood and useful,
of being left alone and able to sleep,
of my children refusing my land
so they will not repeat my life,
of talking and walking with friends,
of completing the work and dying with ease.

I weep for the old land,
for its vast narrowness,
for its profound stupidity,
for its chaos and tenacity,
for its power to possess those of my kind
to devour us to nourish itself
to seize our hearts and throats
and mix our moans with songs—

songs of monstrous grandeur
and merciless devotion,
songs crazed by the cycle of that land.

# June 1989

*to a poet in China*

You were arrested last night in my dream.
Your wife fled to her parents' in the country
carrying your baby, who was asleep
with his small mouth carelessly open.
Your last words were very simple:
"If I don't come back, remember,
I did nothing but tell the truth."
I cried and started shooting.
My rifle spoke elegantly
splitting every lie in half,
blowing out all the false charges,
quenching the eyes of the police
who struck your cheeks
while handcuffing you.

Since June third
my dreams have run wild,
craving to kill the killers
as if their lives were no more than flies.

In the foreign land
we all watched it unfolding:
the capital was darkened
by a red, red night.

On television I saw
a truck of soldiers pass by and shoot
three men who were watching them moving out.
A small girl hid herself in a rickshaw,
but thirty-nine bullets smashed
the vehicle and the life inside.
Behind her stood a placard:
PEOPLE ARE NO LONGER AFRAID OF DEATH,
WHY DO YOU THREATEN US WITH DEATH!
Some blocks away
a young man stopped eighteen tanks
with two bags of groceries.

Here, our flags, our national flags,
have dropped halfway on every pole.
Even schoolchildren stand silent before class.
The whole world knows, except
the Chinese who mourn and celebrate,
mourning for the deaths of murderers,
celebrating the murder of themselves.

History, my friend, is being revised,
just as the blood was scrubbed off
or covered up with grass and flowers,
and the bodies burned to a riddle of numbers.
The killers improvise reasons for killing
while the victims commit a crime
if they are killed.

Everyone says, "Nobody expected
such an end!" An end?
Who knows when it will end?

From fresh stumps hidden in sleeves
deadly hands are growing.
From curses behind doors, from groans in dreams,
an eyeless typhoon is gathering.

*June 1989*

# Faye George

## Amtrak

Somewhere in Carolina to the right of midnight
I remember waking to see a broken warehouse
green as mold in the moonlight.
This is a day brilliant with rust:
heat-radiant freight cars, sun-struck auto parts,
the corrugated rail-side towns.
The train moves down the long leg of Florida;
the land rolls out like an idle wish.
I believe the six-foot sofa in that meadow
climbed out of a jar in Tennessee.
The head steward blows his nose, with a smile.
Our waiter looks weary;
I feel I should get my own coffee.
A hawk drifts like a dark wrinkle in the air.

How many of us do the cows blink out of their fields
each day? How many will return to these pastures,
stiff-legged as egrets, pacing out an easier way?

## The Moon Is in the Eastern Sky

The moon is in the eastern sky.
There are no storms tonight,
no threat of snow.
The thin-lipped bay has eaten
all the clouds had left.

The space between the stars is deeper,
all their violence flawless.
There is no wind;
each tree is perfect separateness.
Each stone has grown a shadow.

I am further from the next house.
My house has grown the shadow
of a woman in a window.
The thin body of the mercury
measures this cold peace.

# Norfolk to Boston

She is too warm in her clothes,
with menses, excitement,
and the Norfolk sunshine.

Two gray heron ply between
the runway and the creek
that curls away like pared rind.

She eyes the blue lights
beading the runway, and catches
at the sapphire on her throat,

turning with thumb and finger
the shape of a memory
to points of new fire.

"The temperature in Boston
is thirty-two degrees."
The captain's voice is sanguine,

pleasantly southern.
She secures her seat belt
and lets go of the leaving—

leaves the city blocked out below,
its spaces apportioned,
finished as a dead thing.

The bay is quiet as an iced
northern pond, colored mauve
in the aurora of morning.

The blue jet flare of an engine
flickers like St. Elmo's fire,
reflected off the water's skin.

Contours of coast roll out
like moist pie crust—thin, thinner,
wafering off into the sea.

This climbing is never routine for her,
the adieu to what is down there
for an hour or forever.

The god that cabins the body
in steel uncages something.
She is free

on an island in this waste,
aware of energy
and the peace of displacement.

# Rain

See how the maple leaves curl
pale side out and sway
like grieving women. The wind
that herds the maple leaves together
cleaves the arborvitae.
A broken limb lies
in lily-of-the-valley.

Rain puddles on the porch.
A light behind the clouds
glosses the deck.
The rain is thorough, like women
who go down on their knees
and scrub until
their thighs bleach gray
and the color runs out of their eyes.

# Welcome to This House

Welcome to this house.
We go barefoot in this place
along the passages
to the mouth of the echo. Stoop low.
Do not disturb the spiders overhead
and in the shadows along the wall.
We do not kill them. They are sacred.
They create the universe
from rock to bone, spinning, spinning.
The bones that line the way
are our fathers' bones.
They must be scraped four times a year
for offerings at festivals, and again
when times are bad
and there is little flesh to eat
from harvest wars.
Sometimes we hold the skulls and dance:
it is our way of making love.

We believe the spiders are spirits.
Everything has a purpose.
The spiders spin stars. We make bones.
We have no fire to keep away the beasts.
We are the beasts,
devouring, dancing, dreaming,
making bones to love,
to warm the cold seepage of stone.

# What She Looked Out Upon

What she looked out upon
through the small grille
of the kitchen window
was the exhausted clothesline

strung across the yard,
its soft and sagging middle
a hammocked emptiness
that crossed her eyes' rest

as a thin shadow
of the depression
she looked in upon,
thinking of what was to come:

the winding down,
the thinning—
of bone, of hair, of skin,
of patience even.

Hoping enough would be left
to finish with some grace
what had begun without thinking.
Thinking how the days rolled out

in laundry and bad news. How the pole
that held the clothesline
held the wires
that pulled the clanging world in.

Most of the time not listening
unless something
caught her attention
the way the moth

between the windows and the screen
now did,
wings flailing
against the vague web.

She could see the spider too,
shroud maker, paying out thread,
little god, moving gingerly along
the avenues of its invention.

# Kathleen E. Krause

## Streets

It's when the sand is washed by the sea,
it's then that my keys don't work.
I come home in a panic, trying not to spell
the wrong words the right way.

Fumbling with the birds,
I drop them again, this time into the reflection
I saw some time ago; that puce sound of
my locked up young, pinned.

My noose is made of crepe or cashmere.
Pouches of air and lavender whiz
through my kind bed where we engrave my names.

## To

I knew I'd have to do something better than that—
looking over the acres, in no rush.
Dry doesn't move.
Thinking back to the drawing room,
her skin had pockets
and her eyes did something.
(These notes are wicked.)
Behind the curtains that closed off
the bay windows
I could see the light from the girls' school
that stayed on till dawn—
a world of tinted yellow.
I could find the rabbits, or pretend.

## Train

That last white drive
felt like tea-butter.
Since then, I've done some things,
smelled a muskrat all worn out.

## Scrape Scrape

Primrose and garland
objects and subjects
religious, perhaps.
Teacher, give me your stockings
and some hair,
some stockings and your hair.
We go to the goats and pigs—
misbehavior, ricochet, animalized.
My doll, eyes rolling,
still and starched,
picked and knotted.

Theory-stuffed brain limbo
and the time we rode horses
along the Gap of Dunloe.
Do this do that,
but what does the word "become" mean?
What makes a sound?

## Portrait

A linen canvas is stretched
in the room of low and work.
The plot creeps in like an owner,
an official, a threat—
a naked.
The subject drapes herself,
lets her thoughts take fluid,
take gaze.
The lopsided one,
the romantic,
jumps from the bed
in a quote, spiraling.

## No Dragon

it is pluck of wing
dose of lispings
animal of gesture makes her way

around the place where water wells
sifting her dusty paws along the shade

fire warmed hands held
swinging now, light lights kindly
on the belly as
games play
a breath but a blow
in the safe ear of seashells
no muscles are needed, though they are here

dots filter through the negatives
the click of a buckle-shoe peeks
at a flare through a bulge
apples are couching
bisque bathes in limbs of rare salmon.

# Foot

Oh cry!
That slender arched foot,
Not just a foot.
Don't look at the face of her
Or do
And it surprises.
She's old.
But cast down again
To that foot
Pulling itself out of its stuffed shoe
Resting sexy and moving.

# Accident

Like close little hairs
resting, we were.

Gutted on a roadside
of nettles, bees, and soldiers,

we finished our buckles
in laps whipped madly.

## Frank and Luna

When this was thought of years ago,
people said it was just like trees in Japan.
We were laughing so much those days.

One particular October evening,
people felt like leaving, just stood up
and went to the bathroom. We found glass

shards later where the boxes had been lifted,
as if a struggle had taken place,
or the beginnings of our lives were touched.

Now Frank and Luna sit alone on their porches.
Alone to each other, but more destined,
more fated than real markings on real animals.

I know only because of coincidence.
As the train pulled away at 5:10 on the dot,
we blew kisses. His face was jammed

up against the window; it even looked like
jam as his lips smeared into the invisible
boundary between us. A lump in the throat

never stopped me before. When I realized
the story's end was near, I excused myself
for the changing pronouns. But you see,

they were meant to be anyone at all,
so how was I to know? How was I to know
Frank would sin and I would be Luna?

# DINTY W. MOORE

# White Birds

Tommy Prendergast is in my kitchen, scratching his bald spot and talking up a storm. He seems to be having an argument with someone, only Tommy is alone in the room. My refrigerator door is wide open and cold air is pouring out. The back door is open, too, and I'm standing outside, about to walk in.

When I do, Tommy says hello and goes right on talking as if I've been there with him all along. He's wearing a blue nylon jogging outfit, and the skin on his face is red from the sun.

"I saw these girls," he says, holding his hand up the way you do to show how tall someone is. "They're about twelve years old and skinny. You know how I mean, don't you Daniel?"

"Close the refrigerator," I say, "Or take something out of it."

He looks surprised, but ignores my suggestion. "Three girls. I'm looking at them, and I notice they're looking at these birds. You know, the big white ones."

"Egrets," I say.

"Yeah, egrets. Over at the lake."

A large lake borders the Garden District of Baton Rouge, and that, I suppose, is where Tommy got the sunburn. The lake is about the size of an airport and the egrets use it like one, gliding in and out according to some schedule only they seem to understand. So far, I'm pretty much following what Tommy is trying to say.

"So the girls are watching the birds?"

"Right, right. They're just watching, and I'm just watching them, and that's when it happened."

"What happened?"

He grabs a can of Old Milwaukee, shuts the refrigerator and sits down finally at the table. "Never mind," he says, "it's nothing." He drains the can and drops his head forward as if he's fallen asleep.

Tommy has been my friend since we were eight, someone I was always glad to see crawling over the fence into my patch of backyard. He was much littler than other kids our age but made up for it by being somewhat fearless. Now, at thirty, he's still a small man, but balding, with a faint mustache. He's a good carpenter, but has never managed to hold a steady job. I've seen his falling asleep act before, more often than I like to admit, so I simply go to the refrigerator, pull out another beer and set it in front of him.

"The girls," I say. "Tell me."

He looks around, confused. "Daniel, how'd you get here?"

"Just tell me about the girls."

"The girls?"

Playing dumb is another of Tommy's favorite games and probably the main reason I'm the only friend he has left. "Get to the point," I say. "Tell me what you have to tell me or give me the beer back and get out."

He sits up straight and looks me in the eye.

"While I was watching these girls, they floated across the water. Then they turned into white birds."

When my wife Laura left me, Tommy was nearly as upset as I was about her leaving. Laura took Tommy seriously, while everyone else in town treated him like a bad joke.

She left because of the baby, or specifically, because there was no baby. We married just last October, when I got my job at the library, and we decided to have a child right away. It was her idea, but I didn't fight it. She was pregnant by Christmas and so happy she would sit for hours propped up in bed, just smiling, like a girl with a secret that she loved turning over in her mind. Laura was as content and as beautiful as I'd ever seen anyone be.

Until mid-February. There was no warning. Just cramps in the middle of the night and the baby was gone within an hour.

I told her not to worry, we'd get over it. But more than just a baby flowed out of Laura that morning. Her whole life seemed to float away. She no longer smiled at anything. She no longer wanted to see our friends. She didn't want to talk. She was twenty-four and had plenty of years to try again, but she didn't want that either.

"We can have another baby," I'd say.

"I don't want another baby," Laura would answer. "I want my baby."

To Laura, the baby was as real as if she had held it in her arms before it died. To me, it was never really anything at all. And somehow she didn't seem able to forgive me for that.

Last month, she moved to New Orleans for the summer, to be with her sister in the big house on Prytania. And to be away from me.

The Tuesday that I come home to find Tommy standing by my refrigerator and talking to himself, he ends up sleeping on my couch. He keeps drinking my beer and repeating the story about the three little girls turning into white birds, and eventually he is too drunk to walk the half mile back to his apartment.

I wake up Wednesday morning to see Tommy, dripping wet and wrapped in a blue towel, sitting on the corner of my bed. "I've been thinking of killing myself," he says.

I pretend I don't hear. You can't stop Tommy from being difficult, but there's no need to encourage him either. He's often talked of suicide, and there are days I reach a point where I wish he'd just shut up and try.

"Let's talk," he insists. "Let's talk right now."

"I'm sleeping. This can wait."

He shakes his head. "No. It can't."

I look at him and realize he might be serious. Something in his eyes hints that, something in the way they don't flinch when he says the word "No." I sit up, put on my glasses and walk to the kitchen. He follows.

"I don't believe you," I say, "but tell me, for the sake of argument, why you're going to kill yourself?" I turn my back on him deliberately and start the water for coffee.

"Because of you know what."

"No, what?" I ask, folding a paper towel into a triangle because I've run out of filters.

"You know."

I turn, and he is pointing in the direction of the lake, like someone might point to a room where an insane relative has been locked away for years. Then he says, "You know, the doctor says I can't have children. He says I'm sterile as a fresh needle."

"You aren't even married," I mumble back.

"It's all the same. I can't have kids, right? So there's no point in getting married. So there's no point in going out with women. So why even bother trying to find a date? So why live, huh Daniel?" He laughs, then goes to my refrigerator and nonchalantly helps himself to some juice.

I finish making the coffee, confused by this latest bit of silliness, and end up thinking about Laura and how she would have taken Tommy much more seriously. Tommy hadn't dated anyone for six years, but she would have listened to Tommy and found a way to help him out. Most people treated Tommy like a stupid adult, but Laura always treated him like a bright child.

All I can do is what I can do, though, and some days it's all I can do just to put up with Tommy. While I'm thinking this, Tommy looks up at me like he's suddenly realized something important.

"You're right," he says. "It's no reason to kill myself."

"Good," I answer, cracking an egg into a bowl. "Let's have breakfast."

When the fried eggs and toast are ready, I make Tommy tell me again what he saw at the lake, and I try forcing him to be specific. It's something I remember my father doing with me.

"The girls just lift off the bank," Tommy explains. "They float, Daniel. They float like angels, right out to the cypress."

"What do you mean, they float?"

"I mean above the water."

"How far above the water?"

"About two feet. They float straight out, and there's some sort of smoke around them."

"Smoke?"

"Like fog or something, but the sun's shining."

"Okay. Then what?"

"They turn into birds."

"What kind of birds?"

"The white ones. I told you that already."

He seems excited, but not puzzled. It's as if he doesn't realize this is impossible, as if he thinks he's seen something rare but totally reasonable. Once, years back, Tommy told me he'd been treated for depression. Later he said it was schizophrenia—but he often changes facts like that, at whim. Another night, when we'd been drinking, Tommy told me he would sometimes hallucinate, that it scared him a little but that he basically liked it. I didn't know then whether to believe him or not.

"How do you know you didn't imagine this," I ask, back at the breakfast table. "How do you know you really saw the girls turn into birds?"

"I saw it."

"You hallucinate, Tommy. You told me. How do you know you didn't hallucinate this?"

He gets up from the table, walks around to my side and stands right over me, looking as serious as I've ever seen him.

"It wasn't like that. I know the difference, and it wasn't like that at all."

I can be foolish at times, and make mistakes, but I look at practical people and they don't seem to be doing much better. So even though Tommy's story is preposterous, I say that I believe him. And when he says he wants to learn more about the birds, to spend evenings at the lake and observe them at close range, I agree to go along. My life hasn't been proceeding so well with me in charge, so how could it hurt to let Tommy dictate things for a while?

We get to the lake about the time the sun starts to lower itself toward the I-10 overpass. I watch the sun, and Tommy watches the birds. One night, our third, a large egret appears in front of us, so large that I assume it's a male. He swoops in, banking to a wide turn and tilting his wings sharply. For a moment, he appears to be suspended in midair, then quickly he stretches his neck and glides to a landing.

Standing in about six inches of water, he draws his wings tight around his body and pulls back his long neck, until he's only half the size he seemed in flight. I glance toward Tommy, and the look on his face reminds me for a moment of the way he would look when we were boys exploring this same lake. I'm glad to see that. I look back at the bird and wonder if he ever worries like we do, if lost children and lost wives ever cause him to lose any sleep.

But the white bird just stands in the shallow water, not letting on to what he's thinking. His eyes scan the surface, his thin legs remain fixed in a firm *V*. Then, without warning, his neck darts forward like a rubber band and he snares a three-inch minnow in his orange beak, swallowing it whole. I can see the lump slowly work down his slender neck, a quarter-inch at a time. Then, he turns and looks at me, his head at an odd angle, as if perhaps he has something to say but can't find the words. That's silly, of course, but it seems that way for the moment. Finally, his wings slap the water and he flies off toward a cypress about twenty yards out in the lake.

When we return to my apartment that night, Tommy stands on my sofa in his bare feet and pretends to be an egret. "Do you have any idea how hard it is to catch a fish? Did you ever try to catch a fish?" he keeps asking.

I assure him that catching a fish by hand, or beak, is not easy.

"And things look different under water," he says, his neck moving from side to side, his eyes patrolling my living room carpet for imaginary minnows. "You look through the water at a fish and it's not really where you think it is."

"Light refraction."

"That's it. Refraction. Birds have to adjust for that. They have to understand physics."

I suggest to Tommy that egrets don't need to understand physics, that they just know instinctively where to strike. Tommy won't hear of it.

"How do you know? How do you know? You don't know what a bird knows and what he doesn't."

He seems about to get angry, so I concede the point.

A few weeks later, Tommy moves in with me. "Closer to the lake," he says, but I know the truth, which is that his landlady has tossed him out. He's not sleeping much now, and he's becoming harder and harder to talk to.

The night he moves in, an oppressively hot Friday evening, I ask him again to tell me about his vision. I'm looking for a clue, some key to what is happening. Tommy repeats lucidly and without significant change the story of the three skinny girls staring into the water, then floating like ghosts out into the lake. But when I quiz him, trying to poke a hole in his delusions, he doesn't want to talk.

"It's not important," he says.

"Of course it is," I argue. "You wouldn't have seen it if it weren't important."

"Forget it."

"Why aren't you interested? Why don't you want to know what it means?" I ask.

"Daniel," he says, reversing roles, seeming as exasperated with me as I always am with him.

"What?"

"I was hallucinating. Just drop it."

Tommy is still fascinated by the birds, hiking day and night out to the lake, but the vision seems to have merely become something that brought him there—like a movie he saw, found interesting, and forgot about a week later. All he cares about now is understanding the birds, and in his own way he probably can. Like them, he spends hours sitting quietly by the lake, watching nature at nature's pace. He differs from the birds in that he cannot fly, and in that he returns to my apartment every night to share the six-pack of beer I buy. But to the extent that a bird thinks, I suppose he's thinking like one. A bird just wants to catch enough fish to live. Tommy just wants to see enough birds.

Something about the three skinny girls and the white birds continues to fascinate me, though, despite Tommy's change of mind. As a youngster, I dreamed of flight and exotic lands, and these birds know both. The girls make me think of Laura, too, and of how delicate she turned out to be. In the weeks before she left, she seemed unable to speak, unable to say what was on her mind. Like the egret that night, the one that stared into my eyes and cocked its head as if wondering how to make its point.

The final night I spend along the water with Tommy is in early August. He's still living on my couch and I'm still trying to put it all together, to make sense of what is happening to Tommy.

It feels like rain, so we grab our sandwiches and drive to the lake in my car. We're sitting quietly on the bank as dusk settles in, Tommy watching a tree full of white birds and me worrying about Tommy, when he catches me off guard.

"Why don't you call Laura?"

I don't answer right away. I just look across the water. I called every other night for a while, when she first moved out, but we ended up either fighting or sitting quietly, not knowing what to say. At the end of every call, I would ask her to quit being depressed and she would tell me to quit saying that.

"You should call her," Tommy says. "It's not right."

"Let's talk about something else."

"You must think about her."

"No, not really."

"You're lying. I know. You think about her all the time. You should call her, make her come back. What if I weren't here? Who would be your friend?"

I should pick up on that comment maybe, be more concerned about what Tommy means, but I'm worrying more about myself. "She doesn't care about me," I say.

"You didn't care about her. She wanted you to love the baby like she did, and you didn't. You know that's why she left."

"I don't know what I know anymore."

"Well, I do, and I think you're acting dumb."

"Why is this any of your business?" I ask, but I know he's right. I know that I need to keep calling Laura, or I will lose her, but knowing and doing are two entirely different things. I almost say to Tommy that I have no idea what to tell Laura when I call, but I notice he's watching an egret that has landed very near us, closer than any egret has dared land before. The bird is particularly beautiful, the eyes soft and distant, the white body thinner and more immaculate than other egrets I've seen. I can't tell really, but I can guess, so I guess this one is a female. She rolls her neck slowly, as if tired and trying to remember something. Then she spots Tommy, and stares at him.

I'm watching her, wondering whether it's easier to be a bird than it is to be a human being, when Tommy lunges. He jumps from the bank into the mud, grabs the bird as it attempts to launch itself away from danger, and, in an awkward twisting of limbs and feathers, falls backwards into the water. But he has the bird firmly against his chest, and when she realizes she's caught, she holds very still. I notice that she seems much bigger in Tommy's arms than when she stood alone on the bank.

I watch as if what's happening is not quite real. I'm in a sort of shock, I suppose. Tommy is in the mud, trying to stand up without losing his hold on the egret, and I'm wondering why the bird doesn't use her beak. She could hurt Tommy and be free if she did.

Tommy manages somehow to get to his feet, and he begins shouting to me. "Open the trunk. Gimme the keys." He's coming at me with the egret wrapped in his arms, staggering as she shifts her weight from one side to the other. He reaches one hand toward me, fully expecting my help.

"Let her go," I say.

"No. Just gimme the keys."

"Let her go, Tommy."

He walks up the short bank and right past me toward the car, figuring, I suppose, that I'll give in to him as I always have before. What I do, though, is something different. I can't let him put the bird in my car, and I can't let him walk away with it, out onto the road. I know only two things for sure—I don't want to see the bird hurt and I don't want to see Tommy in jail.

I walk over toward the car, the keys in my hand, and offer them to Tommy. He reaches out his left hand with difficulty, still fighting the bird with his right. I grab his wrist and use the only wrestling move I know, one I remember using as a kid, one I probably used on Tommy when we were ten. I twist his arm behind his back.

"Let go of the bird, Tommy."

"Please."

"Let it go."

"No. Don't ruin this for me. I want this."

I yank his arm until his hand is bent up over his opposite shoulder, and the white bird breaks free. It hits the ground, landing on its feet, then pushes up and flies quickly over the water. The bird cries out much louder than I ever imagined it could, and it keeps crying as it flies off toward the trees.

Then I look for Tommy. He's on the ground, crying, too.

For the next ten minutes, he won't speak to me. I try to calm him down, and finally I succeed, but he won't come home with me. He eventually walks away and I drive home alone, only to sit awake all night, waiting for him, worrying that it was a mistake to let him leave.

In the morning I get a call. A psychiatric nurse tells me that Tommy has admitted himself to the hospital and has named me as the person to contact. I take over his clothes, but another nurse says Tommy doesn't want to see anyone. Two days later, he's sent to a state hospital, then eventually to a group home. He still lives there, in fact, and works as a carpenter, and writes to me and says he is happy.

I continue to visit the lake for a while, not every night, but often, and I continue to watch the birds. I think about Tommy and his vision and why he dragged me out there night after night. I'm not sure I understand, but eventually I take his advice and call Laura. After the third phone call, she agrees to come see me.

I take her to the lake. I tell her what occurred to me one night while I was watching this one white bird. It was a week after Tommy admitted himself, and I was watching this bird and wondering if it was the one Tommy had tried to capture. What occurred to me was that our baby is not dead, but is out there somewhere, still waiting to be born. Like a small bird, I say to Laura, a small bird hovering in the sky and looking for a place to land. I tell her I want us back together again. And she agrees.

So here we are, spending part of each evening walking slowly around the lake. We watch the birds awhile, then we go back to the apartment and do what we can do, whatever it takes to guide our baby home.

# FRANCES RICHARD

## Asparagus Bed

Rustling private things. Frilly,
chest-high in the sand. Step off
the kitchen porch, saddles of dew
soak her eyelet shoes. Worn crescent
concaves her paring blade, the inevitable star-patterned
colander. She died and the frond
volunteered, wound in
rusted barbwire, festooned rank
to the pasture fence. Independent. Perennial. Cockeyed
in leaf mulch, they push. Sap-white, a slip trimmed
with Sears lace, nacre glow of her thigh
as she bent. It's exhausting, this old gauze of
local growth. Tremble, a breeze and no one
remarking her, cloister of weeds
fill the gully. Where mosquito larvae perish
from poured kerosene and she cuts, cuts.
Their tapered heads, untouched, still
edible, bloomless. The hot season
enters. Long sugars toughen.


## Now You Are

Lying with him in this field.
Ground dry but humidity elemental, and all around the tasseled grass
    perimeter woods a-sway.
The many tones of black: mulch, ooze, plush, constellations, faint
    drumming sound.
You're talking children.
His voice cool syrup merging your pale rucked-up skirt to his pale cheek.
Enzymes calling, electricity reaches for you with faint hands, and now you
    are an oval space, a gap.
Inside which you are standing at a screen door.
Drooling toddler balanced on your hip.
A cellular nostalgia, brainstem hope.
He looms behind, a husband, you're a wife, you hoist the child to show

>   her a rippling world strained silver.
> If you say this is the field: behold, the field appears.
> Because she has no reason yet to distrust either one of you, and now here come headlights
>       strafing the pastoral.

## Infiltration

Along the road beside the loch are rhododendron blossoms reddish-blush
and gravel of crushed shell; the curving mass of your chest
swells your sweater. Wool pilled (lone dead sheep, its gassy belly) and
you telling me how roedeer herd in dripping woods; you hear
the roebuck's sexual cry sometimes across Glen Dubh. *Dubh* means dark
predictably, and what disturbs me is a tenor in the day that shows how
you and I grow similar: here stand sheer hills, their green walls
sweating dew as bathroom tiles would, and there go rabbits, leaping
from the bracken flashing muddy under-fur. I know you watch, crave
proof I love what you love, but I can't want it
veering through me, your perceptions roots I could be earth to.
Close impulse on my tongue, a gritty divot, but *no*. No—
Sink my heels in the damp wells of rubber boots, walk faster—pores take in
the sea-mist and I would thwart even that much infiltration—
would spit out even beauty if I could.

## Story About *Yes*

We sit in her office she had a clipboard it has a blah lustrous
flange. Nubbed
upholstery. Ventilator heating
or coolant sound. I said preamble

then just that you killed
yourself. She nods. All the tenses and.

Distance of carpeted floor.

Breath, then in brisk tones fast
forwarding, jotting, not looking at me, *Did you find her?*

No, transparent
wrong, stupid never. Vanisher

you left for work. I go to morning
preschool and what passes
for world reassembles its whirring gargantuan air heaves all
afternoon you fall fall I
play blocks, eat graham crackers,

drink juice! Zilch
kept, all x-ed, something opened

the body of normal

and splashed in obliterate
*no*. But that stirring. Faint tickle, dark
hair falling, taste of hot plush. Pulse, enormous
caress, shapeshifting
marrow, full, sheer—Explain

that I thought and her office
dilated, I smiled at her, feral
happiness rose in my throat. Before I realized
what her question meant I almost said *yes*.

# Reverie/Plus

Then not on purpose but strangely I quit
drinking milk, it tasted of green stink, bad
muck. Stuck in reverie/plus
some disgrace at the dining room table, Wisconsin Avenue
leafy trees hectic in pattycake
clap. Air winning, always. Wouldn't you like
to go straight out the window like that—
Drifting, hating my cup. Waiting for someone, my grandmother, say, to
take it away from the tablecloth marbled in white
against dense brown, psychedelic
snow pattern melting and changing the dirt. That tablecloth
belonged to my mother or might have, it looked
like her when she was there.

## The 1950s

        Scattered glass, dash and front seat
moiré. His blue-stained hand—why. Hushed and sunny. Leaked
ink, maybe engine jam. Genre of clapboards, blown peonies, fathers' throats

pressing, minutely releasing their neckties. Rows of them. Stand
in spring wind, tarred platform, birds bobolinking
swooped power lines. 7:43 to the Loop, a lack. A day.

        Opens his eyes. Again blank, and in scraps.
Crack the Pontiac. Some lady's fence casting barred shadow. As Mars lights
bloom nil in the placid light, crumpled hinge

groaning, a glaring badge, serge sleeve and cowboy hat, bland meaty
reach. Meanwhile, on the outskirts of town. *OK son. OK
you reckless shit, imagine*

        *how your mother's been feeling—*
What will. Happen. A pressure, as in whiskey, gum spirit of turpentine.
Glasses askew where his cheek presses ridged blue
upholstery, small pencil point in his eye. Bicycle spoke and kids yelling

hardened, homework, private furniture fixed. If he hurries
this: *Tempus,* in other words, *fugit.*
Down to a nub, sharpened minute. Dumb cul de sac.


## Sign

Stand bleakly in the yard.
The finned-yet-bulbous car half cropped away.
Seventeen years old as if that caused you
and explained—
      Pale sweater thrown—deliberately
pinned—and pearl-pale shoulders, empty sleeves, arrested
flap. Newborn clutched and blurry
in layette. It must be hospital
morning, a close frame. Uptilted cradle gesture, prideful private
smile, you could crush

that softness in. If spasm flooded through you and you
        wanted—the napped velvet, petals, seepage, oily rush.
Your undreamed-of manifested
from the inside. As bar windows swim with pulsing,
colored signs—*The Ebbtide, Last Chance*—but your zones
are mostly tonal: saltmarsh, boulders. An empurpled, green-shot, slaty,
constant sea. Mud headlands melting, briars rowdy, vengeful, fairytale.
        Flat bands of squinting sunlight lie
contiguous. Unhusband space and angle, unadorned,
of concrete step. Your outlaw tingle, downcast flash of terrible
new poise, it's axiomatic.
Film across you—


## Cold Seconds

Days when I tore at my hair
but it wouldn't come out. Soles of my feet stung
from slapping the bare stairs I ran up, palms
glowed from slapping the wall. Didn't dare
use my fist. Things waiting to tell
on me if I made them shatter: marble slab
misaligned on the dresser-top, paint on the headboard—
shade of pale mint, like dried toothpaste—crazing
to delicate shards. If one of the ghosts,

say my grandmother's mother herself, had come to bring me
a glass of water, would I have been
soothed? And also loons

laughed intermittently, wild and cryptic through reeds,
mulchy shore, and then cuddling into my sheets I would love
the first cold seconds, before the heat of my body
fanned out and warmed the twin bed.

## Pentecost: Collinwood School Fire, Cleveland, 1908

The children have all gone now
   sprawling into their separate orbits—
  half believing in arms to catch them
three floors below, or maybe the universal
   dream of flight. The others
blindly lurching toward memory's promise
  of light beyond the sooty dark.

  She understands both kinds of faith.
One like air heavy with too many wings,
   flightless, less adult, but blessed
as the room of her childhood
   where a trapped mourning dove beat
   itself against the glass until its small
heart burst, believing, as it must,
  in the infinite, unattainable sky.
One like the enduring touch
   of hands near midnight which read
   all they remember deftly,
each arc of tendon, belly, bone,
   like a note held almost to forever,
or the exquisite throats of swans.

   Though it was hunger, not faith,
  which kept her silent when she caught
the scent of charring wood, the ache
   of it searing her groin
seconds before the bell began, too late,
   its insistent whine—a white sound
   like pain's numb silver spark
an instant before the mind records
   the body's message and forces us

to scream. She's thinking about
   the summer she turned thirteen—
  Sunday morning and fever left her

the only one home, her family
  on their knees at St. Stephen's.
Beneath her brother's bed she found
  a box of photographs. Women like
  flowers, the fleshy petals of their sex
glistening as in dawn light. Women
  like vines, intertwined, the sleek
muscles of their shoulders like small
  waves lapping shore. Outside, sun
  burned the fields hour upon hour

into days until the wheat stood
  like a crop of bone, country of famine.
The starry amaryllis shed its scarlet
  in the unforgiving noon as if to say
  her hands, stroking the buds of her breasts
each night were wrong, and her fingers,
  like honeybees when they light upon
tiers of wisteria, were surely the devil's
  ten children, and that was why she woke
  in autumn to hot blood between her thighs.

Now she leans against the doorframe,
  brass fittings warm against her shoulder
blades, and waits for those long-ago women
  to descend in their robes of flame.
  This time she will not refuse.
She will call them Love, which makes
  a sound like something you'd whisper
to a frightened child who wakes and will
  not sleep. And Desire, too, shall come
  whose skirt is smoke and ash

and the first inclination toward sleep
  which renders the flesh agreeable.
She turns from the noise of sirens, breaking
  glass, the shouts of the man breathing
  through his mask who's powerless to cross
the smoldering, skeletal floor,
  who watches the dark beads of her necklace
begin to glow as fire unlooses her
  clothing—coral blouse, sweater, shoes.
  Until, finally, she opens her lips

to the hymn of fire, its first deep kiss
   passing halfway down her throat
so she is breathless but opens wider, wide,
   her mouth gaping the first vowel
 in her new tongue, which is global,
which means **yes,** which means **more.**

## Sometimes the Dead

How infinitely we come to love the finite—
        the moment summer's first sunset hangs
     its impossible light in a balance while

my lover and I stare like idiots, unable
        to say what we've just learned,
     that lesson of light transubstantiated

into darkness. One day I look at something,
        a shovel, say, and it's not the same.
     It becomes the shovel my father used

snowy mornings when, as a child, I'd lie
        in bed listening to the muted
     huff of metal striking snow like a gasp,

the thud of that bright weight being thrown
        to either side of the driveway, and
     then my father's car stuttering off through

early dark, the way, years later, the ambulance
        did when it took him away from that
     street he'd come to take for granted.

I'm remembering another loss, too, my lover
        feared drowned one summer in Alaska,
     the shore covered with spent salmon

grown monstrous in their slow dying, once-bright
        scales peeling like leprous flesh.
     But wasn't it desire which brought them,

snouts elongated, transformed into scythes
        they used like shovels to dig in stream
    beds a haven for their million eggs

like snowflakes drifting down? And having
        put on this new form, they couldn't take
    it back and so went on a few days, weeks,

throats finally sealed as fate, leaving
        themselves like ghosts of themselves,
    all papery bones and black flesh along the

acrid shore. But there was also the scent
        of blackberries which become for me
    the aroma of comfort the way a loved one's

scarf or handkerchief becomes a connection
        when they are gone. All those hours my
    lover was lost the police muttered apologies

and everywhere the scent of blackberries.
        I kept seeing her boat as it pulled away
    from the dock, a *V* of water opening

under that cobalt sky as she disappeared
        from sight. All that night I believed
    in her hands held up to firelight,

steam rising like incense from her palms, and
        in the morning I walked the shore, listened
    to the metallic buzz of flies shimmering

above the torn wing of a herring gull,
        and then the drone, distant at first,
    of a plane approaching. Its silver body

caught the light, reflected,
        so it looked like an immense coin
    tossed in the lake for luck, and suddenly

her face appeared at a window,
        surprising as Lazarus to everyone
    but me, who had come to live with ghosts

years before when a blizzard buried
        the driveway and I took hold of my shovel
    and felt it change beneath my fingers

into the one my father used to hold.
        And my breath not my own, either,
    though how can I make you believe that?

Whatever we love we love despite
        its impermanence, and maybe more
    because of it. How else would you explain

our fascination with sunsets, the way
        the vanishing light sets fire
    to the down on the throat of the person

you love and you reach out but the fire's gone.
        That is the story of our lives,
    which is loss, though sometimes the dead

come back. When my lover stepped
        from the plane and I wrapped my arms
    around her I held the same flesh

I'd always known. But she was changed
        in the way only those who were feared lost
    and then return are changed.

Like my father who died. Or didn't.

## The Martyrdom of St. Sebastian

Someone had put a scythe to the sweet grass—
    its torn blades, like fistfuls of emerald
 fire, bled into summer dusk the scent of something
half-remembered, while crows drifted
      in wide arcs as if to mimic the farmer
    who paused in his work to watch them thrust
      toward the sun, their hollow feathers
like those which kept the sleek Mauretanian arrows

true as the soldiers kissed each silver tip
  pulled from quiver to bow, to level
    with their squinting eyes on the Palentine
  Hill, each shaft singing against the small
breeze, going deep as love into the young boy's
  flesh, slim thighs, chest oiled with sweat, one
blade ringing against the bones of his left ankle
  like a grim toast, though his executioners were less

    cruel than drunk on sour wine which spilled,
  almost black in the half-light, from earthen jugs,
Sebastian's hands drawn tight above his head
  with three straps of fine leather, one arrow
 driven hard into the pit of his arm, though even
   then he refused to break, would not look away
     from that final, beautiful light which sent copper
spears into the feathery clouds; and when the moon

  began to rise the soldiers left him for dead or
    for the faces of exotic women veiled
 in showers of perfumed hair so that the faithful
  crept out of the sheltering black and cut him
from the wounded tree, brought him back from the light
  he wished to fly into, though he was intent
   on death's certain fame and appeared, weeks after,
    before the emperor, opening his robes to flaunt

  a scar on his groin which resembled a crow, until
    he was beaten with clubs, cast into a common
sewer where he was later found, though this time he
  could not come back. Finally, in death, he was
broken, not by unbelief, but by young men
  with names like swift rivers who fingered the dark
    silk of his hair, then severed him
from himself. Head to the west, heart to the south.


## Each Bone of the Body

    sounds like a prayer, sacrum,
sternum, scapula, as if those
    who first regarded, then named
them, belonged to an ancient cult

       of architects who built temples
which resembled human forms with
       limbs outstretched so that
they faced the stars like stars
       and offered back this planet's
elements as five spokes on a
       spinning wheel.

If each bone of the body is holy
       it is because it gives shape to
mortal love—bowl of the pelvis
       like a cradle, sickles of the
hips like two moons, every angle
       open as the mouth to a kiss,
even though we will all be torn
       one day, from the comfort of
our usual orbits, and broken.

Yesterday, a woman I didn't know
       unbuttoned her blouse slow as the
unraveling of a long summer morning,
       held the violet silk slightly
apart like those statues of Christ
       from my youth with his private
smile red as the hook and eye of
       a surgeon's needle, his crimson
nimbus, cold fingers resting
       against his quiet stone heart
which was forever on fire, wounded,
       crowned with bloody thorns,
and worn like false regret or like
       a ghastly pendant hung
at the precise center of his chest.

Once I believed
       love was like that, a cruelty
which haunted the empire of
       my childhood with the hushed
voices of black-robed nuns
       who spoke of Adam's ribbed side,
how God drove his fist in
       until that first man fell
silent, then snapped off

      a single rib which looked, at
first, like the waxing moon until
      he crushed it beneath his
heels like dust, mixed in blood
      from the season's first kill,
then gave it to the wind for form,
      to the man who called that
new shape Eve, though she cared
      little for his lists of rules
and names, preferred instead slender
      throats of irises, pomegranates
with their skin of fire, orb of
      gold for morning, silver-black
at night, and the circular logic
      of stars. She was judged to be
too much in love with the sleek
      tongues of fallen angels, the
taste of what was sweet and forbidden
      and sin. What could she say
except that she loved the heft of
      her bones, the way her mouth
had wrapped around the promise of
      knowing all there was to know?

In a room whose battered wooden
      floor was always covered with
thick curls of white wax and so
      seemed in perpetual winter,
Sr. Ignatius would read aloud to us
      from a book of martyrs bound
in sanguine leather—those who
      were wrapped in sheaves
of wheat, set as torches against
      night, whose skin was slipped
off like clothes before love—
      stones, arrows, hooks in the
glistening air. Teeth of the lion,
      claw of the bear, the wheel
in flames on the hill. Sebastian,
      Agnes, Catherine, Paul, all
destined for statues and stained
      glass, blood being the coin
and currency of paradise.

Once I believed faith was a gift
    which would help me turn
away from everything that woman,
    her blouse open, was trying
to say. Now I think it is a science
    of probability, as in
**the sun will rise tomorrow** or
    **this woman will stay**
**with me tonight.** And if I'm
    wrong, if faith means I must
turn from the truth of her body
    beneath mine, the late autumn
hues of her lidded eyes,
    then I am content to be damned
to this world where the sky
    will grow heavy with seasons,
wings, or swathes of blue smoke
    rising, and rivers at sunset
will burn but not be burning.

All my prayers will be simple,
    unspoken, the union of bone
against bone. I will pray to
    the body, which never makes
impossible claims of perfection,
    and to this world, which promises
this much this morning—

the sound of rain on slate shingles,
    the scent of last night's
jasmine candle burning down by
    white curtains which float in
the mouth of an open window, and
    the skin of the woman next to me
which turned to silver in the
    moonlight, whose shadow tasted
like the powdered wings of a moth,
    an angel, who will wake to this
gift I offer, a branch of forsythia,
    its fleet fire bright against
the burnt umber of her hair.

I am telling you this despite
    the six o'clock news.
Despite Death who flicks open
    the cover of his expensive
watchcase, turns his collar up
    against rain, who, after all,
has been mistaken
    for that dark child named
Pain with his quick temper,
    stamping feet, who stoops to
tie our nerves in knots as if they
    are nothing more than the
troublesome laces of high-stitched
    boots. I am telling you this
despite Christ's flaming heart,
    the wound in Adam's side,
despite martyrs who upset the
    general equation, who refused
to flee, but lingered instead
    like cheap perfume, then bent
to kiss the cruel angles of strange
    and glittering instruments—
morning star, scimitar, stiletto
    teeth of the iron lady.

I am telling you this because
    it is the only religion
I know to be true, because the
    blades of our shoulders are
almost wings, because, whoever
    you are, we are alive on this
blue planet, because rain has
    overflowed the copper gutters
and the bruised sky looks only
    like itself, which is enough.
Because this is the only life
    we can be certain of. Because
this world, each bone, is holy,
    and never, never enough.

# CARL PHILLIPS

## In the Blood, Winnowing

I.
Before the dumb hoof
through the chest, the fine hair
of wire drawn over the head, snapping
free of the neck's blue chords,

before the visionary falling away
from a body left mumbling to itself,
consigned to the damp sling
of tropic circumstance,

there was this morning now,
in the shower, when you know
you are dying,

you are dying and your body—
a lozenge or a prayer, whatever goes
slim and unimportant when the tongue
has grown overly zealous—

contracts under the steam,
under the light that shows up on your skin
as a deep red the shower's curtain
alone can't account for.

II.
What is it but
yours, the one hand
drawing the scrotum (no longer
yours) back upon itself?
When you come
into the other hand, it's like
spitting on death's breast, on
her spectator shoes,
to distract her.
Trembling in the water,
in the stick of yourself,
you watch the talisman's shadow,

already twisting, diminished against
the tiles, to the pig's-tail stump
of conclusion,

all it ever was.

III.
Stones do not matter.
You are twenty-nine for no reason,
or thirty-seven, your favorite prime.
Perhaps you are precisely that age
when a writer means, finally,
all that he says, a cubed square
of cell after cell containing
all the hounds of childhood,
with their hard buckles and hot
irons, their pins for under
your fingers. Dreams
are of falling
asleep at locked windows,
you are all the stones
that keep missing the glass.

IV.
Nothing stops
for you admiring the hair
that has sprung late
at either shoulder,
for you crushing your face
into the shirts that bloom
like cutaway views of old
lovers from your wall of closet.
It is any morning when the train
rattles over birdsong, the suggestion
of blades coming dry
from the night; brilliantly,
shaft after shaft, the sun passes
over the shit and bone and feather
of yours and other lives on earth,
the canted row houses, children
in their crippled victory gardens,
throwing knives in the air,

and you tell yourself (already
growing hard again over the train's
crosstown difficulties)
that everything counts:

the correct tie,
the bit of skin between sock
and cuff, the man beside you,
strange and familiar as a tattoo
the hand wakes to and keeps
wanting to touch,
refusing to believe
in that part of the world
where things don't wash off.

# Undressing for Li Po

Li Po,
the moon through the vertical blinds
is laying its bars down,
I see black, tapered lives, and
the paler ones in between, all the sticks
of my life left to mend.
Fingering the two flat prayers
at my chest, one pierced with a gold ring,
the other rouged with a broken wedge
of mouth-paint,
I'm remembering your fondness
for wine, Li Po, you desiring your own
reflection, or the moon's, the same thing,

and dying from it.
At the mirror, to the man I love
too much, I am trying to say
that I have no need
for his tattooed body, his
hands at my wrists, the cicatrix
of woes tilting down
from beneath the belly—

that I'm tired
of flesh tumbling over the dwindling sword

of itself,
something like joy.

Li Po, Li Po,
the moon is picking its way
over used swabs and razors, pots of cream,
my face where I left it, on the dressing table.
I am thinking
mountains,
good wine,
plash of exile,
letters to nowhere, the poems,
untrimmed affection,
distance, boats coming
more still than the water
in their wandering.

Li Po, last night,
drunk again, I stood naked downstairs,
just dancing, dancing . . .
I watched my feet recover and lose again
their apricot, moving in and out from
the moon's light,
watched my body lose all particulars
save clean grace, what I'd forgotten.
I imagined dancing with a man seven feet tall,
the moon making a small planet of his face,

I thought of you again, Li Po.

## Aubade for Eve Under the Arbor

To the buzz and drowse of flies coupling over and over,
I wake, find your body still here, and remember it can
be this way always, us in abundance, visitors few,
behind everything a suggestion of more, ready or not,
where that came from.

                       In those spaces of the world that
the trees, bending aside, give onto, I watch small game
settle and move on, barely long enough for me to assign
them their various names: bush-fowl, blue raven, peahen

with her dull hand of a tail scribbling onto the wet grass
behind her the questions I still can't understand: how
long, when is too much not enough—what price desire?

It is easier for me to believe I came from dirt, having seen
what a little spit and a couple of fingers can do, given
the chance, than that anything torn form my side gave rise
to you, despite evenings when, still awake after turning
from you, I have run my hands up my own body and come
close to saying yes, something's missing. . . . I wonder,

this morning, can you say what it is. I roll over, intending
to ask, but can't wake you, seeing you this quiet, and the sun,
through vines that hold back the sky, throwing shadows, in
thin snakes, across you—look, there is one now, at your ear:
tell me, it seems to say, what can you know of the world?

## As from a Quiver of Arrows

What do we do with the body, do we
burn it, do we set it in dirt or in
stone, do we wrap it in balm, honey,
oil, and then gauze and tip it onto
and trust it to a raft and to water?

What will happen to the memory of his
body, if one of us doesn't hurry now
and write it down fast? Will it be
salt or late light that it melts like?
Floss, rubber gloves, a chewed cap

to a pen elsewhere—how are we to
regard his effects, do we throw them
or use them away, do we say they are
relics and so treat them like relics?
Does his soiled linen count? If so,

would we be wrong then, to wash it?
There are no instructions whether it
should go to where are those with no
linen, or whether by night we should
memorially wear it ourselves, by day

reflect upon it folded, shelved, empty.
Here, on the floor behind his bed is
a bent photo—why? Were the two of
them lovers? Does it mean, where we
found it, that he forgot it or lost it

or intended a safekeeping? Should we
attempt to make contact? What if this
other man, too, is dead? Or alive, but
doesn't want to remember, is human?
Is it okay to be human, and fall away

from oblation and memory, if we forget,
and can't sometimes help it and sometimes
it is all that we want? How long, in
dawns or new cocks, does that take?
What if it is rest and nothing else that

we want? Is it a findable thing, small?
In what hole is it hidden? Is it, maybe,
a country? Will a guide be required who
will say to us how? Do we fly? Do we
swim? What will I do now, with my hands?

# The Full Acreage of Mourning

The truth is, *I was at the point of utter ruin.*
Alone. The one tree at last no plum-tree, but
purple, like plums. And all day in the leaves
the little nameless Solomon birds saying who:

*Who has woe? Who has sorrow? Who has wounds*
*without cause?* I am no stranger to wisdom—
*Like a sparrow in its flitting, like a swallow*
*in its flying Like a lame man's legs Like a*

*thorn that goes up into the hand Like an archer*
*who wounds everybody* is love, yes, I know that,
there are books and I have read them, there
are flowers, the ones whose streaks spell out

beautifully **alas!**, all the others marked *You
will be like one who lies down in the midst
of the sea* or *like one who lies on the top of
a mast* in fine print: of each one haven't I

taken to my mouth the thin petal and swallowed?
The truest words are something else at any
given moment can happen, will, has happened.
I could say that *at the window of my house I*

*looked out through my lattice, and I perceived
among the youths a young man* spitting proverbs
like "You can lead, if it is thirsty, any horse
to the water," and that would be but one version.

Another is: Unable to forget, I sought out every
space that I thought might contain you. Each
one I entered. At each I called Come, or Where
now, Little Shield, or Little Sir Refuge, here?

# Blue

As through marble or the lining of
certain fish split open and scooped
clean, this is the blue vein
that rides, where the flesh is even
whiter than the rest of her, the splayed
thighs mother forgets, busy struggling
for command over bones: her own,
those of the chaise longue, all
equally uncooperative, and there's
the wind, too. This is her hair, gone
from white to blue in the air.

This is the black, shot with blue, of my dark
daddy's knuckles, that do not change, ever.
Which is to say they are no more pale
in anger than at rest, or when, as
I imagine them now, they follow
the same two fingers he has always used
to make the rim of every empty blue
glass in the house sing.

Always, the same
blue-to-black sorrow
no black surface can entirely hide.

Under the night, somewhere
between the white that is nothing so much as
blue, and the black that is, finally, nothing,
I am the man neither of you remembers.
Shielding, in the half-dark,
the blue eyes I sometimes forget
I don't have. Pulling my own stoop-
shouldered kind of blues across paper.
Apparently misinformed about the rumored
stuff of dreams: everywhere I inquired,
I was told look for blue.

# Bethany Pray

## In the City

I was used to lack
and called it
honest work.
Small flowers grew
in the narrow yard
because I demanded that much,
standing over them
with a cup of water
in the short hours of sun,
guarding their green fires.

When I am with you,
I forget my hard-earned garden.
We lie curled for a long time
in blackness.
Suddenly my soul comes right up
to my mouth
and speaks out of it.

See, on my collarbone
is a circle
where your lips were,
making me unsuitable
for the subway passage
and wide evenings alone
though I loved them
once.

## Conception

You stripped and stood
in a column of light among the trees
like a lighter tree,
and I admired your incandescence,
your good form.
I lay down
on the pine needles and looked up
to where the treetops formed a ceiling
like stained glass.
When I opened my arms,
your wide chest
pressed down on me—heavy,
like waking after the weightlessness of sleep;
like a door.

A field sloped down the hill
from us, and at the bottom
a line of bathing suits flapped
between two trees, one of them dead.
A little further, cars were parked
in a clump by the barn.
The screen door banged
as people came and went.
On the far side of the house,
your various relatives
talked and drank
and stroked the children's heads.

On that day,
I wanted to enter in
through the frame of your body.
Through the trees came the sound

of your cousin calling out
for a game of croquet,
and we snuck down the hill and joined in.
Still, I remember the first thwack
of the mallet, the colored balls
spilled out on the grass,
the voices suddenly familiar.

# The Nameless

1. *The Naturalist*

When a man I know speaks,
his words seem to have just come in
from outdoors. The grasses' exhalations
sweeten the air,
the flowers he names become unmistakable,
beautiful.
But I'm not a naturalist myself.

2. *Admission*

The outdoors was a room among rooms.
Afternoons I climbed a pine tree
to be unseen and still see.
Like slow fish,
the family passed the windows,
back and forth.

Later, on my back in bed,
I whispered my transgressions
so they wouldn't bloom later
into nightmare. But

my evil wishes went too deep:
like dandelions, always
a pale bit left.

3. *The Torrent*

In the shower,
I ponder how to tell my husband.
How to say it right?

A thousand vanishings bloom in the steam.
Every line I try out
is coy or smug or sad—
The words make a torrent
within which
sings the knot of cells
in its thready voice.
How can I love the nameless?

## Tree

1.
I sang when labor began,
my husband and little daughter
sleeping;

pleased with myself I sang,

and cursed when suddenly
I couldn't sing,
the house too small to walk in;

better, the empty street,
big late-summer leaves wallowing
in mist,

the soft air there and not there,
someplace for the pain
to vault up into.

At the hospital, the pain
was like white birds:
how they gather like a fist

and then unfurl,
dropping,
and rise again as they converge—

larger than the body—
the body
a scrap of newsprint
tossed in that updraft.

2.
Night veils the neighboring houses.
In the kitchen the two-year-old
spits on the table,
and in my arms, the baby shrieks

like a snared animal.
I spin around
with violent intention

but then what-I-am
shatters into nothing, a resumption
of air.

At bedtime,
I hold the children in my arms
and hear the walnuts
thud upon the grass,

as if the falling had become
what held up the world.

# Quartet

1.
Down the covered ramp
she flies, the clear
source of exuberance.
The air is green sea
mantling her shoulders;
around her,
the fleet of grocery carts
rolls together, winking
and clanking.

2.
When the neighbor's cat
scratches her wrist,
three welts rise, each
with its pindot of garnet.
The lines say "iii";
or maybe, "!!!"

on her soft blank arm.
She only cries for a minute,
not blaming me.

3.
Naked from the bath,
she drapes herself in my arms,
her belly sunken
from last sickness.
Save for her smirk,
she could be dead: skin
like translucent stone;
the thighs, land and inert;
feet, a little toed in,
trembling with her pulse.

4.
She climbs in my bed this morning
to run her fingers through my hair.
I know how to keep my pleasure
to myself, and so swing
my legs over the side
and begin to speak
in that dry, dark voice
though I want to cry out,
—Don't stop!—

# In Dream, in the Eden

In the Eden of memory,
the black walnut tree has not been cut down
and waves its fern-like leaves above their heads.
The schoolmates make their way
from grove to pool, throw off
their colored shirts, raise their thin
white arms, white as seashells,
thin as piccolos, and dive.

Their towels draped around their necks,
they wander through the garden

where the mother's sweet voice
quavers and eddies among
the low grasses, the flowering dogwoods.
Ease my burden, she calls,
know my terror,
and they lie down under the branches,
green-shadowed. That is how
I remember it: the many blossoms,
the little fallen soldiers.

# Apparition

—Let me be delivered—I think
at day's end
with my forearms in hot water
and the two pale bright faces
at the table.

When we all sleep,
faith composes our faces
as if dreams were apparitions,
light blowing through the dark chamber
like a god,
lifting aside the bedclothes,
lifting us into a muscular dance with truth.

Why are the stairs tilted
so I can barely pull myself up?
Why the third phantom child crying from the yard?
Don't I love them well enough?

But look at this sky
upon waking, its transparence touched
with white and smaller coral islands,
their edges blurred
with shadow. This
is what I need—oh sheet
of light, oh
blind blue eye.

# Jeffrey Skinner

## Play Dead

Like the black D.J. in New Orleans
who declared his own wake on the air
and the resurrection to follow—five bucks
admission, with the promise of a hundred
to anyone who caught him breathing.
One woman pulled up a chair
before the open casket, and fastened
her eyes on his chest for six hours,
the roar of blues and whiskey all around.
I don't know if she got the hundred;
arriving at my meeting of drunks
before the story's end, I clicked off
the radio with the engine. One man
was missing from our group, the story
on him an old one: he went out
and booked a cheap hotel to drink
undisturbed, telling no one. Then finished
the job with a twelve-gauge. We
spoke in turn, each of us careful to say,
with the precision of a soldier cleaning
his weapon in the night, just how
the story cut. *Play dead:* we were familiar
with that command. We had risen once.

## Come

*Tell me first which opening
and I will.* Her razor slipped in the shower,
a pinstripe of red down her leg.
She was not crazy, her bills were paid.

*There's a lack of freedom in your mind*,
he thought, and wanted to say,
but hung up. All that land beneath the crisscross
of voices, all that American space

beneath wires. . . . Missing the ocean,
he took forever to dip one toe
in Gregg Lake. She sat on the stony bottom
beckoning with a slow water hand.

The sky darkened, yes, as in a bad novel
and Hey!, aren't those crows storming
from the trees like sudden rage
familiar? The same old childhood crows?

No. What goes around just goes.
The phone ringing as she lathers her hair,
he on the other end breathing hard.
All that watered-down blood between them.

# Speak

The five thousand sat back
on the grass, arms around their knees,
wary or expectant, without a clue
what to expect. It was
hard to hear the man speak—
he appeared to be no taller than a cup.
And even those who heard,
their huge faces leaning in to the glow
his body made, could not say
they understood, only that his words
like wine drew warmth from their skin,
the air filled with a mixture
of comfort and sorrow. It was not
until he had finished speaking
that the five thousand woke
to their hunger. And then the bread
tasted like bread, the fish
like fish. Glad to have it, the everyday
miracle of food; but not why
they had come. A man you could hold
in your palm, you could kill
with a careless step,
who nevertheless spoke with human
tones, beautifully, though he made little sense—
that was worth the dust, the long walk.
That was something to see.

## Fetch

Go, bring back the worthless stick.
*"Of memory,"* I almost added.
But she wouldn't understand, naturally.
There is the word and the thing

adhering. So far so good.
Metaphor, drawer of drafting tools—
spill it on the study floor, animal says,
that we might at least see

how an expensive ruler tastes.
Yesterday I pissed and barked and ate
because that's what waking means.
Thus has God solved time

for me—here, here. What you call
memory is a long and sweet,
delicious crack of wood in my teeth
I bring back and bring back and bring back.

## Stay

A clearance sale banner has broken free and risen
momentarily into clouds: EVERYTHING GOES. Cool air,
Canadian import, silvers the look of grass
and branch, each leaf a tuning fork set humming,
each shadow exact, razor-cut. Across the street
Frank rakes his hosta bed; the scritch
of tines jerks up my dog's head briefly. But it's
a known sound, and she sinks back
into the furred rumple of dream. My daughters
have entered their teens intact, whole shells, rarely
found, waiting to be lifted and filled with a new
element, air breathers now. Everyone alive
is arrayed. I don't say joyous, I say singular
constellation. And I want everything
to stay as it is: stay, cloud pinned
over the slaughterhouse on Market Street,
stay voices of men laying concrete on Mossrose.
Stay Sarah, whose body has sifted mine fifteen years.

Stay sober mind, stay necessary delusions.
Stay shadows, air, rake, dog. Good stay. Good.

# Jocelyn

"If they hear desperation in your voice they won't choose you."
      "Who?"
"The minions."

I leaned back. Her mouth smiled, but her eyes
      glistened like viscera—
eyes and mouth from different faces.

Some mixture of revulsion
      and pity puffed up
a thought balloon in my head: *I will help you,*
      it said.

      \*

She was going to play drums with Marianne
Faithful, would fly to Ireland when she got the call.
She withdrew her living allowance, $428.73,
stuffed it in the brandy snifter tip glass

at Twice Told Cafe. Jim, the owner, ran
after her with the cash, forcibly returned it.
Instead, she bought CDs and passed them out
like leaflets to the skateheads on Bardstown.

She knew Don Flood, the local news anchor
was speaking to her in code—"You are the rose
of perfection," he'd say, piercing her soul
from the six o'clock report. She wanted to tell

him she understood, whisper everything
was all right: though they could not be together
she saw the wires that ran into his body. She wrote
letters, but got no reply, so had to sneak

into the studio. Cops took her before she could
see him, say *Don, it's all right;* though they

were apart, she understood: the wires,
his body. She had them too. It was no one's fault.

    *

3:00 A.M.: *"Hey Dad, I'm cooking up
a beautiful cut of Siberian tiger,
care to join me for a bite?"*

When her father arrived
the kitchen
was a box of smoke, the skillet

piled with flaming supermodels
scissored from *Vogue*.
He put out the fire

and drove her to Central State.

    *

They could only keep her a limited time
against her will and, once outside, no one could force her
to take the chemical that kept her steady. She would,

for a while, work checkout at Kroger's and stay
straight—glassy-eyed, her skin fish-belly white.
But soon the world grew unbearably dull,

as if it were all a gray matter of sprockets and gears,
and she'd stop taking the pills, stop in at Baha Bay
for a strawberry daiquiri or two, and the world

snapped back into color and dire significance.
And she knew again the true meaning of traffic signs, could
look into the bus driver's eyes and see his grandmother

suffering the Great Depression, could track
constellations round the North Star with her bare eyes,
feel time on her skin like the spray from a just opened orange.

Those days the sun broke across any surface of water
she heard as music, and bought blank sheets to write it down—
"Cave Hill Lake at Noon, August, 1995." It was

exhilarating: so much meaning!—Every car horn blared
her name, every Dow Jones closing enwrapped, like a fortune,
a rise or fall in her fate; every infant stared and smiled

at her (her!), and she'd wink, and stare back, and only
turn away when mom scowled, the bad mom, the mother eye . . .

    *

I'd throw up my hands: all her poems
were bloody gowned spirits wandering lime halls,
every doctor Dr. Death, Dr.
Lucifer, sewing her brothers and sisters
into cocoons suspended, and slowly . . .

O thread of calcified veins!

"There are brilliant lines here," I'd begin, "But
what is the overall . . . I don't see . . ."

She'd interrupt—

"It's hard being Pilate. I know. And I forgive you.
But it's harder to be Jesus, much harder
to be Jesus Christ."

Her cheek twitched, her right eye drooped;
her lips, cracked white as hardpan earth in winter . . .

"Especially when no one believes, and you want to stop
being Jesus but, of course,
you can't . . . So, do you think

I can finish the thesis by March? I really have to get past this,
and get a jump on my doctorate and,
you know—my life . . ."

    *

Other times she was Elvis. Or Jeanne d'Arc.
Or Gabriel. She exhausted eight psychiatrists, three social workers,
friends, bosses, coworkers, teachers, father,

father . . . How could I help her?
I had felt death, petty and alert, pecking at my own madness
not long ago, and every day stood guard in the shadow of certain thoughts,

and in any case believed
a good percentage of my *fin de siècle* America
was certifiable. It's a bitch, tearing oneself from nightmare

to waking: the cells of waking and dreaming meld
and you cannot help but leave some torn pink fabric in that world.

    \*

I saw her last a month ago. Did I still teach?
She seemed, stretched within her skin, paler than memory,

as if madness were a gas, lighter than air. I said, yes, it's more
of the same and going well, and she nodded, her smile

installed as if by pliers, and stared
at me, until I felt some nerve awaken in the base of my skull.

I could think of nothing
to say, then, having failed;

and smiled and raised my hand like some adolescent
imitating a movie Indian, and turned to walk

to the parking lot at Ear-X-Tacy
where I had come for a CD.

    \*

But which band, what title, what style?
There were thousands to choose from, centuries and diaspora

of disparate cultures, all making a noise
the others were slow to call music . . . I stood before the clerk, my mind

clenched, and long tubes of fluorescent light began to flicker
with incredible rapidity. The boy-
clerk stared, the diamond of his nose-stud glittering . . .

                                            men riding

    camels, scent of clove and dung, the furious

        white music of that star . . .

And *Sorry*, I mumbled, *No, it's nothing. There's nothing I need.*

# JEAN VALENTINE

## Your mouth "appeared to me"

Your mouth "appeared to me"
a Buddha's mouth
the size of a billboard

I thought: of course,
your mouth,
you *spoke* to me.

Then your blue finger,
of course it was your finger,
you painted with your finger

and you painted me with your finger . . .

Then appeared to me flames:
transparencements of every hand and mouth.

## Mare and Newborn Foal

When you die
there are bales of hay
heaped high in space
mean while
with my tongue
I draw the black straw
out of you
mean while
with your tongue
you draw the black straw out of me.

## Mother,

any life you got
it *was* from the wind you got it.
You licked it up off the floor
and chewed it up and put it

in my beak and I wanted more.
I wanted all four winds
and the whole world's floor,
sex, poetry, my right mind,

—*Who do you think you are?*

# The Pen

The sandy road, the bright green two-inch lizard
little light on the road

the pen that writes by itself
the mist that blows by, through itself

the gourd I drink from in my sleep
that also drinks from me

—Who taught me to know instead of not to know?
And this pen     its thought

lying on the thought of the table
a bow lying across the strings

not moving
held


# October Premonition

October premonition

seeing my friend leave
I turn my head up, away

if she has to leave
let me not see her

my leaving mother
leaving my door open a crack
of light     crack of the depression world

# Contributors' Notes

**Doug Anderson**'s recent book, *Blues for Unemployed Secret Police* (Curbstone Press, 2000), was published with a grant from the Eric Mathieu King Fund of the Academy of American Poets. His first book, *The Moon Reflected Fire* (Alice James Books, 1994), won the Kate Tufts Discovery award in 1995. His poetry has received awards from the National Endowment for the Arts, The Massachusetts Artists Foundation, The Massachusetts Cultural Council, Poets & Writers, Inc., and in 1993 he won the Emily Balch Prize from *The Virginia Quarterly Review*. His poems have appeared in *Ploughshares, The Massachusetts Review, Field, The Virginia Quarterly Review, Southern Review*, and many other literary magazines. His critical work has appeared in *The New York Times Book Review, The Boston Globe*, and *The London Times Literary Supplement*. He teaches at Pitzer and Pomona Colleges, in Claremont, California.

**Robert A. Ayres** manages his family's ranching operation in the Texas Hill Country. His poems have appeared in *Cumberland Poetry Review, The Marlboro Review*, and *Southwestern American Literature*, and the anthologies *Outsiders* and *Urban Nature* (Milkweed Editions, 1999, 2000). He lives in Austin with his wife, Margaret, and their two daughters.

**Cheryl Baldi** graduated from Dickinson College and received her MFA in creative writing from The Warren Wilson MFA Program for Writers. Currently a member of the part-time faculty at Bucks County Community College, she lives in Doylestown, Pennsylvania, with her husband and two children.

**Sally Ball**'s poems have appeared in *Ploughshares, Southwest Review, The Threepenny Review*, and elsewhere. She is an Associate Editor of Four Way Books. She lives in Arizona.

**Jennifer Barber** is the editor of *Salamander*, a magazine for poetry, fiction, and memoirs. She has lived in Spain and England, and received her MFA from Columbia University. A selection of her poems, entitled *Vendaval*, appeared in *Take Three: 3*, AGNI New Poets Series, published by Graywolf Press in 1998. She received a Bruce Rossley New Voice Award in 1998.

**Erin Belieu** was born in 1965 in Omaha, Nebraska. She was educated at the University of Nebraska at Omaha's Writers' Workshop, The Ohio State University, and Boston University's Writing Program. She has won the National Poetry Series Open Competition for her manuscript *Infanta* (Copper Canyon Press, 1995), The Academy of American Poets Prize, and *The Nebraska Review* Prize. Her work has appeared in such journals as *AGNI*, *The Antioch Review*, *Harvard Review*, *Prairie Schooner*, *The Formalist*, *The Greensboro Review*, *The Journal*, and *Yellow Silk*.

**Marianne Boruch** has published four collections of poetry: *View from the Gazebo* and *Descendant* (Wesleyan 1985, 1989), and *Moss Burning* and *A Stick That Breaks and Breaks* (Oberlin College Press, 1993, 1997). Her collection of essays, *Poetry's Old Air*, came out in 1995 in the University of Michigan Press's Poets on Poetry series. She teaches in the MFA program at Purdue University.

**Laure-Anne Bosselaar** is the author of two poetry collections: *The Hour Between Dog and Wolf* (1997), and *Small Gods of Grief*, winner of the Isabella Gardner Prize for Poetry for 2001, both published by BOA Editions, Ltd. She is the editor of *Outsiders: Poems about Rebels, Exiles, and Renegades* and *Urban Nature: Poems about Wildlife in the City* (Milkweed Editions, 1999, 2000). She currently teaches a poetry workshop in the graduate writing program at Sarah Lawrence College. Her next anthology, *Never Before: Poems about First Experiences*, will be published by Four Way Books in 2003.

**Kenneth Zamora Damacion** is the author of two poetry manuscripts, *The False Angel* and *Last Note Between Heaven and Hell*.

**Volodymyr Dibrova** is a Ukranian writer, translator, and literary critic. He has published three books of short stories, four plays, and two novels. His novellas *Peltse* and *Pentameron*, translated by Halyna Hryn, were published by Northwestern University Press in 1996. He currently teaches Ukrainian and is a writer-in-residence at Harvard University.

**Sharon Dolin** is the author of a book of poems, *Heart Work* (The Sheep Meadow Press, 1995), and four chapbooks: *The Seagull* (The Center for Book Arts, 2001), *Mistakes* (Poetry New York Pamphlet Series, 1999), *Climbing Mount Sinai* (Dim Gray Bar Press, 1996), and *Mind Lag* (Turtle Watch Press, 1982). She currently teaches poetry workshops at the 92nd Street Y's Unterberg Poetry Center in New York City, and she is coordinator and cojudge of The Center for Book Arts Annual Letterpress Poetry Chapbook Competition.

**Patrick Donnelly** is currently a student in the Warren Wilson MFA Program for Writers. He is a curator of the reading series at the Ear Inn, and Program Assistant of the CCS Reading Series, sponsored by Four Way Books (both in New York City). He lives in Brooklyn.

**John Donoghue** lives in Cleveland, Ohio, and is the author of *Precipice* (Four Way Books, 2000). For the past twenty-eight years, he has been a professor in the Department of Electrical and Computer Engineering at Cleveland State University, and his poetry has appeared in journals including *AGNI*, *Prairie Schooner*, *The Virginia Quarterly Review*, and *Willow Springs*.

**Ellen Dudley** is the author of *Slow Burn* (Provincetown Arts Press, 1997). Her work has appeared or is forthcoming in *TriQuarterly*, *AGNI*, *The Massachusetts Review*, *The Poetry Miscellany*, *Phoebe*, and other magazines. She is the winner of a Vermont Council on the Arts Fellowship and is founding editor/publisher of *The Marlboro Review*. She lives in Marlboro, Vermont, where she is co-owner of a construction company.

**Gary Duehr** lives in Boston, where he is a visual arts critic and photographer, as well as codirector of the performance company Invisible Cities Group. He is the author of *Winter Light* (Four Way Books, 1999) and *Where Everyone Is Going To* (St. Andrews College Press, 1999). In 2001, he was awarded an NEA Fellowship in poetry.

**Linda Dyer** has been the recipient of fellowships from the Colorado Council on the Arts, the NeoData Endowment for the Humanities, and the Vermont Studio Center. Her first book of poems, *Fictional Teeth*, was published by Ahsahta Press in 2001.

**Martín Espada** is the author of six poetry collections, most recently *A Mayan Astronomer in Hell's Kitchen* and *Imagine the Angels of Bread* (W. W. Norton, 2000, 1996). His awards include an American Book Award, the PEN/Revson Fellowship and the Paterson Poetry Prize. A former tenant lawyer, Espada teaches in the English Department at the University of Massachusetts-Amherst.

**Terri Ford** is a graduate of the Warren Wilson MFA Program for Writers. She is a recipient of grants from the Ohio Arts Council and the Kentucky Arts Council, as well as the Kentucky Foundation for Women. Her first book of poems, *Why the Ships Are She*, was published in 2001 by Four Way Books. Her poems have appeared in many small press magazines, including *AGNI*, *Southern Poetry Review*, *Evil Dog*, and *Forklift, Ohio;* she also has a poem in jumbo Braille on a sculpture in the Columbus Library. She was the Ohio Arts Council Writing Fellow at the Fine Arts Work Center in Provincetown, Massachusetts, in the summer of 1999.

**Faye George**'s poems have appeared in *The Paris Review, Poetry, The Amicus Journal, Yankee,* and numerous other journals and anthologies. Her book-length collection, *A Wound on Stone,* was published in September, 2001, by Perugia Press.

**Tereze Glück** grew up in Woodmere, Long Island, and now lives in New York City. She is the winner of the 1995 Iowa Short Fiction Award for her collection of short stories, *May You Live in Interesting Times.* In 1993 she was awarded a grant from the National Endowment for the Arts, and she has been a fellow at the Virginia Center for Creative Arts, Ragdale, the Ucross Foundation, and Djerassi. Her stories have appeared in numerous magazines, including *Antioch Review, Fiction, Epoch, Story, Columbia, The North American Review, The Gettysburg Review,* and others. She has a twenty-four-year-old daughter who is a sound editor and actress in New York.

**Sarah Gorham** is the author of three collections of poetry: *The Tension Zone* (Four Way Books, 1996), *Don't Go Back to Sleep* (Galileo Press, Ltd., 1989), and *The Cure* (Four Way Books, forthcoming). New work has recently appeared in *The Paris Review, AGNI, The Ohio Review,* and *DoubleTake.* Gorham is Editor-in-Chief and President of Sarabande Books, which she co-founded in 1994.

**Ha Jin** has published several books of fiction and poetry. His most recent book is a volume of poems, *Wreckage,* published by Hanging Loose Press in 2001. His work has been translated into more than twenty languages.

**Melissa Hotchkiss** is one of the editors of the poetry journal *Barrow Street,* and a codirector of the Barrow Street Reading Series in New York City. Her work has appeared or is forthcoming in *The Marlboro Review, The New York Times, The Cortland Review, 3rd bed, Gathering of the Tribes, Heliotrope,* and *Whole Notes.* Her book, *Storm Damage,* is forthcoming from Tupelo Press in 2002.

**Brian Kiteley** is the author of *Still Life with Insects* (Graywolf Press, 1993) and *I Know Many Songs, But I Cannot Sing* (Simon & Schuster, 1996). He is at work on a history in stories of Northampton, Massachusetts, *The River Gods.* He teaches at the University of Denver.

**Michael Klein** wrote *1990* (Provincetown Arts Press, 1993), a book of poems that tied with James Schuyler for a Lambda Literary Award in 1993. He also wrote *Track Conditions: A Memoir* (Persea Books, 1998), which was recently optioned for a film, and he is currently writing a book of essays about sex and friendship called *The End of Being Known*. Recent poems have been published in *Fence, Barrow Street,* and nerve.com. He teaches in the Goddard MFA-in-Writing Program in Vermont, the summer program at the Fine Arts Work Center in Provincetown, and is spring 2001 Visiting Poet at SUNY Binghamton.

**Kathleen E. Krause** was winner of *Phoebe's* 2001 Greg Grummer Poetry Contest, chosen by Brenda Hillman. Her work has appeared in *AGNI, Lit, Salonika,* and is forthcoming in *Lungfull!* In the winter of 1999, she guest-edited an issue of *Salonika*. Her chapbook, *Broth,* was published in 1997 by Linear Arts. She lives in Brooklyn.

**Sabra Loomis** has received awards from The Massachusetts Artists Foundation, The Yeats Society, and The Heinrich Böll Foundation. Her book of poems, *Rosetree,* was published by Alice James Books in 1989; a second collection is forthcoming from Salmon Press in Ireland. She teaches poetry workshops for the New York Public Library, the Joiner Center at the University of Massachusetts, and the Poets' House, Donegal.

**Pablo Medina**'s latest books are *The Return of Felix Nogara,* a novel (Persea, 2000), and *The Floating Island,* poems (White Pine Press, 1999). He is also the author of another novel, two books of poetry, a memoir, and a collection of translations from the Spanish of Tania Diaz Castro. He is on the faculty of The Warren Wilson MFA Program for Writers and New School University in New York City. Born in Cuba, he lives in Hoboken, New Jersey.

**Alison Moore** is the author of a collection of short stories, *Small Spaces Between Emergencies* (Mercury House, 1992), which was selected as one of the Notable Books of 1993 by The American Library Association, as well as a novel, *Synonym for Love* (Mercury House, 1995, Penguin USA, 1996). She has received a National Endowment for the Arts literary fellowship and an Arizona Commission on the Arts fellowship in fiction. She is currently the project director for a public outreach program with the Orphan Train Heritage Society of America, Inc. She lives in Fayetteville, Arkansas.

**Dinty W. Moore** is the author of two books of nonfiction, *The Emperor's Virtual Clothes* and *The Accidental Buddhist* (Algonquin Books, 1995, 1997), as well as a book of short stories, *Toothpick Men* (Mammoth Books, 1998). He has written stories and essays for *The New York Times Sunday*

*Magazine, The Georgia Review, Southern Review,* and *Utne Reader,* and is a 1992 National Endowment for the Arts Fellow in fiction writing. He teaches writing at Penn State Altoona.

**Dale Neal** is a novelist, critic, and journalist in Asheville, North Carolina. His short fiction has appeared in *The Marlboro Review, The Carolina Quarterly, The Crescent Review, The Chattahoochee Review,* and other literary quarterlies.

**Frankie Paino** received an MFA in writing from Vermont College in 1990. Her first book, *The Rapture of Matter,* was published by Cleveland State University in 1991. Her work has appeared in many journals, including *The Kenyon Review, The Antioch Review, Quarterly West, Prairie Schooner, The Gettysburg Review,* and *Poetry Northwest.* Her poems have been anthologized in *Poets for Life* (Persea, 1992) and *American Poetry: The Next Generation* (Carnegie-Mellon University Press, 2000). She has been the recipient of numerous awards, including a Pushcart Prize and the 1994 Cleveland Arts Prize in Literature.

**Carl Phillips** is the author of five books of poems, most recently *The Tether* (Farrar, Straus and Giroux, 2001) and *Pastoral* (Graywolf, 2000). His honors include selection as a finalist for the National Book Award, the Morse Poetry Prize, a Guggenheim Fellowship, and the Witter Bynner Fellowship from the Library of Congress. He is Professor of English at Washington University in St. Louis.

**Bethany Pray** received an MFA from The Warren Wilson MFA Program for Writers. She lives in Hastings-on-Hudson, New York, with her daughters.

**Frances Richard** teaches English at New School University and Barnard College. She is a regular contributor to *Artforum* and nonfiction editor of the literary journal *Fence.* Her first book of poems is forthcoming in 2003 from Four Way Books.

**Jeffrey Skinner** has published three collections of poems: *Late Stars* (Wesleyan University Press, 1995), *A Guide to Forgetting* (Graywolf Press, 1988), and *The Company of Heaven* (Pittsburgh Poetry Series, University of Pittsburgh Press, 1992). A fourth, *Gender Studies,* is due out soon from Miami University Press. His poems have appeared in such magazines as *The New Yorker, The Atlantic, The Paris Review, Poetry,* and *The American Poetry Review.* He has coedited two poetry anthologies, *Last Call: Poems on Alcoholism, Addiction, and Deliverance* and *Passing the Word: Writers on Their Mentors* (Sarabande Books, 1997, 2001). He has been the recipient of grants from the NEA, the Ingram Merrill Foundation, the Howard Foundation, and three state arts agencies. In 1997 he was the Frost House Poet in Residence. Skinner currently directs the creative writing program at the University of Louisville.

**Jean Valentine** is the author of eight collections of poetry, most recently *Growing Darkness, Growing Light* (Carnegie-Mellon University Press, 1997) and *The Cradle of the Real Life* (Wesleyan University Press, 2000). She lives and works in New York City.

# EDITORS

**Carlen Arnett** received a 1999 McKnight Artist Fellowship, Loft Award in Poetry. She has also been awarded a MacDowell Colony Fellowship and a nomination for the Pushcart Prize. Currently, she teaches at the Minneapolis College of Art and Design. She is an Associate Editor at Four Way Books.

**Jane Brox**'s most recent book, *Five Thousand Days Like This One*, was a 1999 finalist for the National Book Critics Circle Award in nonfiction. Her first book, *Here and Nowhere Else*, won the L. L. Winship/PEN New England Award. Her essays have been selected for inclusion in *Best American Essays*, *The Norton Book of Nature Writing*, and the *Pushcart Prize Anthology*. She is the recipient of grants from the National Endowment for the Arts and the Massachusets Cultural Council. She teaches in Harvard's Division of Continuing Education in Cambridge, and lives in the Merrimack Valley of Massachusetts.

**Dzvinia Orlowsky** is the author of three poetry collections: *A Handful of Bees*, *Edge of House*, and *Except for One Obscene Brushstroke* (Carnegie-Mellon University Press, 1994, 1999, and forthcoming). In 1992, Minatoby Press published her chapbook, *Burying Dolls*. She is a Founding Editor of Four Way Books and a contributing editor to *AGNI* and *The Marlboro Review*. She received a Massachusetts Cultural Council poetry grant in 1998 and a Massachusetts Cultural Council professional development grant in 1999. She has taught at The Boston Center for Adult Education, Emerson College, Gemini Ink, and the Stonecoast Writers' Conference.

**Martha Rhodes** is the author of two poetry collections, *Perfect Disappearance* (winner of the 2000 Green Rose Prize from New Issues Press) and *At the Gate* (Provincetown Arts Press, 1995). Her poems have appeared in many anthologies, including *The Extraordinary Tide: New*

*Poetry by American Women* (Columbia University Press, 2001) and *The New American Poets: A Bread Loaf Anthology* (University Press of New England, 2000), and in such journals as *AGNI, The American Poetry Review, Fence, Ploughshares,TriQuarterly,* and others. She teaches at Emerson College and New School University. She is a Founding Editor and the Director of Four Way Books.

# ACKNOWLEDGMENTS

*Grateful acknowledgment is made to the publications in which the following pieces first appeared. Unless otherwise noted, copyright of the work is held by the individual writer.*

**Doug Anderson** "North of Tam Ky, 1967," "Bamboo Ridge," "Night Ambush," "Itinerary," "Doc," "Blues," "Xin Loi," and "Rain" from *The Moon Reflected Fire* reprinted by permission of Alice James Books © 1994 Doug Anderson.

**Robert A. Ayres** "The Orchard" and "Alameda Circle" originally published in *The Marlboro Review*. Reprinted by permission of the author.

**Jennifer Barber** "Hot Morning in the Attic" originally published in *96 Inc*. "Oak" originally published in *The Massachusetts Review*. "In the Bosch Room" originally published in Partisan Review. "San Miguel," "Vendaval," "Nights," "A Village I Love," "Letter," "Photograph of My Mother, A Girl in Central Park" and "Summer as a Large, Reclining Nude" published in *Take Three: 3,* published by Graywolf Press in 1998. Reprinted by permission of the author.

**Erin Belieu** "Tick," "Prayer for Men," "The Spring Burials," "Georgic on Memory," "Erections," "The Small Sound of Quiet Animals," "Watching the Giraffes Run," and "Another Poem for Mothers" from *Infanta,* © 1995 by Erin Belieu. Reprinted with the permission of Copper Canyon Press, PO Box 271, Port Townsend, WA 98368-0271, USA.

**Marianne Boruch** "Then," "The Luxor Baths," "On Sorrow" reprinted from *Moss Burning,* Marianne Boruch; FIELD Poetry Series v. 2; Oberlin, OH; Oberlin College Press, © 1993. Reprinted by permission of the author. "Head of an Unknown Saint," "Happiness," "The Hawk," "Tulip Tree" reprinted from *A Stick That Breaks and Breaks,* Marianne Boruch; FIELD

Poetry Series v. 5; Oberlin, OH; Oberlin College Press, © 1997. Reprinted by permission of Oberlin College Press.

**Laure-Anne Bosselaar** "From My Window, I See Mountains" originally published in *Out of the Dark: Survivors of Family Violence* published by Queen of Swords Press in 1995. Reprinted by permission of the author. "Amen," "The Feather at Breendock," "The Radiator," "The Hour Between Dog and Wolf," "Hôtel des Touristes," "From My Window, I See Mountains," "Unable to Find the Right Way," and "The Cellar," © 1997 by Laure-Anne Bosselaar. Reprinted from *The Hour Between Dog and Wolf*, poems by Laure-Anne Bosselaar, with the permission of BOA Editions, Ltd. "The Vase," © 2001, by Laure-Anne Bosselaar. Reprinted from *Small Gods of Grief*, poems by Laure-Anne Bosselaar, with the permission of BOA Editions, Ltd.

**Kenneth Zamora Damacion** "Last Note Between Heaven and Hell" originally published in *Bamboo Ridge*. "The False Angel" originally published in *The Marlboro Review*. Reprinted by permission of the author.

**Volodymyr Dibrova** The Foreword to *Burdyk* first published in *Berezil Literary Magazine*.

**Sharon Dolin** "Jacob After Fording the Jabbok," "Spanish Snapshots," "The Domestic Fascist," "The Visit," "If My Mother," "The Bear," "Pomegranates," and "Confession" from *Heart Work* published by The Sheep Meadow Press, 1995. Reprinted by permission of The Sheep Meadow Press and the author.

**Patrick Donnelly** "Baba" and "How the Age of Iron Turned to Gold" originally published in *The Virginia Quarterly Review*. "Finding Paul Monette, Losing Him" and "After a long time away" originally published in *Beloit Poetry Journal*. "I am a virus" originally published in *Heliotrope*. Reprinted by permission of the author.

**John Donoghue** "Articles of Exploration" originally published in *The Virginia Quarterly Review*. "Physical" originally published in *The Western Journal of Medicine*. "Waiting for the Muse in Lakeview Cemetery" and "Shiela's Auras" originally published in *The Marlboro Review*. Reprinted by permission of the author.

**Ellen Dudley** "Ojo Caliente Suite" and "Kilauea" originally published in *Many Mountains Moving*. "The Bats" originally published in *The Best of*

*Writers at Work, 1995.* "Night Fishing" originally published in *AGNI*. "Leaving Lincoln" originally published in *Sou'wester*. Reprinted by permission of the author.

**Gary Duehr** "Dog World" originally published in *The American Literary Review*. "All the Little Sorries" originally published in *Fine Madness*. "Ricochet" and "Missing" originally published in *Poet's Voice*. Reprinted by permission of the author.

**Linda Dyer** "My Muse: Gravity" and "Conservation of Momentum" originally published by Forklift Press as part of a broadsheet entitled *6,000 Lucyfied Stars*.

**Martín Espada** "La Tumba de Buenaventura Roig," "Colibrí," "Latin Night at the Pawnshop," and "Jorge the Church Janitor Finally Quits" from *Rebellion Is the Circle of a Lover's Hands* by Martín Espada, © 1990 by Martín Espada. Reprinted by permission of the author and Curbstone Press. "DSS Dream," "White Birch," and "When Songs Become Water," © 1993 by Martín Espada, from *City of Coughing and Dead Radiators* by Martín Espada. Used by permission of W. W. Norton & Company, Inc. "Imagine the Angels of Bread" from *Imagine the Angels of Bread* by Martín Espada, © 1996 by Martín Espada. Used by permission of W. W. Norton & Company, Inc.

**Terri Ford** "Better Off" originally published in *Steam*. Reprinted by permission of the author. "Mister Hymen" originally published in *Conduit*. "BP Station Employee Restroom, 2 A.M." and "For the love of an anaconda woman" reprinted from *Why the Ships Are She*, © 2001 by Terri Ford, published by Four Way Books.

**Faye George** "What She Looked Out Upon" originally published in *Poetry* © 1996 by The Modern Poetry Association, reprinted by permission of the Editor of *Poetry*. "Welcome to This House" originally published in *Yankee*. "The Moon Is in the Eastern Sky" and "Norfolk to Boston" originally published in *The Bridgewater Review*. Reprinted by permission of the author.

**Tereze Glück** "The Coast of Massachusetts" originally published in *Columbia Magazine*. Reprinted by permission of the author.

**Sarah Gorham** "Shared Cup" and "Cupped Hands" originally published in *The Paris Review*. "River Mild" originally published in *Poetry East*. "Interim" originally published in *The Ohio Review*. "Honeymoon, Pleasant

Hill" and "Last Day at the Frost Place" originally published in *The Journal*. Reprinted by permission of the author.

**Ha Jin** "Ways of Talking," "A Peach," "Distance," "At Midnight," "In a Moonlit Night," "The Past," "Lilburn, Georgia," "I Sing of an Old Land," and "June 1989" reprinted from *Facing Shadows* © 1996 by Ha Jin, by permission of Hanging Loose Press.

**Brian Kiteley** "I Know Many Songs, But I Cannot Sing" reprinted with permission of Simon & Schuster from *I Know Many Songs, But I Cannot Sing* by Brian Kiteley, © 1996 by Brian Kiteley.

**Sabra Loomis** "Delia" originally published in *Salamander*. "The Trouble I Have in High Places" originally published in *Poetry New York*. "Echo," "Woman and Donkey," "The Bear That He Shot on Their Honeymoon in Montana, That Growled, and Tried to Come into Their Tent," "Coming-Out Party," "Ziffy-Sternal," and "Front Seats" appeared in a chapbook, *Travelling On Blue*, published in 1998 by Firm Ground Press. Reprinted by permission of the author.

**Pablo Medina** "Mortality" first published in *Shout Magazine*.

**Alison Moore** "The Angel of Vermont Street" originally published in *Story* Magazine. Reprinted by permission of the author.

**Dinty W. Moore:** "White Birds" originally published in *Writer's Forum*. Reprinted by permission of the author.

**Frankie Paino** "Each Bone of the Body," "The Martyrdom of St. Sebastian," "Sometimes the Dead," "Pentecost: Collinwood School Fire, Cleveland, 1908" from *Out of Eden*, Cleveland State University Poetry Center Press, 1997. Reprinted by permission of the author and Cleveland State University Poetry Center Press.

**Carl Phillips** "Undressing for Li Po," "Blue," and "In the Blood, Winnowing" from *In the Blood* by Carl Phillips, © 1992 by Carl Phillips. Reprinted with the permission of Northeastern University Press, Boston. "Aubade for Eve Under the Arbor," © 1995 by Carl Phillips. Reprinted from *Cortège* with the permission of Graywolf Press, Saint Paul, Minnesota. "As from a Quiver of Arrows" and "The Full Acreage of Mourning," © 1998 by Carl Phillips. Reprinted from *From the Devotions* with the permission of Graywolf Press, Saint Paul, Minnesota.

**Bethany Pray** "Conception" and "In Dream, in the Eden" originally published in *The Virginia Quarterly Review*. Reprinted by permission of the author.

**Frances Richard** "Infiltration" first published in *The Virginia Quarterly Review*.

**Jeffrey Skinner** "Come" originally published in the *Columbia Poetry Review*. "Fetch" originally published in *The Iowa Review*. "Stay" originally published in *The Georgia Review*. "Jocelyn" originally published in *Crazyhorse*. Reprinted by permission of the author.

**Jean Valentine** "Your mouth 'appeared to me,' " "October Premonition," "Mare and Newborn Foal," "Mother," and "The Pen" reprinted from *The Cradle of the Real Life*, © 2000, Wesleyan University Press by permission of University Press of New England.